THREE FEVERS

Leo Walmsley. (Photograph copyright Peter Woods.)

Three Fevers

Leo Walmsley

Foreword by Stephanie Walmsley

First published in 1932 by Collins

This edition published in 1992 by
Smith Settle Ltd
Ilkley Road
Otley
West Yorkshire
LS21 3JP

ISBN Paperback 1 85825 001 3
Hardback 1 85825 002 1

British Library Cataloguing-in-Publication Data:
A catalogue record is available for this book
from the British Library.

Printed and bound by
SMITH SETTLE
Ilkley Road, Otley, West Yorkshire LS21 3JP

Foreword

This book will take you into another world, where
people are vivid and real, warm-hearted yet un-
sentimental. From the moment one of the local
characters hails the author with 'Now then' – a
Yorkshire greeting – you feel you are moving into a
close knit community.

This is a story of men who live their lives to the
full, taxing their powers of endurance to the limit.
Set in Robin Hood's Bay, a fishing village which lies
between Whitby and Scarborough, it describes the
adventures and rivalries of two families, the Lunns
and the Fosdycks, and the dangerous lives they lead
as they struggle to wrest a living from the sea.

The author keeps himself modestly in the background, never intruding upon the story, sharing
their joys and setbacks. You can sense the deep
admiration he feels for these brave fishermen who
defy danger with an almost reckless gaiety and are
always ready with a quip or wry comment. These
men never brood over misfortune. When catastrophe overtakes them they bounce back with
buoyant optimism like a coble riding the waves.

The story is packed with drama, its characters
strong and forthright. One of the most exciting
scenes is the shooting of lobster pots in a furious
gale-lashed sea. Another is a brilliant attempt to

Book One

CHAPTER ONE

IT was treacherous weather, even for a Bramblewick December. Last night, Sunday, there was a freezing wind from the south-west ; the stars had glittered in a cloudless sky ; the sea was calm, and made no sound. Now, an hour before dawn, the air had an autumnal warmth, the sky was overcast, there was no wind ; yet from the dark north came the threatening thunder of a heavy swell, breaking along the rough foot of Low Batts cliff.

There was no sign yet of the Lunns or the Fosdycks. Their cobles lay drawn up upon their launching carriages behind the breakwater, seeming, in the grey half-light of approaching dawn, like two strange amphibious beasts that had crawled out of the sea during the night to rest. The village was silent. No light gleamed in the rampart of closely huddled cottages which climbed up behind the breakwater wall and along that black shale cliff, which, facing north-east, is Bramblewick's main defence against the winter wind and sea.

Were both families lying in, I wondered ? Did that thunder of swell to the north portend another period of enforced idleness ? It meant at least that the wind had been off the sea during the night. It might mean that the wind would follow the swell, and that before noon the bay would be white with breakers. Yet I knew that nothing but broken water on the landing bar, or that exasperating understanding with the Fosdycks that both boats stayed if one stayed, would keep Henry Lunn ashore ; and while the sky was steadily growing lighter, the sea beyond the breakwater was still only a darkish blur ; the Landing bar was invisible.

I waited, looking seawards to the coming dawn, possessed by that peculiar excitement which grows half from desire, and half from fear. Suddenly there were foot-steps behind me, and at once the quiet of the village was broken by the harsh cawing of two herring gulls which wheeled out of the morning dusk, and alighted on the breakwater wall. Old Isaac Fosdyck was coming down the slipway. Behind him the eyes of his two devoted cats gleamed like living jewels in the dark. He halted, and I said good-morning to him, to which he answered, in his rich prepossessing voice, that was always tinged with a faintly ironic humour :

" Now then." This being the Bramblewick idiom of address.

The cats, too, had stopped, and with arched backs were disporting themselves against his legs. The two gulls re-mained silent on the wall. I asked old Isaac what he made of the weather. He did not look towards the sea. Instead he struck a match and put it to his pipe, and by its light his misty blue eyes twinkled as though he were contem-plating something very funny.

" What do I make of the weather ? " he echoed. He chuckled softly under his patriarchal beard. " Why—it's going to blow north-east. It'll blow north-east before the tide's done ebbing. Aye—and it will blow hard too. It will be winter again."

I asked him if he thought the two boats would be putting to sea : and again he chuckled.

" They're daft enough ! " he answered. " They're daft enough. The Fosdycks won't want to go, but the Lunns will, so they'll have to go too. But they won't catch any

fish," he added, still chuckling. " There's no fish for them
to catch. They'll not earn the cost of their bait."

He suddenly turned to the breakwater wall.

" Now, Joey and Charley ! " he said, in an almost
singing voice to the two gulls. " Are you famished ? Are
you waiting for your breakfast ? "

He put down the bucket he carried, and took from it a
piece of stale fish. The cats continued to rub themselves
against his legs. But the gulls left the wall and, cawing
excitedly, fluttered above his head. He held up a piece of
stale fish. One of the gulls swooped down and took it from
his hand. He held up a piece for the other one, and he
continued to feed them until there was no fish left. Then
he picked up his bucket and chuckled again.

" Well," he said, " I'll away down and have a look at a
bit of line I've got set on the scaur by the Landing ; but I
know there'll be nowt on it. I reckon I'd best take it up.
It's going to come on like it did that day me father and
them was drowned, coming into the Landing. It'll blow
hard. I say it'll blow hard."

He puffed his pipe for a moment or two longer, like an
ancient engine getting up steam ; then, still chuckling
softly to himself, he walked down the slipway to the beach,
from which the tide was rapidly ebbing. The gulls wheeled
off seawards. The cats followed their master to the wet
margin of the beach, stood earnestly watching him for a
while and then, mindful of their paws, turned and slunk
quietly past me for home.

I knew old Isaac too well to be astonished either at his
satellite cats, or at the spectacle of two pet herring gulls
feeding from his hand. I was familiar, too, with his
attitude towards the Lunns and the other Fosdycks, whose
efforts to win a livelihood from the sea appeared to be for

him a perpetual source of amusement. Yet there was no
malice or rancour, or real misanthropy in this attitude. I
took it to be a gesture against the sea itself ; it was as
though his long and tragic contact with it had taught him
the absolute futility of striving to win the material favours
of so elusive a mistress ; and that only in an ironic resig-
nation to this simple truth could a man win something for
the contentment of his soul. Certainly, at the age of
seventy-nine, old Isaac had found contentment.

He was the uncle of Luke and Tindal Fosdyck who, with
the former's consumptive son, Avery, were the only true
Bramblewick men left of the odd thirty who had been
regularly engaged in fishing when I was a boy. The Lunns,
who had emigrated from Sledburgh, a more southerly
village, when Henry was seventeen, were still regarded as
' foreigners.'

But Isaac himself was not a real fisherman. He was ten
years old at the time of that historic coble disaster in which
his father and two uncles were drowned when attempting
to get into the Landing in a sudden north-east gale. His
mother was already dead. He was sent straight away to
sea as cabin-boy on a locally owned brig. On the first
voyage his eldest brother fell from the rigging and was
killed. On his second voyage the vessel foundered with a
loss of two hands, both of them Fosdycks. After that he
served on many other ships, and survived three wrecks and
one collision. At last he became bo'sun of a Burnharbour
brig, the *Nancy Price* ; rose in course of time to be mate ;
invested the savings of all these years in a twelfth share of
the brig, and on the death of her skipper (a cousin) was
offered command. But for some obscure reason he refused
this offer and became ship's cook instead, a berth he held
up to the day that the *Nancy Price* (which was un-insured)

was destroyed by fire in Hartlepool Dock. Then, at the age of sixty-nine he came home, bringing with him the ship's cat (of which the present two were blood descendants), invested a gratuity from the Shipwrecked Mariners' Society in a small and already decrepit rowing boat which, perhaps ironically, he re-named the *Nil Desperandum*, and started fishing, an occupation which had proved as materially unsuccessful as his lifelong one had been.

His aged but remarkably erect figure had now disappeared beyond the breakwater. Seawards of the wall the half-bared backs of the twin reefs or ' scaurs ' which form the comparatively sheltered lagoon known as the Landing, were becoming vaguely discernible. It seemed that the sound of the surf was steadily growing stronger. It travelled with a peculiar clarity on the windless air, as sounds travel in an empty church ; and above its deep monotonous thunder there rose at regular intervals a harsher, more sinister note, as though the moving sea was growing tight and thick, and the sharp rocks were splitting it like canvas.

It was with a measure of relief that I became aware of someone approaching from behind, and, turning, recognized the slender figure of young Marney Lunn. He walked swiftly, with a slight sailor's lurch ; and his feet, shod in rubber deck-boots, made scarcely more sound on the rough paving of the slipway than the paws of one of Isaac's cats. And it was with the suggestion of a cat's indolent agility that he swung round on his heels and stopped, looking seawards, intent upon the weather.

I respected his preoccupation and did not speak.

Suddenly he swung round again, and then, as though for the first time he had become aware of my existence, he said :

" Now then. Got a fag on you ? "

We lighted cigarettes, and jerking with his lips at his, Marney looked once more seawards. I suggested that it looked dirty. Marney grinned derisively.

" Garn. There's nothing wrong with the weather. It's champion. There's no harm in a bit of swell. It's just what you want for cod. It will stir the bottom up, give the fish something fresh to look at. More swell, more fish ! Have the Fosdycks been down yet ? " he added.

I recognized in that inquiry a suspicion of the antagonism with which the two families regarded one another. I said that only old Isaac had been down, and that he had prophesied the wind would blow hard north-east before the tide changed. Marney looked vaguely impressed, but he answered ironically :

"Aye. Isaac *would* have something cheerful to say. He's nothing but an old croaker, that chap. The world's champion. The wonder is he didn't prophesy a hurricane!"

For a minute Marney continued to stare seawards in silence ; then he jerked himself round again.

" Come on," he said. " Give me a hand down with the lines. We'll have to be off in twenty minutes and I haven't made Amy her cup of tea yet. If you took any notice of an old croaker like Isaac," he added, " we'd all be living with a lot of mangy old cats, and talking cuckoo to seagulls. Come on."

Although Marney had served ten years before the mast in the mercantile marine before returning to Bramblewick to adopt the profession of his fathers, he was still only twenty-five. He was good-looking ; gay, abounding with energy and zest for life. He had been married a little over a year, and was the father of a healthy son. It was not strange that he should be unsympathetic with Isaac's serenely ironic outlook on life.

We walked up the slipway into the dock, where Bramblewick's only two streets, Bridge Street and Chapel Street, converge in a comparatively open space ; where the cobles are hauled up in very wild weather, and the lifeboat-house has a convenient site. We turned up Chapel Street, which follows the ridge of the sea cliff, and shortly turned up a dark cobbled alley, where Marney quietly pushed open the door of a tiny cottage.

Out in the alley one had lost the sound of the surf. Stepping inside the little kitchen parlour I was instantly aware of it again, for the cottage was built on the very edge of the cliff, and one could throw a stone from its back window into the sea, eighty feet below. Yet the sound was less sinister now. A fire of driftwood burnt brightly in the grate. A kettle was boiling. Marney turned up the wick of an oil-lamp which stood upon a table neatly laid for breakfast, and looked with a manifestly possessive pride about him.

Even in broad daylight the room was dark, for it had only two small windows. On seeing it first, Marney and his wife had agreed that what it wanted was 'cheering up,' and roses were the most cheerful thing Amy could think of. So they had covered the walls with a paper on which sprays of pink roses were printed on a pale blue ground at the rate of twelve to the square yard ; and a more conventionalised edition of the same theme was repeated in the oil-cloth floor-covering and in an antimacassar laid over a horse-hair sofa, which bore also two red cushions embroidered with yellow roses and leaves of brightest green.

Very few of these roses were visible, however. Against

the north wall stood a mahogany veneer sideboard with a scrolled back, whose top was only a foot from the ceiling, and the space left was occupied by a coloured picture of Grace Darling in a gilt frame. East and west of this were bright representations of two of the steamboats Marney had sailed in, one with Vesuvius in eruption for its background; and on the same wall was an engraving of ' Stag at Bay,' and several photographic portraits. The sideboard had a cloth with an embroidered fringe. It bore a collection of china : three pairs of vases (very precisely ' paired '), a china bust of Lord Haig, and one of Lord Jellicoe to match, a china model of Burnharbour Priory, and one of the Eddystone Lighthouse, with a thermometer in its front. Above the fireplace on the south wall was a varnished oak overmantel which had come as a wedding present from an uncle of Amy's whose hobby was carpentry. There was an oval mirror in its centre. Right and left were diamond mirror panels and brackets which supported more vases, and a model of a full-rigged ship in a medicine bottle, the work of Marney himself. The mantelshelf, too, had a brightly embroidered velvet cloth, with tinsel tassels. There was a vari-coloured rag mat in front of the fire ; and the room contained also a cradle with an embroidered overlay, two windsor arm-chairs with embroidered cushions, a carpet foot-rest, embroidered with roses, and in the recess of the front window was an enormous green plant-bowl decorated with roses, with a geranium plant hiding demurely inside.

Yet the general impression one got was that of warmth and comfort ; and not for the first time I endeavoured to convey to Marney my appreciation. He had quickly set about making the tea.

" Aye," he said, " it's not a bad little spot this. It's

cosy, anyway, and that's the main thing. Now that's what's wrong with old Isaac, in my opinion," he added rather thoughtfully. " Poor chap never got married, and never had a real home of his own. It's only natural that a chap would get queer aloft, with only a couple of old cats to talk to."

" We've just got time for a cup of tea before father and John get down," he added more briskly. " Have one of Amy's cheese-cakes. They're champion. You know it's a bad thing to go to sea on an empty stomach. Any doctor will tell you that."

It was a theory I would not dispute ; but I had a powerful conviction that Amy's cheese-cakes, champion though they were, would not be the most suitable form of nourishment for the voyage in prospect. I was glad that Amy herself at the moment provided a distraction.

" Is that you, Marney ? " came her voice from upstairs.

Marney, in the act of filling the teapot, winked at me.

" No—of course it's not," he answered, lifting his eyes to the ceiling. " What's up with you ? "

" You're not going off, are you ? "

" No," Marney answered ironically, " I've got up specially to make you some tea. Don't make such a noise, or you'll wake the baby."

There was a short silence, in which Marney gave the teapot a vigorous shaking. Then Amy's voice came again, rather tremulously :

" It does sound stormy. I wish you weren't going off. The sea sounds awful. I'm sure there's a storm."

To which Marney answered, with what for once I thought was a slightly unconvincing gaiety :

" Garn. You're only half-awake yet. Weather's champion."

B

When Marney came downstairs again it seemed to me that he was not quite so cheerful. He frowned, and leaning across the table, whispered :

" Be careful what you say. I've told her we're going on to High Batts for bait." And in normal tones, " Hurry and drink your tea. We haven't got too much time if we're to get on to High Batts before the tide flows."

He lapsed into thoughtful silence ; but he proved his confidence in the non-empty stomach theory by consuming three cheese-cakes, two jam-tarts, and two cups of perfectly black tea within the next five minutes. We got up then. He banked the fire, turned out the lamp, and we moved like two conspirators out across the alley into the wash-house, which served also as a store for bait and fishing gear. There were three lines, which we had baited on Saturday. They were coiled on wicker trays or ' skeps,' that looked like Zulu war shields. Marney took one under each arm, I another, and we stepped out again.

His silence lasted until we reached the turning into Chapel Street. Then, with a faint lugubriousness, he said :

" There's only one thing I have against women. They worry about nowt. If Amy had her say we'd never go to sea at all in winter-time. There's no sense in worrying. It's pure daftness. Take life as it comes, that's my motto. If you're born to be drowned, worrying about it won't help. . . . But you ought to have seen that damned kid of mine, snuggling in her arms," he added with a quick return to his gayer self, " that little devil would sleep through a hurricane."

We hurried down past the rows of still dark and silent cottages to the dock, where again we were assailed by the menacing thunder of the north-east swell. But before we had reached the breakwater we were overtaken by Henry and John Lunn, both with lines under their arms.

Of these three men with whom I had joined company, Marney (slender of build, yet lithe as a monkey) was quick, high-spirited, devil-may-care, reckless. John, two years his senior (yet still unmarried), more sturdily built, almost thick-set, was slow, ponderous, moody, seemingly over-cautious. And Henry, the father, still in his physical prime, seemed to combine what was sound in the characters of both his sons with a mature strength, a quiet audacity, a profound experience of life which made their partnership ideal.

All of them were fair-haired, blue-eyed, with full mouths and even white teeth, denoting their remote Scandinavian origin. They spoke the musical long-vowelled dialect of the coast with its rich Scandinavian vocabulary and idiom. But their outlook on life was broadminded and intelligent. Strong in them was the pioneer spirit with which sporadically along the coast a few men of a younger generation were fighting the tragic lethargy which had beset the craft of inshore fishing since the war.

We did not speak. We dropped the lines alongside the Lunns' coble : and I remained slightly apart while the three of them stood together, looking seawards. It was now nearly daylight. The scaurs of the Landing were clearly defined. South, the immense headland of High Batts revealed a misty contour against the overcast and leaden sky. North, the nearer headland of Low Batts stood out in bolder relief, and along its foot the crests of the breakers gleamed like bared teeth through the paling dusk which still obscured the seaward horizon.

John was the first to give his thoughts utterance. He spoke slowly, ponderously, almost with a growl.

" Sea's growing."

" What if it is ? " was Marney's quick comment. " It's a long way from breaking across the Landing mouth."

" It'll be breaking there before the tide turns."

" Garn ! " was Marney's scornful rejoinder. " We're going off, so you can stop your croaking, brother John. You're getting as bad as old Isaac with your croaking."

" I'm not so bad I haven't a pair of eyes in my head, and some sense behind them," was John's surprisingly quick retort. But he as quickly lapsed into his customary gloom. " It's been blowing like hell outside. Sea's grown while we've stood watching. I bet the Fosdycks won't like it. I bet they'll not want to go."

" Hold your jaws, both of you," Henry put in quietly. " You're like a couple of pups yapping. Have they been down yet ? "

" They're coming," said Marney.

A silence fell upon the Lunns. They did not turn until Luke and Tindal Fosdyck were abreast, and then Henry spoke very quietly and very courteously to the elder brother.

" Now, Luke."

" Now, Henry," the elder Fosdyck answered ; and after a slight pause. " Looks as though it's going to blow again."

To which Henry answered non-committally, " It doesn't look too good."

There was a lengthier pause while all five men continued to look at the sea. But I knew that this seeming intentness on the weather was a blind to what was really moving in their minds. The air had become electric with repressed antagonism.

My sympathies in this enduring antagonism between the Lunns and Fosdycks were not altogether one-sided. The

Fosdycks were the oldest Bramblewick family, parish records of them going back for certain to the time of the Dissolution of the Monasteries. It was not unnatural that they should have come to regard that broad sweep of sea stretching between the two Batts as the reserve at least of the Bramblewick fishermen : and that they should have bitterly resented the immigration and settlement in the village of Henry Lunn's father and two other ' foreign ' families.

Yet what must have rankled deeper was that these ' foreigners ' used different gear, employed a different fishing technique, worked longer hours and caught more fish from the bay than they did themselves. And the feeling was not less bitter now that Luke and Tindal were growing old ; that their family, of which the sea had taken such heavy toll, threatened to end at Avery's generation ; while the Lunns, following the war (when the rest of the ' foreigners,' including old Marney Lunn, returned to their native village, while Henry fished in a deep-sea boat, and John and young Marney were sailors in the Mercantile Marine) had started fishing again, with a motor-coble to give them a greater advantage still. Nor again was it less bitter because in the winter there was no one else fishing, which meant that they were dependent upon the Lunns, as the Lunns were dependent upon them, for co-operation in the very heavy labour of hauling the boats up when fishing was done.

Yet Henry, broadminded and good-natured, was capable of understanding, even of sympathising with their resentment. He did not hate the Fosdycks. But he hated inactivity. He hated the restraint imposed upon him by this mutually understood if unspoken agreement that if either family wished to stay the other would also

stay : for there never could be a time when this decision
could be made by him : the " say " was always Luke
Fosdyck's.

The two brothers stood slightly apart from the Lunns.
They were joined now by Avery Fosdyck, whose lanky
figure, wasted by consumption, and pale, clean-shaven
face with its hollow cheeks and deep-sunk eyes made a
striking contrast to the massive, thick-set frames, and
dour, stubborn, grey-bearded faces of his father and uncle.
Neither they nor the Lunns took the slightest notice of his
arrival. We were waiting for Luke's pronouncement.

Obviously he did not wish to go. It was not that he was
afraid. One took the physical courage of the coxswain of
the Bramblewick lifeboat for granted. But both he and
his brother were well past middle age. Their coble, with
its sail useless, was heavy to pull, and the consumptive
Avery would make a poor third hand if, as seemed likely,
they had to make a sudden dash for home. Yet Luke was
aware that Henry Lunn was ready to take a chance. If he
decided against, there was the risk that Henry's forbear-
ance would at last break down, that the hitherto quiescent
enmity between them would become a definite quarrel.
There was the chance that Henry would go out in spite of
him, and chance finding help up with his coble later. There
was the chance that Henry would have a good catch to
send to market on the one o'clock train, while he himself
had nothing. And perhaps it was this last and most
primitive consideration that prompted his reluctant
decision ; for Luke was still a fighter !

" It looks mucky," he growled. " It'll be quick off and
quick in for us. There'll not be time to shoot and haul
more than three lines before it's breaking across the
Landing. What do you say, Henry ? "

Henry Lunn turned smartly round.

"Aye," he answered quickly. "There's no time to waste. Shall we give you a hand down first ? "

As though afraid that Luke might yet repent of his decision, he moved with alacrity towards the Fosdycks, coble. We followed him. Only Avery Fosdyck seemed to linger momentarily, with his hands thrust deep in his trousers pockets, his pallid face turned seawards, with what seemed to me to be an expression of despair.

CHAPTER TWO

It was daylight. The Fosdycks had gone. With Tindal and Avery rowing, and the massive figure of Luke standing in the stern, their coble was already abreast of the two black posts which mark the sudden extremities of the east and west scaurs, and the mouth of the Landing. It rose and dipped steeply to the incoming swell which broke savagely on the scaurs themselves not more than a coble's length on either side. Yet still there was no manifest wind. Away from the scaurs, the sea spread grey and formless to the misty horizon, giving the illusion of a perfect calm. The air was still mild and oppressively close.

Our own coble was now afloat at the shoreward end of the deceptively tranquil Landing. John, with a look of intense preoccupation on his face, was priming the engine. Marney was bending the buoy and anchor of the first line. Henry, with one hand already on the tiller, was watching the Fosdycks' boat.

" They're going to shoot straight out from the Landing posts," he remarked.

Marney gave a contemptuous grunt.

" ' Quick off and quick in ! ' " he mocked. " If I'd been fishing all my life in this spot I'd shoot myself if I didn't know more about fishing than that. Cod run close into the scaur ends when there's a swell. Closer we go in the better. They're afraid of getting their shirts wet. That's what's up with them. . . . Come on, John. Get that damned engine started. You're like an old woman. Here. I'll give her a swing."

Deep in his heart, John enjoyed his brother's raillery, but that engine was as precious to him as a certain infant was to Marney, and he answered gruffly :

" You leave the damned engine alone. Then we'll know whose fault it is if anything goes wrong."

" If I had charge of it it never would go wrong," Marney retorted. " Hurry up. We've seven lines to shoot to their three, and we're not going to shoot in deep water. We're going to put them where there's some fish."

" That's for father to say," John rebuked, seizing the starting-handle. " There's only one boss in this boat."

" And that's me," was Marney's ready answer. " Father only does what I tell him."

" And as you only do what your missus tells you, *she'll* be telling us where to shoot our lines next."

Henry, who had never relaxed his observation of the Fosdycks, suddenly turned to me and winked. But he did not speak. Nor did Marney for once find his usual quick retort to what was clearly a sharpish thrust. Possibly he had remembered that at this moment we were supposed to be on our way to High Batts for bait, for I thought I detected him in a sly glance to the cliff back of the Landing, where the pale light of dawn was now reflected on the windows of his home.

But John, having scored, was discreetly silent. He gave the handle a couple of powerful turns. The engine started without a murmur of complaint. He looked up, smiling broadly at me.

" How's that ? " he said, with a pride that was parental. " On paraffin, too. I'd not be frightened of crossing the Atlantic with an engine like ours."

He put the clutch in. The coble trembled ; then, as

Henry put the tiller over, curved round towards the Landing mouth and the open sea.

At half-tide the Landing measured a rough two hundred yards from its shallow end to the marking posts. On each side of it the protecting scaurs flattened out into a series of parallel but less prominent scaurs. Moving along the nearest of these to the west was old Isaac, carrying a coiled fishing-line in his hand. His two gulls stood sedately eyeing him from a boulder some yards behind.

Henry steered so that he passed within speaking distance of him.

" Now, Isaac ! " he hailed. " Any luck ? "

The old man stopped. I could see that he had been wading knee-deep in the water ; but his eyes were still twinkling.

" Luck ? " he shouted back. " Of course I've had no luck. I've never had any luck since I was born, so it's not likely I'm going to start this morning. There aren't any fish. I say there aren't any fish. I've gone and got my feet wet too. I shouldn't have got me line if I hadn't. . . . And you'll do no better," he shouted after us. " You might as well have stayed in bed, all of you. It's going to blow hard before the morning's done. Sea's growing now."

"Cuckoo ! " Marney commented. "Completely cuckoo!"

" I don't know so much," said John. " There's plenty of folks with less sense than old Isaac. . . . Where are we going to start shooting, father ? "

Father did not answer. Already the boat was feeling the swell. We had passed the bared ends of the scaurs. The crash of the breakers now made almost inaudible the steady *tug-tug* of the engine. Marney was standing up with the buoy in his hand. We had drawn abreast of the posts. The coble climbed a roller that would have reached at least half-way up the breakwater wall, and dipped with an easy crash into its trough. At the same moment the roller split on the sunken scaur-ends close to each side of us, turned over, and went roaring shorewards, leaving a mass of seething, hissing foam in its wake.

We were in the very place of that historic tragedy, and as though Henry had read my thoughts, he waved his disengaged hand to the broken water right and left of us.

" It's a nasty spot, this," he said quietly. " It's all right when you can see where you're going. But when you're coming in in a hurry, you can't tell whether it's breaking right across or not, until it's too late to turn back. That's what happened to old Isaac's father, they say. If it wasn't for this we could stay out almost any weather," he added regretfully.

" And it's a damned good thing we can't," put in John : and, to his brother, " You needn't think we're going to start shooting in here with the swell growing like it is. I want to be feeding my hens to-night, not a lot of crabs. We'll get further out before we start."

" You shut up," said Marney. " You're the engineer, not the navigation officer. Keep below. What about it, father ? You know there's most fish nearest in."

Again father winked, but he said nothing. He kept the coble on a course straight out of the Landing and then slightly north-west until we were about a hundred yards from the posts and the nearest broken water. Then he swung round until we were pointing for Low Batts cliff, and signed to Marney to heave the buoy overboard.

" We're near enough in and far enough out to suit both of you here," he said, smiling. " If it blows up strong while we're off we'll just be able to pick our end up here. The Fosdycks have only just started shooting. Throttle your engine, John. Now, Marney, soon as your buoy is clear.''

One never had any real doubt as to who was boss of that boat. The buoy was trailing out astern. Marney had the first line alongside him. He gave the buoy line a last clearing tug, heaved over the small anchor, and, as soon as its line was paid out, started to shoot. For a while there was no more talking.

It was tricky work. Each line measured four hundred fathoms: and there was a yard-long 'snood' and hook at each second fathom. They were coiled on the wicker 'skeps' so that the baited hooks lay together in a neat heap clear of the line. Even so there was a chance of a hook fouling, either the line, or the boat's gunwale, or even the 'shooter's' hands, which meant that the hook would have to bear the entire strain of the heavy and fairly fast-moving boat.

Henry, when I knew him first, had the reputation of being the smartest hand at shooting on the coast. Now. he admitted, he was not so good as Marney. His fingers had become too stiff. It needed a marvellously quick eye, a dainty touch, unerring judgment. John's ambitions had never lain this way. He was the mechanic, and when occasion arose, the second strong man of the trio. He had a prodigious strength.

There was an immense fascination in seeing these three men at their job; Marney deftly lifting the coils of line, flinging them, with their vicious hooks, clear of the boat. John watching him, with his hand on the throttle, ready to ease down or stop if anything fouled; Henry standing with one sea-booted foot on the stern athwart, the long tiller boom under his left arm, alert, watchful, quietly and supremely in command. He looked like a viking chief with his bristly, straw-coloured moustache projecting above his tightly closed lips, his bright audacious eyes roving restlessly from the boat, across that heaving, windless, enigmatic sea.

Our course continued towards Low Batts, parallel to the rocky shore, and just clear of the breaking surf. But soon the shore began to sweep out north-east in conformity with the strike of the headland cliff, and we turned north-east, riding the swell head-on. The first line was nearly shot.

" Stand by ! " Marney shouted to me. " Don't make a mess of it ! "

I lifted the ' skep ' of the second line alongside that of the first, took off its lashings, bent its beginning to the loose end of the first, and as the last coil of the latter went overboard, moved the empty ' skep ' out of the way, an effort which afforded me considerable satisfaction, but which produced from Marney only a sarcastic grunt.

" Slow," he said, flinging a coil of line into the air as though it was a living snake. " Slow. You're nearly as slow as our John, and there never was anything slower. . . . Keep closer in, father. We're getting off the rock edge here."

The coble rose almost on its end as he spoke, mounting a terrific roller. A petrol can came crashing down from a thwart. Marney swayed, but the next coil, with its baited hook, shot out as clear as the first.

" Sea's growing like hell," John complained. " We'll be lucky if it's not breaking here when we come back. Why can't you have a bit of sense, the pair of you ? You know the Fosdycks will be only too pleased to have the lifeboat out after us, and make fools of us."

Being ' made fools of ' was the one thing the Lunns

really feared, and nothing came so completely within their conception of the term as an active challenge on the part of the Fosdycks to their sea judgment, or their ability to get back to shore unassisted.

But Henry, taking a glance at the Fosdycks' boat, now about a mile to the south-east of us, smiled complacently.

"They'll be back before us," he said. "But they'll know better than try that game on. If they do they'll only have it to launch back. . . . They're queer chaps, the Fosdycks," he added, turning to me. "You'd think that in a place like this, with only two boats working, it would pay you both to pull together. But it seems they can't forget father and them coming here and showing 'em how to fish. And they've not liked us starting with a motor-coble. Yet they've got enough brass to buy a motor if they wanted. If they worked the same way we do they'd catch just as much fish. But they'll go on sticking to their old-fashioned ways until they die, I reckon. They're queer. That's all I can say about them."

"But I could say more," put in Marney darkly, leaning almost horizontal with the boat as she rode another great roller.

"And so could I," added John.

"Then you can both hold your jaws," said father with a surprising severity. "Least said, soonest mended."

Both Marney and John grinned, but they did not speak again for a while. We were now running parallel with Low Batts cliff, still head-on to the rollers which broke, not against, but along the cliff foot ; chasing each other for half a mile before they finally crashed on the shores of the bay itself. They were typical deep-sea waves, very long and regular in their incidence. It seemed incredible that we should ride over them in safety and tolerable comfort, while not more than eighty yards away they could have smashed an iron ship to pieces in a matter of hours.

Would the wind that had transmitted this awful energy to the sea follow on ? The sun had risen, but the sky remained completely overcast. Round the distant headland of High Batts a steamer had appeared ; but its smoke trailed languidly astern, denoting a complete absence of wind. Yet the swell obviously was growing. The noise of it, reverberating from the precipitous walls of the adjacent cliff, was like that of an immense cataract. Over the entire shore of the bay the breakers were throwing up a fine white mist, which almost obscured the land, and the village itself. The unnatural closeness of the air helped to increase one's apprehension about the weather. Yet the business of shooting went steadily on with only that gloomy look in John's eyes to suggest that my apprehension might be shared ; and that look I knew was more or less habitual, and signified a resistance to his brother's recklessness, rather than a fear of the sea itself.

Each line took roughly a quarter of an hour to shoot. The second was now nearly gone. I bent on the third, earning from Marney this time a curt, " That's better."

" Where have the Fosdycks got to now, father ? " he asked, almost in the same breath.

Henry glanced over his shoulder.

" Still shooting straight out. They must be on their second line."

" I bet poor Avery is wishing he was back on shore," Marney remarked thoughtfully. " Now, I'm sorry for that poor devil."

" So am I," put in John. " It's a damned shame him having to go to sea at all, the way he is."

" Aye," agreed father. " The chap seems to be in a very poor way."

" They say he's only got one lung," Marney pursued. " And that's no better than an old sea-boot. Doctor told him that if he went on getting himself wet and cold he wouldn't last the winter. But what's the poor devil to do ? His mother's dead, and he's not married. There's no one to look after him. He can't go on the dole. He's got to earn a living somehow."

" He told me once," said John, " that he wouldn't have been a fisherman at all if he'd had his way. He wanted to be a grocer. But no one would give him a start, not even carrying out. I heard tell——"

" Look out ! "

A sudden shout from Marney caused John instinctively to throw the engine out of gear. A hook had fouled. Quickly Marney's hand shot out and seized the receding line, and he held on to it against the way of the boat while with the other hand he deftly caught the offending hook from a bunch of others it had caught.

" That's one of your lines," he shouted at John when the line was clear, and the boat, in gear again, took an almost vertical plunge down the back of a roller. " You must have been thinking of that lass you were going to meet in Burnharbour on Saturday night while you were baiting in. My lines never foul. Nor father's. It's you who ought to have been a grocer."

" And I might have to be one yet," John answered, " when you two have gone and drowned yourselves ! "

The tragedy of Avery Fosdyck was forgotten in another battle of wits between the two brothers, which went on until Henry, glancing south-east, remarked suddenly :

" Damned if the Fosdycks haven't started to haul.

They're hauling before they've started their third line. Something must have scared them."

" So they are," John muttered slowly. " I wonder what's up ? " And then suddenly he shouted, " I know why. Look at the coastguard station. North cone's up." He turned to Marney. " Now will you say I'm croaking ? "

The coastguard station was built on high ground at the back of the village, and its flag-staff rose clear above the white mist shrouding the village itself. A small, black, conical bag was just discernible, hanging from the signal yard. Its point was upwards, denoting the conventional warning of an approaching gale from the north.

" Now will you say I'm croaking ? " John repeated. " There's evidence for you. We'd best get this line shot, and then start hauling straight away."

" Don't talk so daft ! " was Marney's comment. " We've come out to fish, not to play at launching boats up and down."

Quite unperturbed, he went on with his occupation, while Henry, looking again towards the Fosdycks, said complacently :

" Aye. That's what's turned them about. They've seen the cone, only they could have told it was going to blow without that. I don't blame them for hurrying in with a coble like theirs. So long as they don't expect us to join them. It just beats me why they don't get a motor. Look at us, and where we've got to already. They couldn't have worked this end of the bay this morning if they'd had six men to pull for them."

John shook his head despairingly, and bent gloomily over his engine.

The third line was shot. We started on the fourth, and not by a yard did Henry deviate from that course which

C

was steadily bringing us nearer to the extremity of Low Batts. Yet despite their outward complacence, I knew that both Henry and Marney were aware that we were running into danger ; that every fathom of line shot was a fathom between ourselves and the safe water behind that perilous Landing mouth.

Not a word was spoken while the fourth and fifth lines were shot. We were practically opposite Low Batts point when I stood by to bend on the sixth. But before Marney was ready we cleared the point, and a line of rough, breaker-fringed coast came into view beyond it. And with that line of coast, terminating at the high bluff called Kettlenab, which bears a light of the same name and hides the port of Burnharbour from the south, came in view the open sea, the northern skyline, the wind itself.

For two miles to the north, the surface of the slowly heaving sea was dully polished under the low-lying pall of pewter-grey cloud that obscured the sky. Beyond, divided by a line as clear cut as the contour of that for-bidding coast ; reaching from the coast to the north-east skyline, the sea was almost black ; the cloud above it was almost black, save for one small gap of startling blue sky, across which a wisp of white cloud moved like a ragged sail torn from a ship.

The wind ! One saw it in that wisp of scurrying clouds in that expanse of dark furrowed sea, whose clear-cut margin was travelling south-west, as fast almost as the wind itself. And suddenly one felt it in the air ; not a movement, but a peculiar coldness, as though one had plunged into an icy bath.

I thought that John would be the first to break the silence with which we surveyed that disquieting prospect, but I was wrong. He merely glanced from the sea to his father, whose expression remained completely unperturbed ; and it was Marney, swaying to the wild movement of the boat, who spoke, with a rather uncertain defiance :

" Stand by with that other line."

But it was father who spoke next ; quietly, decisively :

" You needn't trouble. Throttle your engine, John. Hold on your line, Marney. Start hauling soon as she comes about."

CHAPTER THREE

THERE was no alarm in Henry's voice. He had made the decision of a cool gambler who knows the precise limit of his stake. We turned. For a moment we were broadside on to the swell, and the coble rolled violently. But before the next roller came we were facing the land, John had opened his throttle to half-speed again, Marney had started hauling.

For a time we were silent. Despite that we were all conscious of the approaching wind and its significance, we watched the line coming on board with undivided interest. The fascination of a fisherman's life is that he reaps his harvest from an unseen world through whose insecure and perilous crust he throws down his sacrificial gifts for a reward that may be small, or may be great, but is always uncertain. All that he knows of that obscure region beneath him is that it is inexhaustibly rich.

True that we expected nothing of that first line. In normal weather we should have waited an hour at least before hauling. The first few fathoms had not even touched the bottom. Marney's face took on an expression of profound disgust, as hook after hook came up with its bait intact.

" If there's one thing I hate," he grumbled, " it's hauling a line that hasn't had a chance. We might just as well have waited twenty minutes before we hauled."

" You have a look nor'ard, and you'll not talk so daft," said John. " You'll be glad enough of that twenty minutes when we come to the far end of the line. If it's not breaking across the Landing by then it'll be a wonder to me."

"What if it is?" shouted Marney with a sudden cheerfulness. "You can swim ashore and then start that grocery business of yours. . . . Gaff—father. Here's the first, and a good fish, too."

We had drawn under Low Batts again. The coast beyond had disappeared, and with it that threatening expanse of furrowed sea : and the wind itself was temporarily forgotten in the excitement of bringing on board a twenty-pound cod.

"Now will you stop your croaking!" Marney shouted, continuing to haul while father deftly unhooked it. "Here's another. Damned if it isn't its mate!"

A second fish of about the same weight was gaffed and brought aboard, followed shortly by a third, only a pound or two smaller.

"Who says there aren't any fish?" Marney went on gaily. "I told you old Isaac was cuckoo! What's wrong with him is that he's never got wed. It's soured him. And you'll be as bad as him, brother John, if you don't get yourself a wife before long. I'm giving you some very sound advice. . . . They're damned good fish, too. They ought to fetch at least four bob a stone."

Marney was beaming now. Even John looked less gloomy, although he allowed his brother's ' sound advice ' to pass without comment. Henry's face still wore that expression of absolute imperturbability as his eyes roved without rest from the boat to the crashing breakers between ourselves and the cliff ; to the seaward horizon, and to the mist-hung shore.

About fifty fathoms came in blank. Then came a codling which did not need the gaff. The end of the first line was reached without another fish. I unbent the line and stowed it out of the way. Marney had stopped beaming. He hauled half of the next line before swinging another codling on board.

" They're not so plentiful as I thought," he muttered then. " The Fosdycks will have the laugh on us if we don't do better than this. Where have they got to ? "

We looked shorewards. The other coble had nearly reached the Landing posts.

" They're just about in," said Henry laconically.

" And I shouldn't mind if we were too," said John. " Look nor'ard now. It's coming, and no mistake."

Within a space of less than ten minutes the entire aspect of the seaward horizon had changed. From the extremity of Low Batts, as far as eye could reach to the south-east, it was as though that inert mass of low-lying cloud was being rolled up from the line of the sea in dark, horizontal, moving folds, from which drooped folds of paler colour, trailing like an immense opaque curtain over a sea that was dark furrowed and flecked white by the advancing wind.

" It's coming," John repeated. " It's a squall, too. That's either hail or snow behind the wind. . . . Now where should we have been if we'd waited ? It's going to be a devil. I tell you we're not going to get in a minute too soon."

Whether Marney glanced seawards or not, I did not know. He created a diversion at that moment with a shout of, " Eh ! What's this damned thing coming up ? Look out—father. Quick ! "

Henry, gaff in hand, leaned smartly over the gunwale ; but instead of the gaff he reached his bare hand into the sea, and lifted a big lobster out of it clean into the boat.

Again it seemed that the weather was forgotten. Both Henry and John stared at that utterly unexpected crust-

acean, flapping on its back on the boat's bottom as though
it was a bar of gold from a sunken galleon.

"Well, I'm damned!" said Henry.

"If that doesn't beat the band!" said John.

"First I've heard of a lobster being hauled close-in in
December," was Marney's contribution, as he continued
to haul. "And it looks as surprised as we are. I should
think it's gone and eaten something that hasn't agreed
with it, and put its compass wrong."

"I don't know," said John, with a new seriousness.
"They're making lobster pots already at Burnharbour. I
was talking to a chap on Saturday night, and he said they
were all starting for lobsters in February. He'd got a
proper lobster fever on him. Couldn't talk about anything
else but the brass Burnharbour chaps made out of lobsters
last year. If we had a couple of score of fine ones like that
it would pay us better than cod. I reckon we ought to
start making pots now, so we can start fishing when prices
are good."

Marney swung another codling into the boat. He
grinned, but he was taking John quite seriously.

"I thought you'd gone courting on Saturday night,"
he said. "So you went and caught lobster fever instead.
Well," he added, "those chaps did make some brass by
all accounts. There was one boat made nearly a hundred
quid in a week."

"There was one made over a hundred," put in Henry
quietly. "Lobsters were bringing three shillings each all
week."

I was aware that Henry's eyes had an unusual sparkle
in them as he took another glance at the lobster; but I
had still to become really acquainted with those peculiar
and highly infectious fevers, which, as one season declines,

spread among the fishermen of the coast, firing them with a wild enthusiasm for the next.

Nothing more was said about lobsters then. The end of the second line came with a single fourteen-pound cod. The third line was hauled without a fish. There were two lines left. We were more than halfway home ; and still there was no wind. Yet despite that the swell was less noticeable now that we were moving with it, the margin between the boat and the edge of the broken water was steadily decreasing as we moved into the bay. Without their exchanging a word, I knew that each of the Lunns was thinking of the buoy, the Landing mouth, and the squall behind us.

Were the seas breaking across the Landing mouth ? The Fosdycks' coble long ago had disappeared between the posts. Presumably they had safely navigated the passage which had for them that especially tragic significance. Since we had lost sight of them, however, the swell had measurably grown. Ten minutes of a squall on top of it might make the difference between a safe entry and an impossible one.

With the fourth line our luck began to change again. Two more good cod came in quick succession. There was a blank, then a run of about a dozen not big, but respectable fish. Their appearance was greeted in silence, however. Every fathom was bringing us nearer to where the rollers were breaking. As the end of the fourth line drew near with another small batch of fish we were obliged to wait while a breaking roller charged past us, before dodging into its churning wake, and out again before the next one came.

And as the end of that line and the beginning of the last one came on board, came the first warning puff of wind.

No one remarked upon it. No one troubled to look round. We felt its chilly blast, we saw it, like the shadow of a menacing hand, move across the grey water ahead. There was a moment's lull ; then came a stronger gust of icy air that whipped the crest of a nearby breaker into smoke. There was a sharp patter of hailstones. The gust passed over and ahead. Another quickly followed ; and in the short succeeding lull I saw Marney take a quick glance shorewards to where, close by the west Landing post, the buoy had become visible as it rode the crest of what appeared to be an unbroken sea.

But he said nothing. He went on steadily hauling. For several minutes the whole view shorewards was obscured by the driving hail, which pattered like rifle bullets on the thwarts and bottom of the heaving coble. The squall was on us. All round, the sea was whipped white by the wind, which was now continuous, and rapidly growing in force.

There was no fish during that period. Then they began to come in again : a batch of codling, a stray pollack, a conger which required all of Henry's strength and dexterity to bring on board. The hail continued. Only by that steadily growing pile of line by Marney's side was it possible to measure the distance which separated us from the buoy. Yet still Henry's face, reddened by the bite of the freezing wind and the sting of hail, was unperturbed as he helped with the fish, steered the boat and kept up a keen watch ahead. More than two thirds of the last line was hauled when the hail stopped. The land cleared again. We saw the Landing posts, and then the wind-whipped pennant of the buoy, poised for a moment on the crest of a wave that was beginning to break not more than a coble's breadth to the west of it.

John, hanging on to the wood casing of the engine as the boat pitched wildly, gave a shout.

" It's breaking ! Right on the buoy. That means across the Landing too ! We'd best cut away now, and make a dash for it. Cut the line ! "

" Garn ! " Marney shouted back. " We're not going to cut before there's need to, and very likely not at all. We're not going to throw away twenty fathoms of good line and maybe a dozen fish just to keep your shirt dry. You look after your engine. We can look after the boat. Can't we, father ? We've got in when it's been twice as bad as this."

My sympathies at that moment were entirely with John. But Henry answered neither of them. He was staring hard towards the shore. Suddenly he said :

" There's a lot of folks on the slipway. I believe there's somebody waving something. Can any of you make it out ? "

The wind, which had now reached gale force, had flattened the mist from the near-in breakers. The hail shower had swept over the village top, leaving the front and the slipway clear. One could vaguely distinguish, near to a group of figures standing on the slipway, a tall man in yellow oilskins, energetically waving a long pole with a black cloth on its end.

" It's Luke Fosdyck ! " John shouted. " He's waving us to stop. It must be breaking across the Landing. He's——"

Before John had finished, there came from the shore the muffled report of a gun. As we looked, against the dark scurrying clouds above the village there was a bright flash, a puff of white smoke from which shot down three scintillating red stars. And as the stars died there came the muffled report of that second explosion.

I had lived my whole boyhood in Bramblewick and that signal was too familiar for me not to understand it. It was the call-signal for the lifeboat crew. The figure we believed to be Luke Fosdyck was now moving up the slipway. The group had dispersed in the same direction. In a minute or two, the double doors of the lifeboat-house would be opened wide. Men would be rushing down, hurriedly strapping on their life-belts. . . .

" There you are ! Didn't I say they'd do it ? "

I looked at John. But it was anger, not fear that made his shout hoarse. And for the first time in my life I saw Henry really angry too. He was standing up, with the tiller boom under his arm, his oilskin cracking in the wind ; and I heard him mutter between his teeth :

" The damned fools ! Do they think we're kids ? "

And then he suddenly looked towards the buoy, now not more than thirty yards away, and said quietly to Marney :

" Have your knife ready, and cut when I say. Never mind the buoy. It'll wash ashore " ; and to John, " When I say ' go,' let her have it ! "

The buoy had disappeared in the trough between two great rollers over which we had already ridden. It appeared again on the crest of the second one, which broke clean on top of it, hiding its flapping pennant in a torrent of spray. We drew down upon it, Marney still calmly hauling. He swung another big cod on board without waiting for the gaff : another pollack, and two more codling. Then, as another roller lifted the coble up not a dozen yards from the buoy, Henry's curt order came :

" Cut ! "

And as Marney slashed at the line, with one steady glance towards that gap between the marking posts a hundred yards diagonally to our left, Henry put the helm

hard over. We swung round on the very crest of that
breaking sea. We sank sideways into its trough. Its
successor rose above us—began to break.

" Look out ! " Henry shouted.

It caught the low gunwale of the boat before we had
time to rise, and sent a torrent of water smashing over us.
But we were not aware then that we were wet. The coble
rode that wave broadside on, and sank sideways down its
back. And as a third and bigger wave still began to rise to
charge straight in between the Landing posts, Henry put
the tiller over again, and shouted violently :

" Let her go ! "

I did not know then if John obeyed that order. From
that moment we were not aware of any other power than
the sea. We swung round as the wave lifted us. For a
time it seemed we were poised on its absolutely rigid crest,
that the two posts on either side of us were themselves
moving towards us, out to sea. Then our stern began to
sink. The wave appeared to become mobile, it passed on,
reared its crest higher, split, and abandoned us in its
boiling wake, with the posts appearing to move landwards
again as the undertow took us back into the path of the
following wave.

I did not look at that wave. I expected it to swamp us ;
and I was struggling to kick off my sea-boots when, like an
immense hand, it gripped us from behind. We rose.
Again there was that illusion of immobility as the boat
balanced on its crest and travelled with it shorewards.
Again the posts appeared to move while we were still.
But this time the posts passed us. The shallow ends of the
scaurs passed us. We saw the bare rock, east and west.
Then again we began to sink down the back of the carrying
wave. The illusion of immobility went. The wave

advanced, passed on. But it did not break, except on the scaurs alongside us. We sank easily into its trough. We were consciously moving under our own power on the undulating, gale-swept, but unbroken surface of the Landing.

For a while none of us spoke. John throttled the engine. Henry steered in towards the shore end of the east scaur, where the Fosdycks' coble was beached. There was no sign of the lifeboat. The beach between the Landing and the village was deserted, but for a small boy running our way. But as we looked, the Fosdyck brothers with their lifebelts on appeared on the slipway. The engine stopped. We moved gently into shallow water. Our bow touched the bottom. The coble became still.

And then Marney emitted a triumphant grunt.

" How was that for a bit of surf-riding ? Well done, father. You couldn't have done it better if you'd trained at Honolulu. Now what about the lifeboat and making fools of us ? I bet old Luke there is wishing he'd saved his fireworks for next Gunpowder Plot night. Who's got a fag ? "

" Here, I have," said John. " If that damned sea we shipped hasn't spoiled the whole damned packet." He produced from his trousers pocket a packet of Woodbines. " Did you notice how that damned engine picked up when father said go ? I tell you there isn't a finer engine on the whole damned coast. Hallo. Here's our Steve."

The boy, easily recognisable as another member of the Lunn family, had halted, panting, on the scaur close by.

" Eh ! " he hailed. " They were just going to put the lifeboat off for you. Crew were getting their belts on. Mother says if you've got a nice cod you're to keep it for dinner. . . . Eh ! Marney ! " he hailed again.

" What's up ? " Marney demanded.

Steve grinned.

" Your Amy's on the slipway. She's been watching you come into the Landing. She says she's going to murder you for telling her lies. She says you've got to come straight up and change your clothes."

" You can tell her he'll do nowt of the sort," put in John indignantly. " There's the fish to clean and get away by the one train, and the cobles to haul up yet. She ought to have more sense."

" You tell her I'll be up in a few minutes," said Marney quietly. " Aye, and you can tell her something else." He suddenly held up the lobster. " Tell her to get this boiled for our tea. . . . Come on, father," he added briskly, as he got out of the boat. " Let's get the fish ashore. The Fosdycks are coming to haul up. We didn't do so bad after all. But we'd have done better if we'd waited a bit before we hauled."

Henry, unfastening his oilskin, turned his audacious eyes to the gale-swept roaring sea.

" Aye," he said quietly, " that Landing mouth's a nuisance. . . . How many fish did the Fosdycks get, Steve ? " he added, turning to the shore.

Steve grinned again.

" Five codling," he answered.

CHAPTER FOUR

" You know," said Marney philosophically, " lobsters, are paying things."

He twisted the big claws off the specimen we had caught that morning, moved over to the fireplace, and looked about for a suitable weapon.

Amy gave an indignant shout.

" Now you can leave the flat-iron alone. I don't want to spend half an hour cleaning it before I iron your shirts. Use the poker."

" Poker's no use," Marney protested. " What have you done with the hammer ? "

" You ought to know, you had it last. You never know where anything is. You're as daft as they make them."

" Shut up," said Marney, " or you won't get any lobster."

He seized the flat-iron, and cracked the claws on the hearth. On his way back to the table he held out the smaller of the claws towards the hands of his infant son, whom Amy was nursing.

" Eh ! " he said, " will you try a bit ? That will suit you better than milk. Let him try a bit, Amy. It won't do him any harm."

Amy quickly seized the claw and put it on her own plate.

" Sit down," she cried to Marney. " Giving lobster to a child only four months old ! You're not fit to be a father."

" Garn ! If he's going to be a fisherman, sooner he knows

what fish tastes like the better. You've been reading one
of those daft articles in the paper. I know how a kid ought
to be brought up."

" Then it's clear your mother didn't," Amy retorted,
" or she'd have brought you up on carrots. Sit down and
get your tea. I've had enough trouble with you for one
day. I haven't got over it yet, watching you come into
the Landing, and hearing that lifeboat gun. He'll not be a
fisherman, if I've got anything to say about it. I'd rather
he was a sweep."

Marney shared the big claw between us and sat
down. Amy poured out the tea with her disengaged
hand.

" They're paying things, are lobsters," Marney continued earnestly. " We started too late last year. We
didn't get the coble until the end of March, and by that
time prices had dropped. But those Burnharbour chaps
made tons of brass by starting early. It isn't very often
our John has anything brilliant to say, but he said it all
right this morning. Damned if I don't make a lobster-pot
to-night. I think there'll be a few hazels over in the
warehouse."

" You promised you were going to finish that mat for
me to-night," said Amy.

" There's plenty of time for that," Marney answered
brightly. " Can't you see I've got lobster fever ? We're
going to start in January, before even those Burnharbour
chaps make a start. We'll spring a surprise on them all.
If there's one lobster close in like that you can depend
upon it there'll be some more. With a bit of luck we might
clear the cost of all our gear the first week, and then have
something over. They're paying things, are lobsters."

" It tastes champion anyway," his wife conceded. " But

I wish you'd light the lamp, Marney. I'm sick of the sight of the sea to-day. Listen to it now. Isn't it awful ? "

The gale had blown with undiminished fury since its onset. A terrific sea was running. It was now high tide and the mountainous waves, breaking on the cliff immediately below the cottage, rattled the frosted window-panes like heavy gun-fire. Marney lighted the lamp. Before he pulled down the blind of the back window we had a last glimpse across the desolate gale-swept bay to Low Batts, now half-obscured by another driving hail-squall.

" I'd rather be here than out there now," Marney remarked with unusual quietness as he sat down again. " It's going to be a hell of a night. I've never known this spot seem so cosy."

I agreed. Even the roses seemed to exude some genuine cheering quality, and the polished oil-cloth on the floor gave a merry reflection of the flares of the fire. The lamp was on the table. It shone full on Amy's face, and on the child, now asleep at her breast. She came of a Burnharbour seafaring family of remote Scandinavian origin. Her skin was fair and very soft, with the faintest suggestion of a lingering sunburn in it. Her eyes were grey, with long black lashes, and they were set wide apart under a well-shaped, intelligent forehead. Her hair, which she wore bobbed, was brown, but its natural, irregular wave revealed a golden sheen where it caught the light. Her nose was straight, with very sensitive nostrils. She had magnificent teeth and full red lips which gave her a fascinating smile. She was vital and primitive, as Marney was. Their mating had been quick, and the child had sealed a bond between them which would endure the inevitable cooling of the intense passionate attraction they had for each other now.

D

"Give us another cup of tea, lass," said Marney. "Lobster fever makes you thirsty. There's plenty more lobster for any one who wants it. I'm going to have a cheese-cake. Cheese-cakes are about the only thing Amy makes that are worth eating. She's not half such a good cook as mother."

"Then you'd better stay and have your supper at home," Amy retorted. "I noticed all the jam-tarts had gone this morning, anyway," she added dryly. "I suppose you wanted those because you were going to the High Batts to get bait. I only wish they'd made you sea-sick, after telling me such a lie. I'll never believe you again, no matter what you say."

"Garn! A woman will always believe what she wants to believe. If I said you were the best-looking lass in Bramblewick, you'd believe it all right. Although you know there's dozens better looking."

"Then I can only hope they'll use their looks to pick up something more useful in the shape of a husband than I've done. . . . That's your third cheese-cake. It strikes me it's pastry fever you've got, not lobster fever."

"I'm going to make a lobster-pot to-night," said Marney solemnly; and to me, "We'll slip across to the warehouse. If I can't give our old man lobster fever I'll chuck fishing for ever."

When we stepped out, it was to find the street lamps lighted. Bramblewick's streets are too narrow to permit of lamp-posts. The lamps are fixed on iron brackets wherever there is a convenient projection of masonry. The flickering yellow glare of them made fantastic patterns of the uneven cottage walls, and was reflected on the cobbled paving, wet with the slowly melting hail from the shower that had just passed over. Chapel Street was deserted, but in the dock, standing in the storm shelter near the lifeboat-house, was Luke Fosdyck, staring stolidly towards the sea.

We did not pass near enough to speak, but he gave us a quick glance, and Marney muttered :

" He'd make good company at a wedding, wouldn't he ? I bet he'll not mention us in his prayers to-night after this morning's do."

I protested that Luke had only done his duty in summoning the lifeboat crew, and warning us back. Henry himself had admitted as much, after the Fosdycks had come down for the hauling of the boats. Luke had said gruffly :

" Seas were breaking right across the Landing. We reckoned you were blinded by that squall."

" We were, pretty well," Henry had said quietly. " But I've always thought it looks worse from ashore than it really is. I chanced it, anyway. I wouldn't have done it if I hadn't had an engine."

But Marney would have none of my protests.

" Garn ! " he said. " They just wanted to make fools of us, and set the whole place laughing at us. They'd have liked to have seen it put in the *Burnharbour Gazette*. ' BRAMBLEWICK LIFEBOAT LAUNCHED TO LOCAL FISHING-COBLE IN DISTRESS.' I know the Fosdycks, and so does father, only he's too polite to speak his mind. I bet Luke will have a blue fit when he hears we're starting lobstering in January. This is the time they ought to launch the lifeboat ! "

Henry lived on the south cliff, on the opposite side of the dock to Chapel Street, and we had to wait until the wash of a heavy sea had run down the slipway before we crossed. Even then, we had to wade ankle-deep through

the spume, which the wind was driving like snow, far up
the dock. The cobles had been hauled to their bad-weather
berths.

" A queer thing happened here one Sunday night last
March," Marney remarked, as we hurried up the lane
leading to the south cliff. " There was more sea than there
is now, and it was a spring tide. Father had come down
to have a last look at the coble, before he went to bed—
he'd got his best clothes, mind you. He saw a big sea come
right up the slipway. When it washed back he saw
something black moving about. It looked like a dog, and
he went up to it, and damned if it didn't turn round
savage, and try to take a piece of his hand. It was a young
seal ! "

We turned to our right, and sharply to our left again.
Marney continued :

" Well. Father's very tender-hearted, you know, and
can't bear killing things. Thinks he, ' It's come up to get
clear of the breakers. I'll get a sack and catch it and put
it in the warehouse until morning, and let it go again when
the tide's down.' He found a sack in the coble, and came
back. The seal was still there. It tried to go for him again.
barking like a dog. Thinks father, ' I'll drive it up the
dock, and then perhaps I'll get someone to give me a help.'
So he got behind it ; and he was so excited by then he'd
forgot there was a rough sea on. A damned big wave broke
clean over the breakwater, and landed on top of him, seal
and all. It knocked father flat on his belly, and the seal
landed him a hell of a smack across his face. Aye—and
when he got up again, the seal had gone. And so had
father's best Sunday hat ! "

We had reached a narrow flight of stone steps that
climbed to a more substantial cottage than Marney's,

standing just below the ridge of a grassy hill, where a low stone building commanded a view of the sea.

" We'll slip in and see mother first," Marney remarked as we approached the cottage. He opened the door, and we stepped into Henry Lunn's kitchen-parlour.

It was a fairly large room, with windows facing east and west. The south side of it was given over to the purely domestic activities of Mrs. Lunn. On the north side was a mahogany sideboard with an embroidered cloth and many vases, a bamboo whatnot table bearing a fine aspidistra, and a small American organ. If there was a wall-paper it was not obvious, for almost every square foot of wall was hidden by pictures, photographs, almanacks, framed certificates, testimonials, and such other objects as were of family interest, and of such a shape and size that they must hang, and not stand.

There was a duplicate of that famous picture of Grace Darling. There was an engraving of the equally famous ' Stag at Bay.' There were coloured pictures of John's and Marney's first steamboats, an enlarged photo of the *Lucy* (the deep-sea boat Henry had skippered during the war) : and there was a testimonial from a foreign government acknowledging his services in the rescue of the crew of a steamer sunk by a U-boat near Spurn Point.

A good oil-painting of old Marney Lunn (done by a summer visitor) took pride of place above the sideboard ; about which were photos of various members of the family at various stages of their development, from Marney as a baby in arms, to John in the uniform of a naval gunner, in which capacity on board a tramp steamer he had served with distinction for the last six months of the war.

But the most important side of the room was the kitchen side of it, the side which was exclusively mother's. The table was close up to the east and bigger of the two windows, within arm's-length of the capacious oven. Here, at one end, sat Eddy, George and Steve, having tea, while mother, with the cloth lifted from the other end, had already started washing up.

" Now, mother," was Marney's greeting.

" Now then," was mother's.

She did not look up from her task. She handled the pile of crocks with a speed and dexterity which reminded one of Marney shooting the lines. Obviously, he had inherited the most dominant traits in his character from her. She was very small, wiry, restlessly energetic. Even at a meal she seemed never to sit down for a longer space than a minute. And she spoke quickly too : fussily.

" Have you had your teas ? There's still a cup or two in the pot. Or I'll make you some fresh. There's some tarts only been out of the oven an hour. The lads have finished. Father and John have had their teas, too. They're up in the warehouse baiting. How's the bairn ? Did you——"

" We've had our teas," Marney broke in, reaching his hand across the table. " But I'll have just one tart to please you."

He took two.

" Here," he said to me. " Try one of mother's. She's not such a good cook as Amy by a long chalk, but she does her best, don't you, mother ? You'll have to come over some day and get a hint or two from Amy."

I saw just a suspicion of jealousy in mother's eyes, but she smiled good-humouredly.

" You always seem to have room for one of mine,

anyway," she answered : and in the same breath, " What
a going-on there was this morning. I nearly dropped a cup
out of my hand when the gun went off."

" Did you think we were all going to be drowned?"
asked Marney with a grin.

" I've got more sense," she answered readily. " If it's
good enough weather for the lifeboat to go out, it's good
enough for father to get in. You were just coming through
the Landing when I got to the top of the hill. It's blowing
hard now, isn't it ? I doubt if you'll get to sea to-morrow
if it keeps like this. . . . Now, Eddy and George," she
broke off, " if you've finished you can go and bring some
wood in from the coal-house."

Eddy and George, aged thirteen and eleven respectively,
got up and went out. They were rather quiet boys,
seeming to be shaping in the pattern of John. But Steve,
aged ten, had all of Marney's devilry in him, and his eyes
sparkled as Marney felt in his trousers pockets and
produced three cigarette cards, and a crumpled and rather
tarry packet of sweets.

" You're spoiling that lad, always bringing him sweets,"
mother protested ; and to Steve, " Mind you give some to
Eddy and George."

" All right, mother," Steve replied with an ironic grin.
" They'll take them if I don't." He looked critically at
the cards. " Eh—I've got these two, Marney. I've got
four of this one."

" Then you can swap them," said Marney sharply. " I
can't tell what picture's going to be inside a packet of fags
when I buy it. You've got to take what comes. . . . Well
—so-long, mother. We'll go and see what father and
John's up to. They never get anything done unless I'm
there to boss them up."

We stepped out of the cottage, and climbed to the warehouse on the hill crest. Another hail-squall was blowing over, and it was as much as we could do to keep upright against the wind while Marney felt for the latch of the door.

The warehouse was really an old cottage with its two lower rooms knocked into one, and the upper storey made into a loft reached by a ladder. As we entered my nostrils were assailed by the scent of tarry rope mingled with wood smoke. The place was lighted by two hurricane lamps, swung from the rafters. A wood fire burnt on the ancient open hearth, near which was an immense iron cauldron, used for cutching lines and other gear. Nell, a mongrel greyhound bitch which had shared the family fortunes for the past ten years, got up leisurely from a pile of old sacking in front of the fire, came forward, and licked Marney's hand. Henry and John were standing at a bench under one of the lamps re-baiting the lines we had used that morning. Henry turned, and smiled. John did not look up from his task. He seemed more than usually gloomy.

" Well, I'm damned ! " was Marney's first remark. " Haven't you got your lines baited yet ? I've had mine done two hours. Here," he said to John, " you go and see if there are any hazels in the loft. I'll finish that job for you."

" You mind your own business," John growled. " You're always interfering. I can bait a line as well as you."

" Listen to Sunny Jim ! " Marney mocked. " You ought to be down in front of the lifeboat-house with old Luke Fosdyck. You'd make a good pair. What's up now ? "

John left off to take a piece of paper from his pocket. He thrust it out to his brother to read.

" Have a look at that. Then, perhaps, you'll not be so cheerful. I tell you fish isn't worth sending away. It's not worth catching. And there's carriage on top of that."

Marney certainly did look less cheerful for a moment. It was a telegram from the Burnharbour fish salesman to whom the morning's catch had been sent.

" Three bob a stone ! " he exclaimed. " That's the lowest we've had this year. I'd have taken an oath it would have brought five. We'll send the next lot to London."

" What if we do ? " John growled. " We'll do no better. I wish I'd never started fishing at all. I'd be a damned sight better off as a sailor."

" Garn ! " said Marney quickly. " You'd no sooner be on a ship than you'd be wishing you were home. You used to talk about nothing else but how you wished you were back at Bramblewick with a motor-coble. What about that night off Cape Race, when all the boats were smashed and the foc's'le was flooded ? "

" Well, what about it ? " John retorted. " It wasn't always like that, was it ? What about Miami and Montreal and Rio ? We had a good enough time there. And you did have a bit of brass to throw about."

Henry was watching his two sons out of the tail of his eye, but he did not make any contribution to the argument. Immediately after the war, the deep-sea boat he had skippered had been sold : his mates had taken berths in drifters, and, with old Marney too old for fishing, he had been obliged to take a shore job at Bramblewick. He had hated that job. I had seen him, on an evening, standing on the cliff edge, staring dejectedly out to sea, and I had known that his hands were itching for the kick of a coble's tiller. I often wondered to what extent the knowledge of their father's unhappiness had influenced John and Marney in giving up the Mercantile Marine. They were both splendid sailors. While they had been together on several voyages they had both held bos'uns' berths on big tramp steamers, and neither would have had much difficulty in obtaining officers' certificates. I knew that Henry himself would not have directly influenced them in their choice. But I was aware that he was sensitive on the point, and I thought that Marney was aware of this too. He was the unfailing champion of ' fishing ' against ' sea.'

" Garn ! " he said. " The sea's all right for those who like it, but you don't, brother John—so you needn't argue. You were always complaining when I sailed with you, fair weather or foul. What about that time you gave a chap in Miami five quid for a gold watch, and when you got back on board discovered he'd wrapped you up a Woolworth watch instead ? I've told you what's wrong with you. You ought to get wed. You'll never be happy until you do. If you don't find yourself a wife soon, damned if I won't find one for you. It strikes me you've got it into your head you're the Prince of Wales ! "

John at last grinned, and stopped his job to light a cigarette from Marney's.

" When I want to get married," he said, " I'll get married. And I'll not want your advice or anybody else's."

John, as a matter of fact, held very positive views on the subject of matrimony. It was a very serious step to take, in his opinion. A chap ought to set about it same

way as he would getting a new coble : and you wouldn't
buy a coble just because she had a nice coat of paint on
her, and dazzled your eye. You wanted something you
could depend upon in all weathers. You didn't want to
find out, when you'd paid for her, she wouldn't sail into
the wind, or that her engine wouldn't pull when her nose
was down. A wife's first place was in the home. To hell
with all these modern ideas about a woman being the
equal of a man ! John's wife would know who was boss
from the start. . . . Give and take, of course. But a
woman these days should be glad to get the chance of
having a man to look after. This fortunate female of
John's choice was to be good-looking, but not flashy :
strong, healthy, a good cook and housewife, fond of music,
but not wanting to be dashing off to the Burnharbour
pictures every Saturday night ; and, it went without
saying, faithful. But he had confided in me once his
rather bitter conviction that he had met only one woman
who ' fitted the bill,' and that was his own mother.

The subject of John's matrimonial future had dropped,
however, and with it the more dangerous subject of
' fishing ' versus ' sea.' Marney had climbed the ladder
into the loft. Suddenly a number of short planks and a
bundle of hazel sticks came clattering on to the floor.
Marney came down again, picked up a couple of planks,
and moved towards the fire. He winked at me, and said
in an undertone :

" Now, you watch. I'm going to give father lobster
fever in ten minutes."

" Where's the hammer, father ? " he said aloud, to
Henry's back.

" How do I know ? " Henry answered. " John had it
last."

" No, I hadn't," said John. " You had it fastening up the fish."

" You had it after that, nailing on the label."

" I nailed it on with a marline-spike. I couldn't find the hammer. You can't find anything in this menagerie when it's wanted."

It was a family failing, this mislaying of vital tools, but Marney had a compensating gift of improvisation. He rummaged among a heap of gear in one corner of the warehouse, and produced a rusty saw, and a long iron bolt. With a fish-box for a bench, he set to work sawing the plank into strips about two feet long, and three inches wide.

" What are you at ? " said Henry suddenly.

" I'm making a chicken coop," Marney answered. " I'm going to start keeping hens. They're paying things, are hens, aren't they, John ?—if only you can make 'em lay eggs. You get on with your baiting, and don't bother about me."

" I know what he's at," said John wisely. " It's that lobster that's done it. He's going to show us all how to make a lobster-pot."

" Then you'd best leave off what you're doing and come and take a hint or two," Marney said dryly. " If we have any more pots like those you made last year, there'll not be a lobster left anywhere. They'll all be frightened away. Now, father did know how to make a decent pot when we were kids. But I think he must have forgotten how with being ashore all that time. Those he made last year weren't up to much. They didn't fish as well as mine."

He had laid the cut planks on top of the box in the shape of a rectangular, gridded frame, and was now preparing to nail them together. I noticed that father was working quicker at his line, which was nearly finished.

" Aye. And who taught you how to make a pot ? " he said, without turning round.

" You did," Marney admitted ; and between blows of the hammer, " But that's not saying anything. Everyone's got to learn. You made your pots too big. We want smaller pots if we're going to work a lot of them. They're paying things, lobsters. They're the best paying fish there is. I'm going to make this pot an inch smaller every way than last year's."

" You might make a better pot than me," said Henry, " but you've never made one yet as good as grandad's."

" Did you hear that ? " Marney cried, with pretended indignation. " Do you remember, when we were kids, how him and grandfather used to argue about their pots ? Father was always telling him his were no good."

" Yes. I heard," said John, non-committally. " I heard all right."

The frame was almost completed. Henry had finished his line, and was fastening the covering of the ' skep.' John had only about thirty hooks to do. Marney hammered in the last nail, and stood up.

" There used to be a brace and bit knocking about this spot," he said. " Any one know where it is ? "

" I haven't seen it for weeks," said father.

" Last I saw of it, Steve had it," said John. " He was making a scooter with a pair of old perambulator wheels he'd found on the beach."

" Then you can buy a new one next time you go to Burnharbour," Marney said philosophically. " He borrowed my knife for the same job, and I've used it for a saw ever since."

" Why didn't you take it away from him ? " father demanded of John.

" If I had, I'd have found a handful of tin-tacks in my sea-boots next time I had to put them on in a hurry. It was Steve who put that live crab in my bed. He wants a damned good hiding from somebody, that kid. If I'd acted like that when I was his age, I'd have got it all right."

" You leave Steve alone," championed Marney. " He only put that crab in your bed because you broke his mouth-organ. You were lucky it wasn't a lobster. Never mind the brace," he added, thrusting one end of his improvised hammer into the fire. "This will do better, and it won't split the wood."

Henry wiped his hands on a piece of sacking, came over to the fire and sat down on a capsized bucket. He picked up the lobster-pot ' bottom ' and eyed it critically.

" It's not a bad idea," he said, " making them a shade smaller. And we ought to make them with a flatter top so that they'll stow better in the coble, when we're shifting ground. Here ! Give me one of those hazels. I'll show you what I mean."

Marney quickly snatched the ' bottom ' away.

" You leave it alone. You can just sit still and see how a pot should be made for once. I've heard you say many a time that a chap's never too old to learn. And John had better watch, too."

Henry grinned. He had an intense respect for Marney, and this constant leg-pulling rarely ruffled his good humour. He took a paper bag of sweets from his pocket and handed them round. Sweets of the stickiest kind were his only vice. He did not smoke or drink. By this time the end of the iron bolt was red-hot. Marney made the first of the six holes which were to hold the ends of the bent hazels to the 'bottom.' Henry watched with ever-increasing interest. John, however, his line finished, had gone out.

"I don't care what any one says," Henry remarked, without, however, taking his eyes from the pot. "No one ever made a pot as good as grandad. Aye—and no one could catch lobsters like he could, or any other sort of fish; except salmon maybe, and that's only because he never troubled with salmon. I've known him come in with six score of lobsters when the other cobles hadn't a score among them. And mind, he was always trying new ways of doing things, and fishing where other men never thought of fishing."

"They used to call him 'Any Weather Lunn,'" put in Marney with a quiet family pride.

"Aye. He was afraid of nowt," father continued. "The first time he went off really fishing, he wasn't older than Steve. He'd been begging his father to let him go for a long time before that, but his mother wouldn't agree. They were long-lining then, his father and his uncle, and a big chap called Ned Sayers, who weighed about sixteen stone, and was as clumsy as a cart-horse. Well, they were leaving their lines all night then, in deep water, and to catch the market they had to go off about three o'clock in the morning. There's no slipway at Sledburgh. The cobles are hauled up on the beach, and they push 'em down, and jump in the last moment. Grandad, being little, got in before they launched. It was dark, mind you, and it was freezing hard, one of the coldest spells there's ever been on this coast. He was sitting in the stern. They got the coble moving; she touched the water, father and uncle jumped in first, and then came Ned, and down went his sea-boot, with great hob-nails on it, right on grandad's bare hand, that was laid on the thwart."

" He's got the marks yet," said Marney, taking the bolt from the fire again.

" Two bones in his hand were broken," Henry continued, " and that wasn't all. The next thing that clumsy devil did was to tread on the boat-hook, and its sharp end jumped up and caught grandad a nasty cut just over his eye. He had so much pain, he must have nearly fainted. But he didn't cry out. He knew if he told them, they'd go back, and that would mean missing the market, and, anyway, he didn't want to be robbed of his first real fishing trip. So he kept his mouth shut, and it was too dark for them to see what had happened. It was his eye that troubled him most. It bled so much. But it was freezing so hard that the blood froze, and his hand went so numb he lost all feeling in it. It was daybreak when they found out. There were blood icicles hanging from the end of his nose and chin, and a lump of frozen blood lying like a brooch on his guernsey. But by that time they'd got their lines hauled. . . . Now don't go and make those holes too big."

" I'm not making them too big," Marney protested. " Those hazels are thick. They're too thick. When we go and get some more we'll only cut thin ones. If it's bad weather to-morrow I think I'll have a walk up to Brewster Wood, and cut a bundle. And there ought to be some wood washed up, with this sea."

" What's the idea ? " said father suddenly. " We're not going to start lobstering before the end of February, and not then unless it comes extra fine weather."

Marney returned the bolt to the fire.

" It's a queer thing," he said with quiet sarcasm, " how

different father is from grandad. Did you hear him say just now how grandad was always trying new ways of doing things. Now, I reckon father's just about as old-fashioned as the Fosdycks."

" Old-fashioned—me old-fashioned ? " father cried hotly. " It's the first I've heard of it ! "

" Now you needn't get your shirt out," said Marney smoothly. " You know I'm only speaking the truth. It's an old-fashioned idea that lobster fishing at Bramblewick begins first week in March. It was the same at Burn-harbour until last year. And look what happened. Those chaps made hundreds of pounds."

" Burnharbour's not Bramblewick," father protested. They've got a harbour. And those chaps are using big boats. They can get in and out when they like. We've got that Landing bar to think about. Look at to-day ! "

" Well, look at to-day," Marney retorted. " We caught a lobster, and I had some of it for my tea. And we caught some cod, and they brought three bob a stone, less carriage : and John's talking about going back to sea again, he's so fed up. I say, same as John, we ought to start making pots now, and start fishing in the middle of January."

" Aye—and lose every pot you've made straight away!"

Marney, as he took the bolt from the fire again, gave me a wink.

" To hear him talk, you wouldn't think father nearly broke the heart of the British Navy during the war, by fishing every night among the mine-fields. You wouldn't think he was the chap the Germans put on their black list, with orders to their North Sea U-boats to sink the *Lucy* at sight. And there he is, afraid of losing a few lobster-pots, afraid of dropping his old-fashioned ideas."

E

" There's some old-fashioned ideas have sense in them,"
Henry answered, quite calm again. " I reckon that
lobster-pots are worth at least eight shillings apiece and
you've got to think twice before you chuck that away. A
hundred pots are worth at least thirty pounds with the
rest of the gear."

" And what's that if you can make a hundred quid in a
week with starting early ? "

" There's always two sides to every argument," father
admitted thoughtfully, putting another sweet in his mouth.
" But we'll not start until the middle of February, and not
then unless the weather's a miracle. January is a worse
month than November in this spot."

The remaining holes in the pot ' bottom ' were completed in silence. Marney had an instinct for knowing how
far he could carry an argument with his father without
starting to lose ground. He put the ' bottom ' on the table
again. There was a hole at each corner, and one at each
side, in the middle. He took one of the hazels, cut a piece
about a yard in length, and bent it carefully into a U.
Then he forced its end into opposite holes, and fitted two
more similar U's ; so that the pot took shape as the
skeleton of a miniature house, two feet long, a foot and a
half wide, and a foot in height.

Working with his customary dexterity, he nailed on a
thinner straight hazel to make the ridge of the ' roof,' and
another straight hazel at each side for the ' eaves.' He
held up the completed framework for his father's
inspection.

Henry made no comment, however. He got up,
rummaged for a minute in another corner of the warehouse, and produced a ball of twine, and a wood netting-
' needle.' He sat down and began to fill the needle with

twine. Meanwhile, Marney took a piece of twine from his pocket, and stretched it from leg to leg of the hazels, close down to the ' bottom,' to form a holding for the net.

" Keep the meshes middling big," said father at last, handing over the needle.

" Who's giving the lesson, me or you ? " Marney demanded. " I know how big they ought to be."

He sat down on the box, put the pot on end between his knees, and began the netting. Once he had got it started, the needle flashed so quickly one could scarcely see it. The net began to grow from the bottom of one end of the pot upwards to the roof, leaving the sides bare.

" He's not a bad hand with a needle," said Henry. " My fingers have got too stiff."

" Garn ! " said Marney. " You're naturally slow, like our John. You don't give your mind to it."

Marney did not look up from his task. We watched him in silence, as though hypnotised by that flashing needle : until suddenly the warehouse door was opened, letting in the full sound of the sea and the wind, and a puff of smoke blew furiously from the fireplace. It was John, washed and in a clean guernsey, and carrying a concertina under his arm.

" God ! It's fit to blow a house down outside," he said, dragging another fish-box towards the fire. " I've just been talking to the carrier. He says there's been a hell of a do at Burnharbour this morning. A motor-coble's been smashed up. The *Esmeralda*. Tommy Long and his two brothers, just south of the pier. They just missed being drowned. A sea washed 'em up on to the scaur."

" The *Esmeralda* ? " echoed Marney, without pausing from his task. " Why, that's a brand-new boat."

" Aye. And they hadn't got her insured either. They've lost everything ; about seventy-five quid's worth of gear and a fine lot of fish."

" It's very bad luck for them," said Henry slowly. " Real bad luck. They're all three very decent chaps, are the Longs. I'm sorry for them."

" It was another brother of Tommy's that was drowned only two years ago, salmoning, wasn't it ? " asked Marney.

" Aye," Henry answered, " while you chaps were away at sea. He was drowned a mile south of Kettlenab, and his body washed up right in the harbour, not more than a hundred yards from where he lived. It was a queer thing that. It looks almost as though he had been trying to get home for burial."

No one spoke for a moment or two. Then Marney said rather thoughtfully :

" Is it eight days or ten days before a body floats in salt water ? "

" Ten," said Henry. " When your uncle Joe was drowned at Sledburgh, he was up ten days to an hour almost. I'm sorry for Tommy Long, losing his boat. Was the lifeboat out ? "

" Aye. But it had to go north to help two cobles in," John answered. " It beats me," he added, with a touch of his usual gloom. " All this bad weather, and us only getting three bob for those cod."

John unfastened the catch of his concertina.

" You're making that pot damned small," he commented.

Marney did not answer. John struck a chord, and then smiled broadly as he observed his father's concentration.

" Lobster fever, eh ? " he said ironically.

" You're making those meshes a bit too small," said Henry, likewise ignoring his eldest son. " You're using twice as much twine as you need."

John winked at me, and began to play a popular song. John was never really gloomy when he had a musical instrument in his hands. He played with considerable skill. Marney by this time had netted one end of the pot, and was going along the roof.

" If you've got nothing better than that muck to play," said Henry suddenly, " you'd better give me hold of it, and start making a pot."

John stopped.

" It's clear you've got lobster fever. Why don't you make a pot ? What do you want ? ' Abide with Me ' ? "

" It would be better than that muck," father replied, glancing round at the remains of the planks and hazels. " There'll not be enough wood left, or I would."

" We're going to start making pots in earnest to-morrow," put in Marney. " Father's just about agreed we should make a start fishing, first fine spell after Christmas."

" I haven't agreed anything of the sort ! "

" Garn ! You will do by to-morrow when you've slept on it."

" It's a damned good idea," said John. " No one would have thought of it, if it hadn't been for me ! "

" You ? " said Marney. " You were just talking about going back to sea ! "

" I'll not go if I can make more brass ashore," John answered.

He began to play " Abide with Me." Nell lifted her eyes soulfully, made a faint howl, then closed her eyes again. He played " Rock of Ages," and " Jerusalem the Golden," and two of Moody and Sankey's fervently mournful compositions, and by then Marney had completed both ends and the ' roof ' of the pot, and was putting a row of . ' starting ' hitches on the square left half of one side.

John put his instrument down, and became intent upon the pot. From the ' starting ' row a funnel of netting began to shape. This was one of the two ' spouts,' the most intricate and important part of the whole apparatus.

" There's one thing certain," Henry remarked, " and it doesn't matter whether me or grandad or Marney is the best hand at pot-making. There isn't a finer pot for catching lobsters than our sort. I don't know who invented it. I believe it never was invented. It sort of grew from one pattern to another, until it naturally got to be the best. I know that grandad was the first to bring it to Bramblewick. It will catch ten times as many lobsters as those the Fosdycks use."

The ordinary Bramblewick pot whose design had not varied since the earliest records was larger than the one Marney was making ; and it had four hazels (or ' bows ') as against Marney's three. In his the ' spouts ' led in on diagonally opposite sides, and the bait would be suspended from a string in the middle. In the Bramblewick type the spouts were directly opposite each other and were joined at their inner openings, making one hole, leading down-wards. Two baits were used.

" Their pots will catch more crabs than ours," said John. " You've got to allow that."

" Only because they've got two baits," said Marney quickly. " If you were a crab, and you came across two pots, one with one lump of fish, and the other with two, it stands to reason you'd go where there was most to eat : that is if there was a big crowd of you, and you were all

famished with hunger. But there never is a big crowd of
lobsters. One bait's as good as a dozen for a lobster, or
for four lobsters. They're not so greedy as crabs. And a
lobster likes to get his food quickly, or he'll not trouble
with it at all. Getting into one of the Fosdycks' pots
makes them so bewildered that they give it up as a bad
job. They'd as soon chew a lump of seaweed ! "

Marney put the last row of meshes on the spout, pulled
its orifice into the pot, and stretching it towards the
opposite side, made it fast. He began the other spout. In
ten minutes it was completed. There remained two
diagonally opposite spaces in the sides. These he covered
with ordinary netting from the bottom to the ' eaves ' of
the roof, and the last row of meshes went on to a short
stick. Knotted to the ' eave,' that stick stretched its
net, and closed the space. Unknotted, it fell down,
making an ingenious door, for baiting, and the removal
of the catch. There remained only the bait-string, a
double cord tied from the roof top at the centre, vertically
to the base. Marney placed the completed pot on the
fish-box, then stood back, like an artist from a canvas, and
surveyed it critically.

It was beautiful, as most things made by primitive man
for a primitive purpose are beautiful. It satisfied one, like
an entirely successful architecture. One felt that the
relation of the base to the bows, the curve of the bows, the
arrangement of the lateral stays, had been conceived and
made with an exact knowledge of the material and the
conditions of service to which the apparatus would be
submitted. The netting was beautiful ; the meshes were
as regular as the scales of a fish. There was beauty in the
various knots, each tied for an exact purpose, for which
no other knot could serve as well.

Yet Marney, the artist creator of it, did not look pleased. Suddenly he seemed subdued.

" It's a queer thing," he said quietly, as he lighted a cigarette. " It's a very queer thing. I've never made a pot exactly as I wanted it. There's always something about it I don't like."

" What's up with it ? " said John. " I can't see anything wrong with it."

" You wouldn't," said Marney laconically.

" Only fault I can find is that the meshes are a bit small," said father. " Twine's expensive stuff. Apart from that it's as nice a little pot as I've ever seen."

Marney gave a contemptuous grunt.

" It's a mess," he said. " I wish there was enough stuff to make another. If I can't do better than that I'd better join the Fosdycks."

There was a pause, during which we all contemplated the lobster-pot. Then Henry remarked quietly :

" Have any of you been up in Brewster Wood lately ? "

" I have," said Marney. " I was up there with Nell only last Friday. She got a rabbit."

" Did you notice if there were many hazels ? "

" Any amount. Enough to make a couple of hundred pots. I'm going there to-morrow if the sea's still rough."

" Then I think I'll have a walk on to High Batts and see if there's any planks washed up. You'd best come with me, John."

John laughed.

" You haven't got lobster fever, have you ? " he asked ironically. " Oh, no ! I thought we were going to tar the little boat, if it was too rough to go off."

" Give me that concertina, and don't have so much to say," father answered.

Henry took the concertina, and with his eyes still on the lobster-pot, played *pianissimo* the opening bars of " Abide with Me." Then, chapel fashion, he stopped and started again, singing the air in a very pleasant baritone. John joined in the bass. Marney contributed a rather husky, but musical tenor.

Another squall was passing over : the hail pelted on the tiles ; the gale howled fiercely in the cavernous chimney ; the sound of the sea was louder now that the tide ebbed, baring the scaur-ends.

Henry played slower than John had done. They sang with a religious fervour : but the plaintive sensuous harmonies of that hymn, attuned with the sounds of the storm, were as remote from chapel religion as the clear song of a lark is remote from a city slum. The lamps hung high and behind. The red light from the fiercely glowing fire shone full on their faces and on the lobster-pot which stood between them like a symbolic effigy of pagan worship.

Thus, I thought, those audacious sea-robbers who were the forebears of this family of fishermen had gathered round their fires of driftwood on the shores of this same treacherous coast, a thousand years ago ; bragging of their exploits, of their prowess in fighting and hunting and fishing ; talking of weapons and boats and gear ; of winds and currents and reefs ; chanting invocations to their fierce gods.

Not once, while he and his two sons sang through three verses of that hymn, did Henry Lunn take his eyes from the lobster-pot which Marney had made. And when he stopped playing he was still staring at it.

" I wonder what the Fosdycks will say if we start lobstering in January," he said thoughtfully.

" Never mind the Fosdycks," Marney answered. " Let's have ' Lead Kindly Light,' before we go and get our suppers. It's the finest hymn there is. What do you say, brother John ? "

" No," said John. " Give me ' Eternal Father.' It's got a champion bass."

CHAPTER FIVE

IT was Friday in the last week in January, and the fourth day of a phenomenal spell of fine weather. The wind, at its strongest not more than a light breeze, had blown consistently off the land. For four days the sun had risen from a dead calm sea into a sky as pellucid as the sky in midsummer. Even the sea air had been warm and dry. That wind, starting to blow gently an hour after dawn, had the savour of earth and grass and trees in it. The pastures sweeping down from the moor edge into Bramble-wick Dale were tinted with a new green ; and on the dark hills themselves, patches of old bracken gleamed, as though the gorse bloom was out in the full power of spring.

We had fished every day. We had tried the Low Batts ' shoot ' again. We had tried the scaur-ends of the bay itself. We had ' shot ' along the foot of High Batts, and this morning we had ' steamed ' due east to a ground called The Chimneys, given the lines an hour, and what we had caught had not brought the total catch for the week to more than a dozen stones. The cod had gone. The haddock had gone before, as John remarked gloomily. " the damned things had ever come " ; and the odd skate and ling, and whiting (also, as John remarked) " were not worth the nails to pack them up ! "

It had been a depressing week. We had finished the last lobster-pot on the previous Saturday, the climax to an effort which had occupied every hour of our non-fishing time since the first onset of lobster fever. Counting four relics from last season which had been repaired, there were one hundred and twenty pots in all. On Saturday afternoon we had carried ninety of them to a space alongside the lifeboat-house, lashed in each pot a quantity of iron ballast, and stacked them. And since Saturday I had not heard one of the Lunns mention the words lobster, or lobster-pot, or lobster fever.

Even Marney's high spirits seem to have evaporated during the last two days, at least when in the company of his father and John. In the boat, shooting and hauling had been carried out in almost complete silence. Father's orders were curt, monosyllabic. John's face had worn a perpetual look of gloom. Father, we had discovered to-day, had toothache : yet this obviously did not completely account for his depression.

I met Marney at the bottom of Chapel Street shortly after dinner. We were to bait his lines, but a bag of mussels, which had been ordered from Burnharbour, had not arrived yet, and we sauntered down the slipway on to the beach. The whole bay was dead calm ; and despite its low winter altitude, the sun had an inspiring warmth. We walked in silence under the wall of the old coastguard station, which forms the southern bulwark of the village, until we reached the foot of the low clay cliff surmounted by the Lunns' warehouse. Here we descried Henry, standing just outside the shed door, with his hands thrust in his pockets, looking across the bay. We stopped and watched him. He did not move, but he did not appear to be really intent upon that seaward prospect. His whole attitude suggested a profound mental preoccupation.

Marney suddenly gave a grunt of disgust.

" I get fed up with our old man when he gets into one of these damned moods of his," he said. " You don't know

what to make of him. Grandad used to be the same. He'd
go for days, and you'd scarcely get him to open his
mouth."

" I know he's got toothache," Marney pursued. " But
that's no reason why he shouldn't decide where the fish
are to be sent. They've missed the one-o'clock train as it
is. If I had a tooth that was giving me hell, I'd go and
have it out. But father's never been to a doctor in his life,
and he swears he never will. And there's the fish packed,
and he won't say if it's to go to Burnharbour or London,
or anything."

We continued to watch him. He did not move.

" I can't stand people who can't make up their minds,"
Marney went on. " If you don't want to do a thing, say
so, that's my motto ; and if you *do* want to do it, then let
folks know. And it isn't as though we don't know what
he's thinking about ! "

Marney suddenly turned seawards.

" Look at it ! Look at it ! " he cried disgustedly. " Ideal
lobster weather. Those pots ought to have been taken out
to deep water on Saturday afternoon. Then they'd have
been water-logged, and ready to bring close in on Monday.
We'd have earned fifty quid at least, by now. And there
you are. He's got it into his head we're going to lose them,
and yet he can't help thinking what we're missing by
keeping them ashore. He won't say where the fish are to
be sent in case he decides not to send them at all but cut
'em up for bait."

Marney was silent for a time. Then he said suddenly :

" Come on ; we'll go up, and see if we can't make him
speak one way or another."

We retraced our footsteps to the dock, but instead of
turning directly up the cliff lane, we carried on towards

the lifeboat-house, where old Isaac stood contemplating our pile of lobster-pots. His cats were disporting themselves in the sunshine on top of an upturned boat close by.

He greeted us with his familiar ironic chuckle.

" Now then," he said, " I see you've got your pots all ready."

" Aye," said Marney, slightly on the defensive. " Have you got any fault to find with them ? "

Isaac chuckled.

" They're all right. I say they're all right, so long as you've got them, but they're not much good when they're gone. I made thirty pots last summer, and I lost the lot the first time I took 'em to sea, before they'd even caught a crab. And you'll do the same if you start fishing this time of year. Winter hasn't started. There is plenty of bad weather to come before it's any use for lobsters."

" Don't talk so daft ! " said Marney, looking at the pots with something like a return to his high spirits. " Nothing venture, nothing win. You ought to know the truth of that, years you've been at sea. You should look on the bright side of things and not be so doleful. Did you get that codling I put in the coble stern for you ? "

" Aye, I did. And I was very pleased to get it. I made it into a fish pie with some tatties, and I had it for my dinner."

" They say Isaac's as good a cook as any woman in Bramblewick," Marney remarked.

Isaac gave a self-deprecating shake of his head.

" I'm no good at anything fancy : but I'll make a fish pie, or a suet dumpling, with any of them. I used to make a dumpling twice a day for my cousin, Joe Fosdyck, when he was skipper of the *Nancy Price*. And that's why he never stopped ashore long. His missus used to make 'em

as thick as cement, and poison his inside. Joe couldn't
live without his dumplings."

"Now I bet you'd be only too glad to have someone to
make dumplings for you, instead of always fending for
yourself," said Marney, expressing a long-held theory.

"Would I—would I?" Isaac promptly answered.
"Not while I've strength enough to get myself out of bed.
And when I haven't, I'd as soon be dead."

Marney had opened the door of one of the pots, and
was making an adjustment to the bait-string.

"One of John's pots," he remarked dryly; and turning
to Isaac again, "What do you make of the weather? Is
it going to blow another gale?"

"It as likely will as not," Isaac answered readily.
enough to be a blizzard before the week's out."

We left him, and made our way to the south cliff.
Marney was silent and thoughtful again. Henry had
moved from that look-out place of his; and as we drew
near the cottage, he suddenly appeared at the doorway,
holding a hand to his cheek, and with an expression black
as thunder.

"Where have you put the pincers?" he shouted,
catching sight of Marney.

"I don't know. Aren't they in the warehouse?"

"No. They're not in the warehouse. There's never
anything to be found in this place when it's wanted. Look
and see if you can find them."

"What do you want them for?"

"Never mind what I want them for," father retorted
hotly. "Find the damned things."

For a moment Marney seemed nonplussed. Then
suddenly he dived into the coal-house, reached to a dusty
ledge under the tiles, and produced in relays two very

tattered ' blood-and-thunders,' a ball of new string, some
hooks, a mouth-organ, the long-lost brace and bit, and a
very rusty pair of pliers.

" That's Steve's magpie's nest," he remarked to me
sotto voce. " He'll play hell with me if he finds out I've
robbed it."

He thrust the ' blood-and-thunders ' into his pocket and
handed the pliers to his father.

" What are you going to do with them ? " he repeated.

A horrible suspicion of father's purpose had already
crossed my mind. He ignored Marney's question and
turned and walked quickly to the warehouse, which he
entered. He banged the door behind him.

" God Almighty ! " said Marney under his breath. " Not
those things !"

We stood, staring in silence at the door of the warehouse as if indeed it had been the execution house in a
gaol, and we had just witnessed the entry of a sombre
procession ; as though in a moment we would witness the
hoisting of the black flag. And then, to our unspeakable
relief, the door was opened and father appeared holding
the pliers in his hand, smiling benignly.

" I've done it ! " he cried triumphantly. " It came out
as easy as a tin-tack. I wish I'd known. I wish I'd
known ! That thing has been giving me hell off and on
ever since Christmas, when I broke it cracking a nut. I
haven't had a wink of sleep with it the last two nights.
And coming out as easy as that ! Have a look at it ! "

Not altogether to my surprise, Marney's face had gone
very pale.

" I don't want to see the damned thing ! " he muttered.
" Chuck it away. What about that fish ? Have we to
label it to Burnharbour or London ? "

Father, reluctantly it seemed, disposed of his trophy, then he came out into the sunshine, and stood where we had seen him standing before. But there was no dejection in his manner now.

" Fancy it coming out as easy as that ! " he said, without, however, taking his eyes from the sea. " I'd scarcely got a fair hold of it. And I nearly went out of my head this morning with pain, while we were at sea."

" For God's sake, shut up about it," Marney protested. " You've nearly made me sick as it is. What about the fish ? Can't you say, one way or another ? "

For several minutes Henry did not speak, but continued to stare across the tranquil bay. Then very quietly he said :

" We'll lose them. We'll lose them for certain."

" Not if we put them out in deep water on the mud," said Marney quickly. " They'll be as safe as houses, no matter what sort of weather comes. The glass is steady. There's no sign of the weather breaking yet. Even old Isaac wouldn't promise a change. If we'd got them soaked we could have been fishing all day to-day. We'd have got a hundred lobsters easily, and they'd fetch at least three bob apiece."

" I know all about that," father remarked.

" Then if you do, say the word, and let's get away now. They'll fill with crabs to-night, and crabs will be worth catching, too. We can run them close in to-morrow, and take them back to the mud before night. Shall I start cutting the fish up ? "

Again there was silence. Then Henry slowly turned.

" I don't fancy it," he said. " It will be against my judgment if we go. We've got very little ballast in those pots, scarcely enough to sink them until they get soaked.

F

If it comes on bad weather before they get water-logged they'll move for a certainty. . . . Where's John ? "

" He won't be far off," said Marney ; and, sticking relentlessly to his argument : " You don't need John to make up your mind for you. What is it to be—yes or no ? You're boss, you know ! "

Henry smiled dryly.

" Oh—am I ? " he said. " Only when there's someone to blame, I reckon. Well, don't blame me this time. Thirty quid's worth of gear, remember ! The Fosdycks will have something to laugh at us for, if we lose it all. . . . Go and find John," he added with sudden alacrity. " We'll want both boats. You two can take one lot in the *Emma*. Me and John will take the rest in the coble, and tow you out. If only I'd known that tooth would have come out like that ! "

I had seen Marney do a job quickly, but never had I seen him move as he did from that moment. He did not speak. He opened the warehouse door, seized an armful of coiled ropes (these were technically the ' tows ') and pointed to another coil for me to carry. We took them down to the breakwater, and placed them alongside the coble, where the box of fish lay under a sack. Marney wrenched the lid off with the engine spanner. John suddenly appeared ; but Marney anticipated his question.

" Get your sea-boots on," he said, without looking up. " There's still some more ' tows,' and the buoys and anchors to fetch down. Get hold of Eddy. We'll have to carry the pots to the slipway bottom. Tide will be nearly up by the time we're ready. Get a move on. We'll cut the fish up."

John did not move.

" You're in a mighty hurry," he said, with all his old

cautiousness asserting itself. " When's all this happened ?
Last time I saw father he nearly bit my head off. What's
happened ? "

" Never mind what's happened," Marney answered.
" We're going off, so don't start croaking about it. Get
the gear down. And if you trip over something that looks
like an elephant's tusk, lying near the warehouse, don't
fetch it here, coz it's father's tooth. Come on, man.
Move ! "

John departed. We fell to, cutting the fish into lumps
the size of a man's fist, with two nicks in each lump to
take the bait-string. Father appeared, carrying another
coil of ' tow,' Eddy behind him with two buoys. Then
shortly came John, moving with an unusual speed,
carrying two more buoys, an anchor, and still another
coil. Henry had got into the coble, and was clearing it of
all unnecessary tackle. We suddenly heard the voice of
Luke Fosdyck, addressing him in surprised and querulous
tones.

" Now, Henry. Are you going to take your pots
off ? "

" Aye," Henry answered, " they might as well be off as
lying in the dock."

" The sea's nice and smooth, anyway," Luke said
slowly ; adding, after a slight pause, " While it lasts."

The coble hid Luke from view ; but nothing could hide
that old antagonism, striving to get the better of his good
manners.

" We'll certainly be lucky if it lasts," Henry replied.

" You'll be the first *I've* known to start lobstering in
January. . . . You'll be wanting a help down, I reckon.
Are you going to take them all off at once ? "

" No. We'll take the other boat with us. But we can

manage that ourselves if you'll give us a hand down with the coble."

Again there was a pause ; then we heard what seemed to be a reluctant :

" Well, I'll go and get Tindal and Avery."

Marney gave me a nudge as we saw Luke walk slowly up the dock.

" You can almost hear him praying for a hurricane, can't you ? "

" Hold your jaw," shouted Henry. " We're not going to have any of that. Where's the engine spanner got to ? "

CHAPTER SIX

It took us an hour to carry all the pots and other gear down and launch the two boats, and stow the pots into them ; and another half-hour elapsed before we got under way. No other method of movement than towing would have been possible with the *Emma*. She was a twenty-foot sailing-boat which the Lunns had purchased second-hand last summer, and the pile of pots rose six feet above her gunwale, giving Marney scarcely room to move the tiller. The coble, carrying twice as many pots, was piled just as high.

"God ! " said Marney, as we gathered way. " There'd be some fun if we were caught in a gale, loaded like this."

But there was no hint that he anticipated any such doubtful form of amusement. He was as excited as a schoolboy out on his first bird-nesting trip of the year.

"Look at the Fosdycks," he said, glancing over his shoulder to the quickly receding slipway, where the two brothers and Avery stood stolidly watching us. " It's a wonder they're not down on their knees praying. If only we'd done this last Saturday. I suppose we might have done if Steve hadn't hidden the pincers where father couldn't lay hands on them ! "

With a quick glance at the coble to see that we were towing true, Marney felt in his pocket, and produced the two tattered ' blood-and-thunders.' He looked eagerly at their title-pages.

" A bit of luck," he remarked. " I haven't read either of these." He very carefully put them away again. " You know," he went on very gravely, " some of the yarns that come out in this paper our Steve gets every Saturday are champion. You can't beat them for excitement."

He made a slight correction to the *Emma's* course in sympathy with that of the coble.

" They're champion," he repeated. " There's one running at present about a detective chap who's on the trail of a master-crook they call the Grey Spider. Well, in the last bit I read, he'd found that the gang had their headquarters in a lonely house down in Cornwall, up on a cliff something like High Batts. This detective chap is afraid of nowt. He's all on his own, mind you. But he climbs over the garden wall of this lonely house—after dark, and with a hell of a thunderstorm raging ; and he walks up, cool as a cucumber, to the front door. There's one of those old-fashioned bells that you pull. He sees it in a flash of lightning, and he pulls it. He's no sooner done that, than a great skinny grey hand reaches down from a hole that's appeared above the door, gets hold of him by the nape of his neck, and pulls him clean inside. That's where it leaves you. Wondering what in hell's happened to him. . . . You know it beats me how these writing chaps think out things like that."

We were passing between the two marking posts. I asked Marney if he did not think our own predicament on that (to me) memorable occasion was not as exciting as the detective's. I was promptly squashed.

" Garn ! That's not what I mean by excitement. There's nothing exciting when you know what's coming. It's the mystery of this Grey Spider chap that grips you.

The unknown. The chap's uncanny. You never know what he's going to do next."

We had left the posts astern : and Henry had set a south-easterly course, a little seawards of High Batts point. It was the finest afternoon of the whole week. The sky was cloudless. The lowering sun had still enough heat in it for us to keep our coats off. The land-scented wind made no more than a ripple on the level surface of the sea, staining it a deeper blue. Marney left go of the tiller now, and we began to bait all the pots we could reach without disturbing the rather delicate balance of the stack. We carried thirty pots, forming collectively one ' fleet.' Each pot had two fathoms of rope secured to it. The ends of these short ropes were attached to the main rope (or ' tow ') at intervals of ten fathoms, so that a ' fleet ' would fish a belt of sea-bottom six hundred yards in length.

" I don't quite know where father's aiming for," Marney remarked, after we had steamed about halfway across the bay. " But I reckon we'll be going to a spot we call Muddy Dooks. It's deep water and mud, and pots will weather a hurricane in it once they get soaked. But we won't get any lobsters there. Only crabs. It's too far from the rock. If only we'd done this last Saturday ! "

This matter of soaking was of vital importance. Owing to the large proportion of wood used in their construction, new pots were extremely buoyant ; and before this buoyancy was overcome, the imprisoned air in the wood had to be forced out by water pressure, a process which took from twelve hours to several days, according to the depth of the sea. Taking off pots for the first time, therefore, was an especially risky business. To shoot them

on the shallow rocky ground where we had caught our
surprise lobster would have been a risk too big even for
Marney to take. Even now I was aware that he was more
than usually observant of the weather. But the sea and
sky continued to give no hint of any approaching change.
The miracle, which Henry had long ago made the con-
dition of an early ' start,' had happened.

We had ' steamed ' for nearly half an hour when we saw
Henry stand up and look landwards, shading his eyes
against the sun.

" That's it," said Marney, also looking landwards.
" Muddy Dooks ! The safest spot for pots on the whole
coast. You'll find the Fosdycks fishing here half-way
through the summer. Safety first. That's their motto.
. . . That's it. South end of Brewster Wood, opposite
the quarry."

I tried to pick out that landmark, but before I had
succeeded the coble stopped, so that with our own ' way '
we drew alongside.

" You can take this berth," Henry said to Marney.
" There'll be enough wind to move you until you can get
at your oars. We'll go farther east, but not far. We'll
have them pretty close together."

The towing-rope was cast off. The coble steamed ahead.
Marney took the first buoy, and when it had drifted its
line clear of the boat, he let its anchor go and started to
pay out the first long section of the ' tow.' While the
wind drifted us slowly east, he took hold of the first pot ;
and as soon as the boat began to tighten on the anchor,
he lifted it up and cried :

" Here goes ! First pot of the season. Fill yourself with
crabs to-night, honey dear, and we'll let you have a go at
the blue-blacks to-morrow. Good luck, honey ! "

He threw it overboard. For a moment it appeared to be floating, as though it hesitated to take the plunge to the dark regions of Muddy Dooks. Then it sank slowly, slowly, festooned with pearly bubbles, until it disappeared. Marney took hold of the next pot ; and when the wind tightened us on the ' tow ' again, gave it his benediction and let it go.

That benediction, and the variations he bestowed on each virgin pot as he delivered it into the sea, was a true benediction. Between Marney and his gear, his boat, his lines, his tools, was a deep, personal association. They were, in a sense, his living mates. And when the last one had gone, followed by the second anchor and buoy of the fleet, and the coble (having shot two fleets in the same time as our one because of the engine) drew alongside, we remained slowly drifting while we looked at the buoys of the three fleets in benedictory silence.

Then Henry looked at the land again, without shading his eyes, for the sun had set, and said quietly :

" I think we're about right here. We ought to be fair in the middle of Muddy Dooks. If the weather only holds through the night they'll be safe."

" They'll be safe enough," said Marney. " We ought to be out to-morrow by five o'clock, run 'em into Low Batts and keep them there all day. There'll be thousands of lobsters about, weather like this. We'll see old Luke Fosdyck turn green, when we've got a box to send to the station to-morrow night. Come on, John, with that engine. We've still got our lines to bait. We'll want some fish to-morrow as well as lobsters. Now what's up with you ? " he added. " You look as though you'd swallowed a bad mussel ! "

We all looked at John, whose face had suddenly assumed an expression of tragic despair.

" What's up ? " Henry echoed.

John made a dramatic gesture with his hands towards the floating buoys.

" What's up ? " he repeated tragically. " Do any of you know what day it is to-morrow ? "

" My God ! " said Marney. " Saturday. It'll be no use our sending anything to market."

" No, it won't," said John ; and with an impressive quietness, " If it's Saturday to-morrow, it's Friday to-day. Friday," he repeated. *"Friday.* Unlucky day ! "

There was a full minute's silence in which all three Lunns stared at those buoys floating on the level sea, as though they expected them instantly to disappear from sight for ever. Then Henry spoke.

" Well. I know what father would have done, if he'd found out he'd shot his new pots first time on a Friday. He'd have hauled 'em up and taken them ashore again. And for two pins I'd do the same myself. I've had a feeling all the time there was something wrong. Why didn't any of you think about it before ? "

Again there was silence. It was Marney who broke it this time.

" Don't talk so daft," he said ; but with a defiance that did not seem to be very convincing. " It's all daftness about Friday being an unlucky day. It's no more unlucky than any other. I'm not going to start hauling again. Get your engine started, John, and for God's sake don't act so daft ! "

John's hand hesitated on the starting-handle ; but Henry continued to look at the buoys irresolutely. Yet Marney, himself not wholly proof against the fear of that superstition, at least had the courage to defy it ; and he used the surest weapon of all.

" Aye," he said slowly, " we'd make a fine picture, wouldn't we, going ashore with our pots scarcely wet ? What would the Fosdycks say ? "

Henry turned abruptly.

" Start that damned engine. Let's get home."

CHAPTER SEVEN

THERE was no sound of swell to give warning of that record January gale. At ten o'clock, when Marney and I had taken a final stroll down the slipway, the sea was dead calm, the sky starry, the wind still gentle and off-shore.

" Champion," Marney had said. " If it only keeps like this another six hours, those pots will be safe, no matter what happens. It's just daftness about Friday being an unlucky day. We'll as likely as not get a hundred lobsters to-morrow, when we bring the pots close in."

I was living alone in a furnished cottage at the back of the village. At two o'clock I was awakened by Marney shouting at the foot of my bedroom stairs :

" Eh ! Look lively ! It's come on bad. We've got to move the cobles up ! "

The miracle was that I slept through the storm so long. Even in thc lee of the breakwater the wind was so fierce one could scarcely keep one's balance. It was snowing : a fine hard blizzard snow. The seas were breaking over the wall and swirling about the coble wheels. Father and Luke Fosdyck were already down. John and Tindal came close behind me, followed by Avery, who as we took hold of the Fosdycks' coble was obliged to lean against it while he recovered from a violent fit of coughing. We had only to move the boat a distance of fifty yards ; but we could scarcely get a purchase on her slippery snow-caked sides, and before we had got her moving a sea crashed over the breakwater on top of us. I heard Avery Fosdyck curse. He had come down without his oilskins or sea-boots, and the sea must have drenched him to the skin. John, too, was unprotected. It was not, however, until we had hauled both cobles abreast of the lifeboat-house that I heard him growl sardonically :

" Friday—by God—Friday ! "

The cold was too intense for us to loiter and discuss that topic which was uppermost in all our minds. But as we parted, Marney said to me :

" Old Luke will sleep happy after this. But we haven't lost them yet, Friday or no Friday. We'll wait and see."

The gale blew with increasing fury throughout the night. It was still snowing heavily at dawn ; but when, half an hour later, I joined Marney on the slipway, the sky had cleared but for a gigantic mass of storm-cloud on the north-east horizon ; and the sun shone with cold splendour on the snow-bound village and coast. The tide was down. The bared scaurs were like reefs of jet between the dazzling white cliffs and the white surf of the gale-swept bay.

" It's a devil ! " said Marney, between his teeth as he looked to the south-east, where, buried under that roaring welter of sea, lay our precious pots. " And this time yesterday you could have sailed a paper boat out there. Come on. Let's have a walk on to High Batts and see if any wood's washed up. Old Isaac will be down in a minute, and I'm damned if I want to hear him croaking this morning. He gets on my nerves. We'll be first-on if we hurry ! "

To be ' first-on ' along that three-mile stretch of beach between the village and High Batts, with a north-east gale blowing, was always an exciting business. One never knew what treasures would be left stranded at high-water mark. I remembered the time when the entire beach was

scattered with plums and cherries from a fruit ship that
had gone to pieces at High Batts : when the village school
was empty with so many boys away ill with fruit poisoning.
I had seen the wooden framework of a grand piano washed
up in the first cove south of the village ; and I remembered
how three of us boys had found a bundle of ship's papers
with one of them relating to a consignment of revolvers.
We had kept those papers hidden in the cliff in a cave of
bushes, where we would light a fire on Saturday afternoons
and play a fine game pretending we were gun-runners in
a revolutionary country.

Marney ran to the coble and procured a length of thin
rope. We were half a mile along the beach, when, glancing
back, we saw the figures first of old Isaac, then of Luke
Fosdyck, moving down the slipway.

" We've beaten Luke this time, anyway," said Marney
gleefully. " I bet he's come down with the main idea of
seeing if any of our pots have washed up. I should think
that would please him more than if he found a bar of gold.
He'll not follow us. If he's hoping for firewood he'll have
to go on to Low Batts, and there won't be much there
with the wind north-east. And those pots won't wash up,
anyway," Marney added defiantly. " We'll find they
haven't stirred an inch when we get out to them again.
And they'll be full of crabs ! "

He did not say any more about that vital subject then.
We had reached Garry Beck, the first of the two little
moorland-born streams that flow into Bramblewick Bay
through ravines in the coast cliff ; and we hurried into
the cove it formed which was laid thick with drifted weed.
There was a chance that we had been anticipated from this
point onwards by someone from the near-by farms ; but
to our joy we found the sand and snow innocent of

footprints. We rummaged eagerly amongst the weed, found a few pieces of wood, and pushed on quickly to the next stream, Browe Beck, and its cove, where again our first concern was to look for tell-tale foot-prints.

" We're first-on all right ! " said Marney. " There's too much for us to carry here. We'll lay it up, and get father and John to come for it later."

It was unwritten law of Bramblewick that the man ' first-on ' could ' lay-up ' at least one back-load of wood at the cliff foot ; and that, provided it had two stones laid on it, it would be considered sacred until the tide had ebbed and flowed twice. We made two such piles of the odd planks which lay among the weeds ; and prepared to cross the half-frozen stream to the next stretch of beach. Suddenly, however, we noticed a bird, standing in the running shallows of the stream. It did not move as we approached. Marney stole upon it and lifted it up with his two hands. It was a guillemot, and a glance was enough to explain its apparent lack of fear. Its breast feathers were clotted thick with oil. Marney dealt with it in the one way humanely possible. He mercifully broke its neck. We crossed the stream and pushed on, but I could see that the incident, familiar though it was, had upset him.

" You know," he said suddenly, " if I was on one of these oil-burning steamers, and I saw the engineers cleaning out their oil tanks close in to land, I'd let 'em have it. I reckon hanging would be too good for a chap who could do that sort of thing. You can't call me tender-hearted. I'm not like our old man. I'd kill any-thing that was harmful, or that I wanted to eat, or I could make brass out of. But I'm damned if I'd torture anything. You can't think of anything more awful than being a seabird, like that one I just killed, having to catch all your food by diving, and having your feathers plastered up with that muck, so that you can neither dive nor fly. Slow starvation. Think of it ! Swimming over a shoal of herrings, perhaps, not more than a foot below you, hungry as hell, and not being able to get a bite at one. It wouldn't be so bad if they could kill themselves ! But they just go drifting about the sea, or wash up in a storm like this, and stand about while they die of slow starvation ! "

We counted a score of these tragic by-products of human progress within the next half-mile, all fortunately dead ; most of them so encased in congealed oil as to be mummified. But we also found part of a mahogany cabin-door with a heavy brass lock on it ; some planks of such dimensions that they might have been sawn specially to make lobster-pots ; and a very useful fish-basket, which had probably washed from the deck of a passing trawler.

It had started to snow again. The whole of the northern end of the bay, and the village itself, was blotted out by a squall ; but immediately to the south the shadowed cliff of High Batts, too precipitous in its heights to give hold for snow, rose stark against a patch of bright blue sky, arched by a stupendous mass of grey-white storm-cloud. That headland, whose foundations of rugged iron-stone reached out seawards like the fore-paws of an immense sculptured lion, seemed to offer a sentient defiance to the raging wind and sea. It gave one a disquieting sense of the frailty and insignificance of man. For thousands of centuries, since the great Arctic Ice Drift pressing relentlessly down the valley of the North Sea had sculptured its lionesque contours, it had looked out across the sea, bearing upon its treacherous surface the fragile crafts of venturing man. It had seen the rude coracles of the Early Britons, the galleys of the Romans, and of those audacious robber-colonists, the Danes. It had seen the ships of the Elizabethan adventurers, the white-sailed East Indiamen, the whaling fleets, the busy brigs and schooners of the nineteenth century, outplaced in their turn by the steam tramp, as the fishing lugger had been outplaced by the trawler, the frigate by the iron man-of-war.

It had looked out upon the traffickings of the war, when the great merchant convoys, protected by airships and cruisers, had passed daily, hugging close to the land; when its cliffs had reverberated to the thunder of gun-fire and the explosions of depth-charges, mines, torpedoes, the blowing up of ships; when, upon its imperishable foundations, the sea had thrown the bodies of drowned men as at the feet of an omnipotent eternal god, to whom the passing of a generation of mankind was no more than a puff of a soft summer wind.

Immediately north of High Batts Point was a deep, narrow cove called Spinney Hole, where, at high water, the tidal current sweeping north across the bay made a series of fierce eddies. The beach of the cove, still hidden from us by a spur of the cliff, was a favourite place for wood and other treasures; and we approached it with re-quickened interest, confident from the virgin sand about the spur that we were still 'first-on.'

" The last time I was in Spinney Hole," said Marney, in tones that whetted my already intense excitement, " I found a great lump of candle-grease, weighing about two stone. I reckon it must have washed out of that German submarine that lies just this side of Muddy Dooks, something to do with her electric batteries. I took it home and put it in the warehouse; and about a week later, mother played war with me, as Steve had melted a

G

great lump of it in her best saucepan, and made candles
out of it, so that he could sit up reading at night. That
kid's got brains ! It seems he learnt how candles were
made in an object lesson at school. He used some of
father's best cotton line for wicks. Mother wouldn't have
found out, if the tatties she cooked hadn't tasted of
paraffin. I once found a whole box of Sunlight soap in
Spinney Hole, and a crate full of oil-lamp chimneys, a
gross of 'em, all the same sort, but they wouldn't fit any
lamp in our house. There were dozens of mines came in
here during the war ; and a German officer without
a head."

We had passed the bluff. The beach of Spinney Hole,
covered almost to the water's edge with snow, lay before
us. We noticed at once a large black barrel, a small spar,
part of a broken hatch, and a sufficiency of firewood to
make a further search a waste of time. We hurried towards
the barrel ; but before we reached it Marney stopped,
looking towards the cliff foot.

" My God ! " he muttered, " look at that ! "

Lying between two large stones, but with its black
pennant conspicuous against the background of snow, was
a cork buoy. We moved towards it. Marney picked it up,
and gazed at it in silence. There could be no doubt as to
its identity. The initials H.L. were burnt deeply into its
topmost cork, which was brand new, like the short piece
of frayed and twisted rope which trailed from the lower
end of the pennant stick.

" It's from the fleet we shot," Marney muttered at last.
" The first buoy. You wouldn't have thought it possible,
new rope like that. It must have been dragged down and
fouled another ' tow,' and chafed through."

I did not speak ; but Marney must have guessed the

question in my mind, for he added, after a moment's contemplation of the rope end :

" No. It doesn't mean we've lost them. There's another buoy to that fleet, remember. But on Muddy Dooks ! You wouldn't have thought they'd have moved at all."

Again he was silent. Then, putting the buoy down again, he said :

" We're not going to walk home with that damned thing. We'll hide it in the cliff, and come and get it when it's dark. If the Fosdycks see it, it will be all over Bramble-wick before night that the Lunns have lost their pots. We'll be the laugh of the village. Come on, let's look at the barrel and pick out the best of the wood."

The barrel was empty and was too awkward a thing to carry. The spar was waterlogged and useless. We collected the best pieces of driftwood, made a bundle each, and started for home, Marney carrying the buoy under an arm. But his high spirits were damped. The gale was now in our teeth. It was still snowing and freezing hard. It seemed that there was not a patch of unbroken water between the scaur-ends and the horizon.

" I'd as soon be carrying a dead body back as this buoy," Marney muttered, as we turned the spur of the cliff again. " Not as though I believe the pots have gone," he added quickly. " Only it looks so daft. It looks as though we didn't know how to fish. I don't know what father will say about it. We'd better not tell him. We'll come and get it to-night, and hide it in our wash-house until we've been off and seen what's happened."

We walked for a while without speaking. Then Marney, turning his face sideways to me from the wind, said in rather gloomy tones :

" The queerest sight I ever saw at sea was in a north-east

gale like this. It was in the war. We were coming from the Baltic to Hull with timber, and there were four other steamers and an auxiliary cruiser which was supposed to pilot us through the mine-fields. We were just about six hours' steam from Spurn Point ; it was blowing like hell, when we heard an explosion, and we saw a Norwegian schooner about a mile on our starboard bow blow up and go under about as quick as you could light a fag. We had to bring to, while the cruiser wirelessed for some mine-sweepers to come and see if there were any more mines in the way. She daren't leave us, of course, and there was too much sea for her to put off her boats to try and pick any one up. By and by, we began to see wreckage floating down on us ; and, you'd hardly believe it, coffins, hundreds of coffins, some floating flat, some popping up and down on end, like a lot of great seals poking their heads out of the water. I've never seen a queerer sight in all my life. The schooner had had a deck cargo of ready-made coffins, and damned if we didn't see a man trying to get into one of them, as though it was a boat. But he was gone in a flash. They were all drowned, all those who hadn't been killed when the mine went off."

The recital of this ' queer ' experience, with the wind almost drowning Marney's voice, did not tend to dispel the depression which the finding of the buoy had put upon me ; but it seemed to cheer Marney up immensely.

" No ! " he shouted, turning his face to the wind again ; " those pots will be there when we go for them. I don't care if it blows twice as hard as this. They might have moved a bit, but we'll get them. I only hope we don't meet father before we get to Browe Beck. There's no other safe spot where we can hide the buoy, this side of it."

We did not meet father. The buoy was safely concealed

under a bush up the valley of the beck. With our load increased by the door and some of the wood we had laid up, we fought our way against the freezing gale past Garry Beck, and along the last strip of beach between it and the village without encountering a single person. The slipway, too, was deserted.

" Come on," Marney shouted as we approached, " let's hurry up, before any one sees us and starts asking a lot of damned questions."

We hurried as fast as our loads would permit ; but even as we set foot on the bottom of the slipway, Luke Fosdyck came round the end of the breakwater wall from the direction of Low Batts. It was Marney's unshakable conviction that he had been waiting round the end of the wall for our return. Certainly his appearance was perfectly timed. He carried a small bundle of firewood over his shoulders, and under his arm a cork buoy identical with the one we had been at such pains to conceal.

There was no possibility of avoiding him. He gave us a hail. We dropped our loads. He came up.

" Isn't this one of your buoys ? " he shouted.

I could feel Marney fighting down his anger ; but his voice was quite steady when he answered :

" Aye. So it is. Where did you pick it up ? "

" Half-way on to Low Batts," Luke answered, putting it down at Marney's feet. " I thought I saw another one washing up, but I couldn't be certain. It'll be from those pots you took out last night, won't it ? It's a brand-new buoy."

" Aye. It's a pot buoy," Marney answered, still self-possessed. " It beats me how it came off."

Luke Fosdyck gave a laugh, and there was no mistaking the satisfaction in it.

" It doesn't beat me," he said. " There's no pots made could stand a sea like this. You'll never see them again, I know, until the ballast smashes out of them and they wash up in bits. You can give 'em up for lost. Nobody can fish for lobsters at Bramblewick this time of year. It's a waste of time and money until March."

Never in the history of that antagonism between the Lunns and Fosdycks had an open quarrel been so imminent as at that moment. As Marney told me later, if Luke had been a younger man there would have been a fight, and I knew what it cost him to answer quietly, as he picked up the buoy :

" Well, we don't know they're lost just because a buoy's come adrift. It's very good of you to have fetched it in for us. Thank you. I see you've got a nice load of wood."

Luke glared at our own heavy bundles. We walked up the slipway in silence, and we parted from him in silence. And it was not until we were half-way up Chapel Street, almost knee-deep in snow, that Marney gave vent to his feelings, which he did with a remarkable constraint.

" That's one up on the Fosdycks," he muttered. " But we'll see who wins next."

CHAPTER EIGHT

THAT gale, which wrought havoc on sea and land between the Tees and Humber—wrecking two big cargo boats, sinking a trawler and two drifters (with a total loss of seven men), destroying a promenade pier, obstructing roads and railways with colossal snowdrifts, wrecking stack-yards, chimneys, telegraph poles—lasted for twenty-four hours. Shortly after Saturday midnight the wind dropped completely. It continued to freeze with Arctic severity until late on Sunday afternoon. Then, suddenly, the wind freshened from the west ; a violent thaw set in. By midnight a westerly gale was blowing. At dawn on Monday, nothing remained to tell of that record storm but the havoc it had made, a few unmelted drifts on the slopes of High Batts, and a long, lazy swell, breaking on the scaur-ends, but leaving the Landing mouth navigable. The gale from the west had died to an absolute calm.

We put to sea in silence that morning. We returned in silence, late in the afternoon. We had shot the lines first along Low Batts. Then we had 'steamed' south to Muddy Dooks. Not one of the six buoys was visible. We had dragged a grapple over the length and breadth of Muddy Dooks for two hours. We had gone back, hauled the lines, and dragged for another two hours ; but beyond a length of bulwark rail, belonging to one of the numerous ships mined or torpedoed in the bay during the war, we had hauled up nothing. The pots had vanished.

I had tea with Marney that afternoon. Amy, rising to what otherwise might have been a depressing occasion, had baked a new batch of tarts and cheese-cakes ; and there were delicious brown scones, hot from the oven. Marney had distinctly cheered up by the time the meal had ended. It was not until then that Amy, who had, I thought, deliberately refrained from mentioning the matter, in sympathy with his feelings, remarked :

" Well, it's a bit of bad luck, losing all those brand-new pots, after all the expense, and not having caught anything in them, and with a bad cod season like it's been. I wish you'd never caught that lobster that set you all out of your heads. We'd have the money now that's gone in buying twine and rope. I think it's awful."

" Don't talk so daft ! " Marney replied quickly. " You've got to take things as they come in fishing. It's a gamble, same as anything else to do with the sea. Nothing venture, nothing win. If they've gone, they've gone. Worse things than that might happen. This house might tumble into the sea. I've heard it cracking. The kid might get smallpox, or swallow a darning-needle. Besides, we haven't lost those pots yet. They're some-where ! We'll grapple every yard of Bramblewick Bay before I give them up."

" You always were hopeful," said Amy ironically.

" If I hadn't been I wouldn't have married you."

" You wouldn't have done that if I'd had my wits about me."

" Hold your jaw, and give me another cup of tea. These are the best cheese-cakes you've ever made.

" No," Marney went on. " It isn't losing those pots that riles me. It's the Fosdycks having the laugh on us. Did you notice old Luke, when we came in ? I bet he and Tindal spent the whole afternoon up on the cliff with their glasses watching us to see if we struck them. And if it wasn't for their whiskers they'd have kissed each other when they saw us give it up. I tell you what," he added, suddenly banging his cup down on his saucer, " if I had ten quid in the bank, I'd go down to Burnharbour now, and buy a fleet of pots, if only to show the Fosdycks how to catch lobsters this week. I'd give anything to turn the laugh on them."

" Well, you haven't ten quid," said Amy, " so you needn't smash the china. What you want is a bit of sense. You'd only go and lose them if you got them. More money thrown away. It'll be the workhouse for us before long. I'd have done better if I'd married a sweep."

" Garn ! I'll be buying you a fur coat out of lobsters before long. You wait and see."

" I'm likely to wait, anyway," Amy replied. " I've had plenty of practice."

This was banter, robust but good-natured ; yet under it all one detected an undertow of serious contention. It was not that Amy was upset by the direct financial aspects of what had happened. It was something far deeper, something entirely primitive. She was fiercely proud of Marney; jealous for his reputation, and, more subtly, for their marriage partnership. She would never boast about his courage, his contempt for danger, his professional skill at sea, or in making gear. She called him ' daft ' on every conceivable occasion. The last thing she would admit to any one, least of all to Marney himself, was that she considered him without equal as a man, and that their partnership was perfect. And it was the sense that Marney, by his over-eagerness, was responsible for the loss of the pots ; that father and John in their hearts were blaming him ; that Marney would be the special butt of the village gossipers, particularly the women, that upset her more, perhaps, than it upset Marney himself. It was a challenge to their marriage, to her own primitive judgment. Strongest of anything in her attitude towards him now was the incentive, the goading almost, to action.

" I don't want you hanging about the house," she said when tea was finished. " You can clear off and see father, while I get the things cleared up. But mind you get back before supper-time. That's seven sharp, I'd have you know. I don't want it spoilt, waiting for you."

On our way to the south cliff, we overtook Steve, looking rather sorry for himself, and holding a hand over one eye. He tried to avoid us. Marney, however, was too quick for him ; and seizing him by the neck of his guernsey he pulled away that hand.

" What's up with you ? " he demanded. " Who's given you that black eye ? "

Steve was doing his utmost to repress the tears that were rapidly filling both his eyes, and he did not speak.

" Have you been fighting ? " Marney pursued. " Who's done it ? Can't you speak ? Who's done it ? "

Steve's lip quivered.

" That's my business," he succeeded in saying, in a way that was incredibly Marney's. " I can fight if I like. He didn't beat me, anyway. I gave him more than he gave me."

" I'll give you another black eye if you won't tell me who it was ! "

" Then you can give me another," Steve retorted.

" What were you fighting about, then ? " said Marney in more conciliatory tones. "Who started it ? "

" He did," Steve answered.

" Who's he ? "

" I'm not going to tell. He said the Lunns were all

damned fools, as they'd lost all their new pots. He said father didn't know how to catch lobsters or anything else. He said our coble was no good. He said everybody knew you were daft, and that our John frightened an old woman to death playing his concertina, and a lot else. So I hit his nose for him. Then we went down on to the sands and had a proper go, with our guernseys off. And he wouldn't have given me a black eye if he hadn't put a stone in his hand. And you needn't go and tell mother I've been fighting. I don't want a good hiding on top of everything else. I'm going to tell her I've fallen down some steps."

We felt that Steve's courage for that approaching interview with mother would be fortified by a visit to the local confectioner, and we subscribed, accordingly.

" It doesn't take long for things to get round in this spot," Marney remarked bitterly, as we hurried up the lane. " I shouldn't be surprised if the Fosdycks have been round from house to house, spreading the glad tidings. I wish I'd been Steve. I'll half-kill that kid who hided him when I find out who it is."

We went direct to the warehouse. John was at work on his lines. Father was sitting in front of the fire, splicing a new grapple-iron on to a length of rope. John took no notice of our arrival. Nell got up from her sack, and made her usual acknowledgment. Father gave his usual smile. But the atmosphere was decidedly tense, Marney's cheerfulness painfully forced. Nor was his first remark, under the circumstances, discreet.

" I've just heard old Luke's been taken to the asylum," he said. " He's laughed himself silly."

John turned his head round.

" Yes. I've laughed myself silly, too," he growled. " I've laughed so much since last Friday, if I laugh any more I'll be paralysed. I've only got to think about those pots to start all over again. Ninety brand-new pots, and all that new gear, and not a damned fish out of them. It's so funny it beats me how any of you can keep your faces straight."

It was the first remark we had heard John make since we had started grappling in Muddy Dooks ; but it gave one the feeling that he had a great deal more to say, and Marney immediately took the defensive.

" Now don't start croaking ! " he said. " If we'd found them, and caught a lot of lobsters to-day, you'd be boasting that we wouldn't have started for another month if it hadn't been for you. What's done is done, so let it be. And we haven't lost them yet, have we, father ? "

Henry, too, had refrained from commenting upon the disaster throughout the afternoon. He spoke now, very quietly and slowly :

" I hope we haven't. But I think we have."

" Then what are you bending on a new grapple for ?" Marney asked. " Are we going to go on looking until we find them ? "

" Aye," father answered. " We're not going to give them up. At the same time it's my opinion they'll have washed out miles, with the tide where it was when that gale came on."

There was silence for a time ; during which I saw Marney glance uncomfortably from his father to John, and back to his father again.

" Well," he said suddenly, and with the self-consciousness of a delinquent schoolboy confessing his sin, " it's my fault if we've lost them. You said we would the day we took them out."

Father turned abruptly from his task.

" Hold your jaw ! " he said sharply. " I'm not wanting you to take the blame for what's my business. If I hadn't wanted those pots to go in last Friday, they wouldn't have gone, so understand that. If there's any one to blame it's me."

Again there was a pause, more hushed than the first. Then John, playing the unexpected part of peacemaker, said :

" There's no need for you to get your shirts off about it, trying to find out whose fault it is. We lost those pots because we took them out on Friday, damned fools that we were ! You can't kid me there isn't some reason for so many folks thinking Friday's unlucky."

Henry turned to his task again. But his anger had not cooled.

" I'd have fetched 'em back when we found out if it hadn't been for what the Fosdycks would have said."

" Aye," put in Marney, " but you wouldn't have thought of that if I hadn't put you in mind of it."

Father angrily threw the rope down on the floor, and stood up.

" I tell you once and for all it's my fault," he shouted, " so say no more about who's to blame. I'm not bothering about that," he went on, still vehemently, " I'm thinking about the Fosdycks having the crow over us ; about what we might have done with those pots this week if it had kept fine like this. And as it is we'll very likely spend the whole week grappling, and still be no better off. And those chaps laughing up their sleeves at us the whole time. I'm thinking what it will be best for us to do."

" Well, and what are we going to do ? " asked Marney very quietly.

Father did not answer ; but he walked across to the

seaward window, and stood staring at the black panes of
it. Then he turned round.

" How many pots have we got left ? " he demanded.

" It's either twenty or twenty-one," Marney answered.
His eyes had suddenly lit up.

" How many pots did we make that one day when we
were all four at it ? "

" We made sixteen."

" Have you got any wood over at your place ? "

Marney's eyes were positively gleaming now.

" I've got enough for about a score of pots, if that's
what you mean. I've got about enough hazels, too ; and
there's enough to make another score of pots here. I reckon
we could make twenty a day, if we went all out," he
pursued excitedly. " I reckon we could make sixty before
the week's out, if we didn't bother with the lines. . . .
God ! The Fosdycks would turn green if we had ninety
pots fishing next week."

" Yes. And we'd turn pink if we went and lost the
damned lot again."

That remark came from John like a cold douche.

" And what about new ' tows ' ? " he went on. "Another
ten quid to fork out. And six more anchors ; not to
mention buoys and ballast ! "

There was silence ; but not for long. The fire of lobster
fever, blazing hot in all our blood again, was not to be
quenched by John's habitual pessimism. It was father
who answered very quietly :

" If it's a matter of brass, that my business. And as for
losing them—we won't. We still don't know for certain
we've lost the first."

He turned to Marney.

" Where's that last bundle of hazels we cut ? "

" It ought to be in the loft."

Quickly, Marney climbed up to the loft. Father moved to one corner of the warehouse, and started rummaging among some planks piled there. Hazels began to clatter down from the loft.

" Where's the saw got to ? " Henry demanded.

" I saw it last in the wash-house," said John. " But Steve's had it since then."

" Are there any nails left ? Hurry up and finish that line, or leave it. One of you go and find the saw and the hammer. We ought to get half a dozen bottoms nailed up before supper."

Marney had already descended from the loft. He ran to the door, and went out. In a minute he was back again with two saws, a real hammer, two iron bolts and a box of nails.

" How much twine have we left ? " father demanded of him.

" We haven't any."

" Leave that damned line as it is," father shouted at John. " There's time for you to catch the five-o'clock bus to Burnharbour if you hurry. You can carry six balls of twine back with you, and order a hundred-weight of rope and some cork to come by the carrier to-morrow. Look lively ! Get them to make the twine into a parcel. We'll not let the Fosdycks know we're going to start making pots again."

John turned from his line.

" You're in a mighty hurry all of a sudden," he complained. " How the devil do you think I'm going to get washed and changed in ten minutes ? "

" I don't expect you to," father answered dryly. " Go as you are."

" You're not going courting," said Marney, who had already sawn two planks. " You'll have to be back on the seven bus, and begin work. You're now speaking to Henry Ford, not Henry Lunn. Mass production, brother John. For God's sake, get a move on ! I've nearly finished one bottom."

John shrugged his shoulders, and wiped his hands. But he went out with alacrity. The work of making sixty pots in a week began in earnest. It was hard, tiring work. The saws were blunt. Most of the wood was wet. A fish-box balanced on an uneven floor did not make an ideal bench. Yet one felt a wild thrill in it all ; an inspiring sense of conflict against a redoubtable enemy, the sea. And we were going to turn the laugh against the Fosdycks.

It was warm in the warehouse. We stripped almost to our waists, and worked like demons. We organized ourselves for mass production. Marney and I sawed all the available planks. Henry began nailing. When we had done sawing, I burnt the holes, while father and Marney bent and nailed the hazels in. We lost all sense of time. We were taken by surprise when the door opened to admit John, carrying a large brown-paper parcel.

" Hallo ! " cried Marney. " Here's John back. What time's it got to ? "

John came forward to the fire, threw down his parcel, and surveyed the result of our feverish efforts with equal surprise.

" It's just half-past seven," he said. " By God ! Six— seven frames. You must have been hard at it. . . . Eh ! " he added to Marney, in unusually brisk tones. " You'd; better start netting. You're quicker at it than us. I'll do that job. Do you think we'll get a dozen done to-night ? "

" I should think we'll get a score done, now you've come

to help us," Marney replied ironically. "You sound as though you'd got lobster fever again."

"I've got some news, anyway," John answered, starting work. "Three Burnharbour boats have taken their pots out this morning, and one came back to-night with eighty odd lobsters. They fetched three shillings apiece. I should think we could have caught a hundred if we'd found our pots and got them inside."

No comment was made on this piece of news; but it was like oil poured on an already blazing fire. We didn't even trouble to look up when the warehouse door opened again, and a voice cried:

"Do you know it's nearly half-past eight?"

We did look up then, or at least Marney and I did. Amy was standing just inside the door, carrying the baby in her arms, and looking extremely cross.

"I've had supper waiting an hour and a half," she went on indignantly. "And now, I've had to carry the baby all this way to fetch you. It's enough to give him pneumonia. Are you coming, or aren't you?"

Marney grinned, a little sheepishly.

"I'll come when I've finished this pot. Sit down. The kid's all right. It would take more than that to give him pneumonia. I won't be a minute."

"Yes. I know your minutes. Your supper's completely spoilt."

There was suddenly a subtle change in Amy's voice.

"Whatever are you doing?" she demanded.

She came forward. Marney said nothing.

"Have you started making another lot of pots?"

Marney did not look up from his task; but he said quietly:

"Aye. We're making another lot, in case we don't find

H

those others straight away. We're going to make the
Fosdycks grin on the other side of their faces."

Amy was silent. But I saw in her eyes what I expected
to see—approval. For a while she watched the netting-
needle flashing in Marney's hand. Then, turning to go out,
she said quietly :

" Well, your supper won't be worth eating if you wait
any longer. I'll put it in a basket and ask Steve to bring
it across. But mind you're back before ten. I'm not going
to sit up for you half the night."

" I'll be back," said Marney. " And don't forget to put
a couple of cheese-cakes in."

" Aye," put in father, " and if you're going in home,
tell mother to send a pot of tea, and a bite of something
for us. We've got no time for supper. . . . What size
lobsters were they that brought that price ? " he added,
addressing John.

" They weren't as big as that one we caught on our lines
just before Christmas."

" I should think that a score like that one would make
about three quid," said Marney thoughtfully. " I tell you,
they're paying things, are lobsters. Has anybody seen my
knife ? "

CHAPTER NINE

For three consecutive days the wind blew off the land—the sky was blue, the sea was calm—for three days the weather was ideal for lobster-fishing. From Burnharbour news came through that seven boats had made a start; that big catches were being made; that prices were keeping phenomenally high—for this wind which made smooth water of the North Sea was a gale on the south and west coasts of England, and the market demand for lobsters was insatiable.

But we had no time for gazing at the sea for thinking of the gear we had lost, the money we might have made if we had been fishing. One Burnharbour boat was fishing in the bay itself, and had its pots close in to Low Batts, in the very place where our pots would have been. John brought in this interesting piece of intelligence. Father, however, was not upset about it.

"Good luck to them," he said. "Some of those Burnharbour chaps have had as much as they could do to make ends meet this winter. They don't know that ground the same as we do, anyway. There'll be plenty of lobsters left when we make a start. The only thing is if we all do well there'll be a glut, and prices will drop for a certainty. We can't help that."

The presence of the Burnharbour fishermen certainly gave new stimulus to our efforts. Yet Henry was perfectly sincere in wishing them good luck. In his opinion there was fishing 'room' for everyone: and so long as a man did not claim more than his fair share, and did not interfere with another man's fishing, the better he did for himself the better in the long run for everyone.

" I only hope the weather doesn't turn mucky with their pots close in like that ; otherwise they'll be in a worse mess than we are. There's not a better spot on the coast for lobsters than Low Batts, but there's not a worse for being nabbed in bad weather. It's not safe to leave pots there all night, this time of the year."

The weather turned ' mucky ' on Thursday night. The wind freshened soon after dusk, backed to south-east, and before dawn on Friday another fierce north-easter was blowing. It was a strange coincidence that it should happen on Friday : yet it was to prove, so far as our fortunes were concerned, the fallacy of that superstition.

On Thursday morning every Burnharbour boat had brought in a big catch. The price of lobsters had dropped from three shillings to one and three. In that gale, which lasted until Sunday night, every boat but one lost every pot it had in the sea, and that less unfortunate one, the boat fishing at Low Batts, saved only a single fleet, which had been fishing in deep water. The rest, smashed as though a steam-roller had passed over them, lay strewn along the bottom of Low Batts cliff on Monday morning. And on Monday we were informed that the Burnharbour fish salesmen were willing to pay three shillings and sixpence for good-sized lobsters. But there were no supplies. All the Burnharbour men had started making pots again.

The gale had left a fairly heavy swell. We were out on Monday, shortly after daybreak, however, and returned before noon with two baskets of cod. We did not pack them. We did not re-bait the lines. We had finished fifty-two pots. The frames of the remaining eight were ready for netting. We worked at them, with only two short breaks for meals, until half-past ten that night ; and by then we had eighty-two pots, complete with ballast, tows, buoys and bait, to turn the laugh against the Fosdycks. The wind was off the land. The swell was rapidly falling : and lobsters were still worth anything up to three shillings apiece !

At four o'clock on Tuesday morning, Marney shouted at the foot of my stairs :

"Eh! Hurry up! We want to get off before the Fosdycks see us."

We did not imagine that the Fosdycks were in complete ignorance as to what we had been doing since last Monday. The fact that we had not fished on those first three fine days was significant. But, as Marney remarked gleefully, " we had them guessing." To turn the laugh against the Fosdycks, it was enough that we should catch lobsters out of Bramblewick season, and sell them at an out-of-season price.

The weather was fine but frosty. Fortunately there was a moon. We brought the gear down first on hand-barrows and piled the pots at the slipway foot. We moved quietly, and the black shadows thrown by the moon helped to give a conspiratorial air to our actions. We launched the coble, checking its weight with a hawser. Its iron wheels made a terrific racket, which the dark, deserted alleys of the village seemed to echo with doubled intensity.

" They'll know we're going off now," said Marney, " but they'll not guess what for, until they hear the *Emma* ; then they'll be down, I bet, to see what's up."

But he was wrong. We launched the *Emma*. We stacked both boats with pots, as we had done that fatal Friday ; and as soon as the flowing tide gave us enough water to float, we made the *Emma* fast to the coble and got under way. The slipway was still deserted when we left it.

The moon was low now. There was no sign of the dawn. We steered due east, between the Landing posts, and then north-east for Low Batts, whose cliffs in the pale light of the waning moon loomed mysteriously against the starry seaward sky. Marney was very excited.

" No Muddy Dooks this time," he said, as he lighted a cigarette. " The pots won't get waterlogged so quickly, close in like this, but there'll be scarcely any tide to move them, so it amounts to the same thing. Mind, they're new pots, and they'll not fish their best yet. But if we only get a score to-day, we'll have wiped out what we've paid for twine, and given the Fosdycks something to think about. Three-and-sixpence apiece ! I tell you, lobsters are the best paying things in creation !"

We steamed almost to the point of Low Batts. Then, so close in to the cliff foot that every sound we made was echoed back from it, we parted as we had done on Muddy Dooks, and the shooting began ; and as before Marney threw each pot into the sea with a benediction.

" Good-bye, honey ! Two blue-backs for you ! "

" Good luck ! You're one of John's. Don't frighten em away ! "

" Now for you, honey. Best pot I've made this year. Six for you ! "

" Another of John's. You look a cripple, but you ought to catch a crab ! "

" Three lobsters for you, honey. They're worth three-and-six apiece ! "

There was no wind and very little tide to help us this time. The eastern sky was paling when we had done and the coble came alongside. We waited for a minute or two, as before, straining our eyes through the slowly melting morning dusk for a sight of the buoys. Then Marney remarked quietly :

" And now, what ? Breakfast, and straight back ? "

Henry did not answer for a moment. He turned and looked south-east. Then he said slowly :

" No. We're not going home on a fine morning like this when we've some pots adrift. These will not be worth hauling for three hours yet. Start the engine, John. We'll go and have a look at Muddy Dooks."

We made the *Emma* fast alongside the coble, and Marney and I got into the latter. It took us half an hour to steam across the bay ; and by the time we had started to grapple for the missing pots, it was nearly daylight. Shortly, we saw the Fosdycks' coble clear the shadows of the distant village cliff, move out through the Landing posts, and begin to move slowly in our direction. We were ourselves " steaming " very slowly, to keep the grapple on the bottom. Henry, with one hand touching the tell-tale rope, remarked :

" It will puzzle them a bit, this. They'll see we're grappling, but they'll not be certain what we've got the other boat for."

" Not unless they can see the other buoys," said John.

" They'll not do that ; the cliff will hide them."

" If we could strike the lot we lost, and take 'em back, along with two score of lobsters from the others, I should say Luke Fosdyck would drop dead. I think we ought to steam farther east, we've grappled all this before."

We steamed east, we turned and steamed west again ; we steamed diagonally across the area of that fishing ground which had behaved so treacherously ; but we waited in vain for that shout from Henry to say that the

grapple had found something in the shape of lobster-pots
or 'tows.' The Fosdycks had shot their lines shorewards
of us. They were now hauling. Henry suddenly started to
haul on the grapple-rope.

"Full steam ahead!" he cried to John. "Those pots
aren't here. Let's go and have our breakfasts."

We steamed in so that we came within hearing distance
of the Fosdycks. Old Luke was hauling. Tindal and Avery
were at the oars.

"Are you getting anything?" Henry shouted, without
a suspicion of malice.

Luke, one could see, was finding it hard to repress his
curiosity regarding the *Emma*. He growled back :

"They're scarce. Sea's gone too smooth for 'em again."
Then he added, "Have you been looking for those pots of
yours?"

"Aye," Henry shouted back. "There's no sign of
them yet."

"And I doubt if there ever will be," was Luke's
comforting response. "I doubt you've lost them for
ever."

"I vote we go and have a haul now," said Marney, as
soon as we were out of hearing. "We'd have time to haul
and get back, before they're ready to launch up. If we get
some lobsters we could lay them out for Luke to see."

"Don't talk so daft!" said Henry. "New pots like
those! We'll be lucky if we get anything to-day. . . . But
we'll maybe have a look at them after breakfast," he added
with a quietness that did not disguise that he was as
excited as any of us.

The tide had ebbed from the foot of the slipway when
we got back. We anchored the coble, and launched the
Emma behind the breakwater. The Fosdycks had not yet

reached the Landing mouth. We stopped at the top of the slipway to have a final look at them.

" Don't take long over your breakfasts," Henry said briskly as we parted. " We'll very likely get off without them seeing us at all. And you'd better bring a bit of grub with you. We may be out a long time."

" You come and have breakfast with us," Marney said to me. " Then we'll know where everybody is. Hurry up. There's old Isaac coming down the dock."

We successfully avoided Isaac Fosdyck. The other Fosdycks were at breakfast themselves when, twenty minutes later, we waded out to the coble and got under way for Low Batts. The weather was dull and cold, with a promise of rain. But there was no wind, and the sea continued to be smooth. None of us spoke until we were more than half-way to the place where the pots had been set. Then Henry remarked with a still unconvincing complacency :

" I think we're wasting time hauling new pots as quick as this. I think we'd better shove her head round for Muddy Dooks again, and grapple until the tide flows."

" What for ? " shouted John abruptly. " We can do that when we've hauled if we want to. We've heard a lot about lobsters the last few months. I'd like to see one for a change."

" John's got lobster fever," Marney remarked. " Don't annoy him, father. It won't take us long to see what's in them, anyway," he quickly pursued. " Which fleet shall we haul first ? That one we shot from the *Emma* ? "

" Aye. It will be the first we come to. I can see the buoys now. Straight ahead."

We were excited as only fishermen can be excited. Henry put the boat neatly alongside the first buoy.

Marney seized the buoy with a gaff, lifted it on board, quickly coiled in its rope until he got the weight of the first pot which, as we were fishing on rock, had no anchor. John stopped the engine. Marney stepped back into the middle of the coble. Henry and John took hold of the ' tow,' and began hauling in earnest. Suddenly the intense silence was broken by Henry.

" Here we are."

Marney and I looked over the side. The water was clear. We could see the first pot quickly ascending. Its rope cleared the surface. Marney seized it, while Henry and John continued to pull on the main ' tow.' Marney reached his hand down. The pot broke the surface. He lifted it on board, and remarked laconically : " Nowt."

The bait apparently was untouched. Marney looked at the pot for a moment, then handed it over to me.

" Stow it well for'ard," he said. " There's another twenty-nine to come yet."

Father and John said nothing as they continued to haul. The second pot appeared. It was also empty. Marney handed it to me without a word, and leaned over to lift up the third, which also was dealt with in silence. Four more pots were hauled before any one commented on the situation. Then Marney said with that semi-defiant air he invariably assumed when things were going bad :

" We haven't struck them yet."

" It strikes me that Burnharbour chap must have cleared them out," said John.

Henry said nothing until three more empty pots were hauled. Then :

" There's more lobsters here than a dozen Burnharbour boats could clear out. I tell you we haven't given them a chance. You can't expect new pots to catch lobsters straight away. We'd have done better if we'd left them alone."

A gloom was rapidly settling upon us. Another six pots were hauled and stowed in the forepart of the boat, with our catch still at zero. Even Marney was gloomy. There was an entire lack of conviction in his voice when he said :

" Well, there's still the other two fleets. We may strike them yet. Are you going to put this fleet back where it was ? "

" We might as well," said Henry. " There ought to be plenty of lobsters here."

" Aye. There *ought* to be," said John. " But *we're* not going to catch them."

He was right. It took us half an hour to reach the last pot and the end buoy. We had seen neither crab nor lobster. John started the engine. We swung round and shot that fleet roughly where it had been before.

" And now for number two," cried Marney, with a slight return to cheerfulness. " We'll do better this one."

" I don't think we will," said John. " I don't think there'll be a lobster in it."

This was purest pessimism : John at his worst : but it was an accurate forecast. The second fleet yielded precisely nothing. We shot it where it had lain before.

" Shall we bother with the third fleet or not ? " said father then. " It's only a waste of time ! "

" There won't be anything in it," repeated John, more gloomily than ever. " I'm fed up with this."

" Then we'll damned well haul it," cried Marney, almost angrily. " If only to give you something new to croak about."

We steamed to the third fleet. Marney gaffed the buoy, hauled as far as the ' tow,' then surrendered the ' tow '

to father and John. The rope of the first pot appeared.
Marney hauled, and seizing the pot itself, lifted it on
board. It contained a very large lobster.

The effect on our spirits was instantaneous.

" There you are ! " shouted Marney excitedly. " Didn't
I say so ? " He laid the pot on the coble seat, undid the
door, seized the lobster and held it up triumphantly.
" There you are ! God ! It's a beauty, too ! "

" If we could get a score like it we'd do well," said
Henry.

" Three-and-sixpence a time ! " said John, looking
round as he hauled. " It is a beauty ! "

John's face suddenly lighted up.

" Eh ! " he shouted. " Do you see whose pot that is ? "
We looked at the pot itself for the first time.

" It's one I made," John acclaimed triumphantly.
" You take a good look at that pot before you stow it,
Marney. Then, maybe, you'll know how to make a pot
that will fish. Hurry up. There's another coming. Whose
is it this time ? "

" It's one of father's," said Marney, reaching down for
it. " It's empty."

There were only twenty-two pots in that last fleet. It
beat the first two fleets in yielding that solitary lobster.
Gloom had settled on us once more by the time the last
pots of it were hauled. We turned and shot it again in
complete silence. And when that task was done, we set
off for Muddy Dooks. We grappled for two more hours,
working gradually seawards of the place where we had
shot the missing pots. We fouled either a rock, or another
wreck, and lost a grapple, but we found no trace of lobster-
pots. It was now well past noon. We had eaten the food
we had brought. Henry said suddenly :

" Well, I reckon we can give those pots up for lost. I knew it ! They've washed out to sea. We'll go and haul the others again, and if there's nothing in them, we'll take them out to deep water, and get home. The Fosdycks won't be very pleased, waiting all this time for us to launch up."

" They'll be pleased enough," said John, " particularly if we go ashore with only one lobster. I've got a feeling we're going to lose this lot of pots, too, before they've paid for themselves. I shouldn't be surprised if we lose them to-night."

" For God's sake hold your jaw," said Marney quite crossly. " It's asking for bad luck, talking like that. I bet we get a score of lobsters this time. Why shouldn't we ? "

No one offered an answer to that question.

" Open her out," said father.

We steamed back to Low Batts. We began again with the fleet that Marney and I had shot. We hauled three pots for nothing ; then a pot with two crabs in it. Two more pots came up empty. The next had two lobsters. The next two, the next four. There was not a pot in the rest of the fleet which did not contain either one or two lobsters. Curiously, neither Marney, nor John, nor father commented on this extraordinary change in our fortunes. It was as though something magical was happening, and that speech would break the spell. We shot that fleet once more in the same place, and steamed on to the second one. The first pot we hauled had three lobsters in it. It was John's pot. But John said nothing. Only his eyes indicated that feverish infection which possessed us all.

That fleet yielded thirty-five lobsters, and at least a dozen crabs. The last fleet, of twenty-four pots, brought the grand total of lobsters up to seventy-three. We re-shot that fleet. John, without waiting for orders, opened the engine throttle, and Henry put the tiller round for home. It was not until then that any one spoke.

" We'll go in and help the Fosdycks with their coble, and have a bit of tea. Then we'll come out again and shift the pots into deep water for the night. We might get a few more."

Father tried to say this with his usual complacence, but he completely failed. His voice was shaky. His eyes were lit with exultation.

" Those lobsters must have started to feed on the flood tide. But it's queer we did so badly with the first haul, and got a lot like this the second."

John pronounced this with the lower part of his face wearing that familiar expression of gloom ; but his voice, too, was shaky, his eyes were bright.

Marney said with a supreme effort at complete indifference.

" Well, it shows there *are* lobsters here in January, if any one's got a mind to catch them."

And then it seemed the effort was too much for him.

" Now, what about the Fosdycks ? " he suddenly shouted exultantly. " Now who's got the laugh ? Seventy-three lobsters out of eighty-four new pots ! Now, who says the Lunns don't know how to fish ? I'm going to put them all in a box, and lay them in front of old Luke Fosdyck when we go ashore, and count them over one by one in three-and-sixpences ! "

" You'll do nowt of the sort," said Henry quietly. " We've had a bit of luck, and that should be enough for us. It's all I want. I don't want to crow over anybody."

" You didn't see old Luke's face when he dropped that buoy at my feet," Marney protested.

" Aye. And you managed to look the other way, when he hailed us this morning," said John. " He was grinning like hell."

" Hold your jaws," father answered. " I see what I want to see ; and you two would do better if you did the same. Luke and Tindal are both old men, and it's not for us to start plaguing them."

" All right," said Marney. " I'll put out the biggest lobster we've got, and give it to Luke for his tea. How would that suit ? "

" Aye. And perhaps he'd take you to the pictures next Saturday night," put in John.

Father ignored both remarks. He glanced back to Low Batts and said :

" I shouldn't have thought we'd have struck them like that bang off. But it's a rare spot for lobsters, Low Batts, if the weather keeps all right for you. If they'd been old pots instead of new ones, we'd have got a hundred. We might pick up another score after tea. We'll keep what we've got on board till we launch up. I don't want the Fosdycks to see them. It will only cause bad feeling."

As we passed between the Landing posts, we could see the Fosdyck brothers coming down the slipway. They began to walk down towards their coble as we drew in to the shore and, as we grounded, Luke waded out towards us. He looked puzzled, curious, and vexed.

" Me and Tindal thought you weren't coming ashore till midnight," he growled.

Henry smiled apologetically.

" We've only come in to give you a launch up," he said. " Don't trouble about us. There's bound to be somebody about when we come back again."

Luke waded a little nearer.

" So you've put some more pots in ? " he said gruffly.

" Aye," Henry replied. " We took 'em out this morning."

" Did you get any lobsters ? "

" We got a few. More than I expected from new pots. I reckon we were lucky. Are you ready for launching up ?"

Luke came nearer and, putting his hands on the coble gunwale, peered inside. The lobsters were in a large basket near where Marney was standing. The last time I had looked at this basket an oilskin was stretched carefully across it, hiding its contents. The oilskin was now lying on the coble bottom, hiding nothing but one of Marney's feet, and Marney was smiling innocently.

For a moment Luke said nothing. He seemed to be swallowing something. Then he said slowly :

" You've done well if you've got all those."

" Aye," said Henry, again apologetically. " It's not a bad haul, all things considered. But we might go a week and not do so well."

" And you might lose all your pots again, too, before you have another haul," Luke rejoined with asperity ; " like that first lot. I reckon it's a month too soon to start lobstering here. And I'll say it again. You'll lose more than you gain."

Henry said nothing. Luke turned away, and waded towards his own coble. We all got out. Marney was smiling. John was smiling. Henry, deliberately had turned his face towards the sea. And on the dry scaur close by, another of the Lunns was smiling. It was Steve, with one of his eyes still bearing the traces of his recent fight in vindication of the honour of his house.

CHAPTER TEN

" FISHING," said Marney, " is just like a game of snakes and ladders. You throw a dice, and make so many moves along the board, and maybe you find yourself on a ladder, and up you go. Next throw may land you on another ladder ; and then, just when you're doing well, and hoping for a throw that will land you on top of the board, damned if you don't hit a snake, and come down to the bottom, and have to start all over again ; while the chap who's missed every ladder, and hit almost every snake, lands home."

" We've hit plenty of snakes, anyway," said Amy. " We don't want to hit any more ! "

" We struck a damned good ladder this week ! "

" And a lot of good it will do us, if you go spending money like you did this afternoon. You spent more than three pounds. You spent over five shillings at Wool-worth's ! "

" What of it ! " said Marney recklessly. " You wanted a new coat, didn't you, and that stuff to make a best dress for the kid ? And I wanted a new hammer, and that chisel and brace and bit ? And we wanted a primus stove, so that I shouldn't have to bother lighting the fire on a morning when the fine weather comes ? What's brass for, if not to spend ? Put that coat on, and let's have a look at it. I wish you'd got that green one with the fancy cuffs. I like clothes with a bit of colour in them. Something bright. Come on. Put it on ! "

" I'll not put it on," Amy answered decisively. " I've

got the things to wash up. I don't see new clothes that often I can afford to make a mess of them. That coat's for Sunday best."

It was Saturday evening. Marney and Amy had gone to Burnharbour by the one-o'clock bus, leaving the baby with Marney's mother. They had brought back with them, in addition to the parcels that covered half the table, some cooked ham, a pork pie, a bag of cream buns, and an assortment of violently tinted confectioner's cakes.

We had indulged in an exciting tea. The cakes, however, had slightly misfired ; and Marney had been obliged to call for a more familiar delicacy.

" These shop cakes look all right," he said, rather wistfully, " but they're not a patch on home-made pastry, even if it's stale. Aren't there any cheese-cakes left ? "

Marney had gathered all the latest gossip from the fish-quay. It seemed that lobster fever was running as high at Burnharbour as it had done before the gale. Everybody was frenziedly engaged making new gear to replace what had been lost in that catastrophe.

" Aye," he went on, returning to his philosophic theme. " It's just like snakes and ladders. Look at us. We go and make all those pots. We look as though we're going to make a fortune out of them, by starting before Burn-harbour chaps. We go and land on a snake, and lose the lot. Burnharbour chaps start, and hit a ladder. Then they hit a big snake, and go back to starting-point. Then we have another throw. And we have a week's fine fishing, and a fine market, because the other chaps are thrown back. Next week they'll all be out again with as many pots as they've got made, and what will happen ? Prices will come down, and stay down, until another gale comes on sudden, smashes a lot of gear, and makes lobsters scarce again."

" So now you're hoping for another gale," said Amy quietly.

" No, I'm not. I don't want anybody to lose any gear. I'm just giving you the plain facts. If every Burnharbour boat is fishing next week, then lobsters will only fetch a quarter of what they've done this week. I'm not hoping for bad weather. But there's no getting away from the fact that fine weather cuts both ways, and that lobster fishing's like snakes and ladders, up and down, up and down, and the main thing from start to finish is the weather."

Marney was not being pessimistic. He was, as he had said, " merely stating the facts." We had ended a week of record fishing. Our average daily catch, from Monday until this morning (when we had moved the pots out to deep water for the week-end) had been ninety-six lobsters. Two small Burnharbour cobles, which had not started at the time of the great catastrophe, had been fishing since Tuesday, and had done very well. Prices had crept slowly down ; and it was only to be expected that they would go lower still when the whole Burnharbour fleet was fully equipped again, provided that the weather remained favourable.

We had watched the weather throughout the week, like outpost sentries on an exposed flank. The pots were waterlogged ; but on that rich, Low Batts fishing ground it was impossible to use anchors ; and an hour of a north-easterly swell would be enough to set them moving, to drive them into the surf and smash them as the pots of that Burnharbour boat had been smashed the night of the gale. Every night we had taken them out and anchored them on the deep water muddy ground where they were resting now.

"Anyway," said Marney, as Amy started to clear up the tea-things, "we've had a damned good week, and I shan't grumble, no matter what happens next. We lost a lot of brass over those first pots, but we've made more than we lost with the second. And we've turned the laugh properly on the Fosdycks. Old Luke hasn't spoken a word to me since last Tuesday. He didn't even say thank you, when I offered him a boiling of crabs. He's simply praying for another gale to come on sudden and smash up our pots."

Marney, I believed, exaggerated the ill-will of Luke. That the elderly brothers were jealous of our week's success, there could be little doubt ; but it was a wholesome, professional jealousy. Even Marney would not impute to them a genuine meanness of feeling. As for old Isaac, he had maintained his customary philosophic detachment. He expressed no astonishment at our catches. He had chuckled with gratitude when Marney had given him some crabs, and a bucket of stale fish for his cats and his two gulls. But he had not refrained from 'croaking.'

"It's all right ! " he had said. "You can catch lobsters when you've got pots, and the weather's all right. But you'll not catch any lobsters when you've lost your pots. And you'll lose them, I say you'll lose them for certain, where you're fishing now."

Marney had settled himself comfortably in front of the fire, and had begun to examine his purchases. I blessed the Woolworth hammer. But I wished he had bought half a dozen ; for I had small hopes that this one would be available next time it was wanted.

Suddenly the door opened and Steve walked in, a little out of breath and manifestly excited.

" Hey, Marney ! " he cried. " Did you fetch it ? "

Marney looked at him in feigned surprise.

" Fetch what ? "

" You know what," said Steve breathlessly. " That paper. *Don't* say you forgot it."

Marney gave a gesture of dismay.

" Well, I'm damned. I knew there was something I'd forgotten. Why didn't you remind me, Amy ? Never mind, Steve. I've got two cigarette cards for you."

Steve for a moment looked heart-broken. Tears were welling in his eyes, but he fought them back manfully.

" I bet you remembered everything else," he said, glancing ironically at the parcels. " It's just like you to forget that, when I've been looking forward to reading it all week. I don't want any cards. They'll only be ones I've got."

" Stop teasing him," Amy interrupted. " You know you were trying to read it all the way back in the bus. He's got it in his coat pocket, Steve."

Marney felt in his pocket, and said suddenly, with mock surprise :

" By Gum ! So I have. I'd clean forgotten all about it. But I haven't started the ' Grey Spider ' yet. I'll let you have it to-morrow."

Steve made a lightning move forward, but Marney drew the paper out of reach, and stared at the lurid illustration of the Grey Spider's latest horror printed on the cover.

" You're not going to have this one until you lend me last week's."

" I can't let you have it," Steve protested. " Father's got it, and he won't let me have it until he's finished. He was reading it out aloud to mother all dinner-time. He said he wanted to see if there was any bad language in it, but I know different. I'll lend it to you as soon as I can get it off him, Marney," Steve added persuasively. " I'll spit over on it ! "

Without calling upon Steve to make this time-honoured and most solemn form of attestation, Marney surrendered the paper. At the same time he drew Steve's attention to the heap of confectioner's cakes.

" You can take all those, Steve," he said.

But Steve was already dashing out of the house like a terrier with a stolen joint. Marney pulled out a half-finished rope mat from under the sofa, spread it across his knees, and started work on it. Shortly, Amy sat down, and, with the child feeding at her breasts, began mending a pair of Marney's stockings.

Here was the climax to our week's conflict with the sea. Outside, it was cold and very dark. Here was warmth, the red firelight, and in our hearts the quiet glow of victory. Yet as Marney sat, apparently engrossed in his fascinating homely task, I knew that he was listening to the faint noise of the surf on the scaur-ends, as a savage listens to the sound of distant war-drums.

CHAPTER ELEVEN

OUR material luck continued. With a blank of one day, when the wind blew south-east, raising a very nasty cross swell, we fished every day of the following week. Lobsters were phenomenally plentiful. Until Thursday, the market remained high. Even on Saturday, by which time most of the Burnharbour boats had come into action, and record catches were made, the price averaged one shilling and sixpence per lobster. We were making money. All the arrears of the cod-fishing season, and that initial disaster of the lost pots, had been comfortably wiped out. Marney and Amy took another trip to Burnharbour on Saturday afternoon. He bought another hammer, the first having been sent away in a barrel of lobsters whose lid had been nailed down with that mysterious unloseable iron bolt. John had bought himself a new concertina. Steve, Eddy and George all appeared on Sunday in brand-new suits. Yet on the following Monday morning, when, just before daybreak, we put to sea again, John was as gloomy as I had ever known him to be ; and Marney was anything but his usual cheerful self.

We were running out direct for the deep-water ground half a mile due east of Low Batts Point. It was not such a safe ground as Muddy Dooks was reputed to be. Between it and the land was a fierce tide race, which Marney had christened Worry Guts, an unholy place to be caught in, in spring tides and a northerly wind. But it was conveniently near to the lobster ground, a point of considerable importance, while we were practising this safety-first method of fishing.

" I thought things were too good to last," John growled, soon after we had left the Landing. " Every damned boat in Burnharbour will be lobstering this week. Lobsters won't be worth catching."

John, too, had been in Burnharbour on Saturday night. It had been a habit of his for the last six months to catch the five-o'clock bus and return by the special late bus, which ran on Saturday night for Bramblewick patrons of the ' pictures.' That John went to the ' pictures ' Marney had frequently expressed an optimistic doubt. Marney himself had been a regular patron of that late bus, when he had been courting Amy. But John was dark. Certainly there was nothing in his manner to suggest that his latest visit had been a very happy one.

" They've been having every Tom, Dick and Harry on to lobster-pot making this last week," he went on. " Some of their big boats will be fishing as many as two hundred pots. They'll bring prices down to nothing. There'll soon be not a lobster left close in."

" Well, that will put prices up, anyway," said Marney, not very enthusiastically.

" Aye," John retorted. " You can always get big prices for things you haven't got to sell. What the hell's the good of that ? "

" Don't be so damned miserable," Marney answered. " There's always something to be caught and sold if you've got a mind to do it. And prices haven't dropped that much yet. Look on the bright side of things, brother John. Isn't old Luke praying for another gale to smash up all those Burnharbour chaps' pots, to give Bramblewick men a chance ? You know there'll not be a real glut of lobsters until the Fosdycks start. That will be the time for us to complain."

Henry grinned at this. There was no doubt that the Fosdycks could catch cod. Henry had never pretended that it was anything but the motor-coble that gave him the advantage in this respect. And at salmon fishing (at which the Lunns hitherto had never tried their hand) it was generally admitted that Luke was without equal along this coast. But the Fosdycks had never done well with lobsters. Of late years they had scarcely bothered with them, confining their activities to the less risky, although less lucrative, catching of crabs.

" I don't know what you're grumbling about," Henry put in. " We've had one of the best runs of fishing I've ever known. And it looks as though we're still going to have fine weather. What do you want ? "

" I know what I want," said Marney.

" What's that ? " said John.

" I want another gale," Marney answered quietly. " There's been too much fine weather for my liking."

I saw a quick, thoughtful look in Henry's eyes, as he looked to the north-east. But John, slower to grasp the subtle significance of Marney's remark, turned angrily on his brother.

" Don't talk so damned daft ! What do you want bad weather for ? To smash up another lot of pots ? I don't want another gale."

" Then stop complaining when it's fine," Marney answered dryly.

There was nothing in the appearance of the sky or sea at present to suggest that Marney's subtle wish would be fulfilled. There was a wind, very light, from the south-west. The sky was overcast, but only with innocent-looking rain-clouds. There was a swell, but it was from the south, and scarcely noticeable. The worst the weather promised was a freshening of wind from the south-west, with a drizzle and fog, possibly rain. Not at all bad weather for lobster fishing, considering that it was still winter.

The subject dropped. We had reached the pots. John and Henry hauled. Marney took the catch from each pot, then handed the pot to me to stow, for our run into the lobster ground.

There were no lobsters here on muddy ground. But many of the pots were literally full of crabs ; so that the netted ends were bulging out with them. Marney was contemptuous of crabs. They were fine ones. But such is the law of supply and demand, they were scarcely worth the cost of packing and sending to market.

There were other things in the pots to interest one, however. Starfish, deep crimson and turquoise, sucked tight upon the remains of the bait. Egg-sacs of octopuses, like elongated toy balloons of pellucid blue, festooned the netting.

" They're fine things for nature study, are lobster pots," Marney remarked, observing my interest. " Particularly if they've been a long time without being hauled. You find all sorts of things in them."

" Aye," put in John, with an unexpected grin. " Even hens' eggs."

" We got any amount of hens' eggs at Sledburgh once," Henry went on with perfect seriousness. " Good ones, too, only some were a bit cracked."

I suspected that I was having my leg pulled, but I was wrong.

" They came from a ship that had her back broken on a scaur," Henry continued. " One of her holds had nothing but eggs in it. The crates broke up, and the eggs washed out, and started to roll about the sea bottom. They went into our pots, just like seaweed or anything else washes in, with the tide."

" It shows they were fresh eggs or they wouldn't have remained sunk," said John informatively. " That's the best test for a hen's egg."

" Father once found a guillemot's egg the same way," Henry continued. " Aye. And I know of a chap who found a set of false teeth in a lobster pot. That was queer, wasn't it ? "

" Somebody must have dropped 'em overboard, being seasick," suggested Marney.

" They more likely came from someone who was drowned," said John morbidly. " Were they gold ? "

" Aye. They had a gold plate."

" I wish we could catch a dozen sets instead of these damned crabs," said Marney. " They'd pay better than lobsters ! "

We had travelled far from nature study, and along a rather gloomy track.

" I often wonder," Marney went on rather thoughtfully, as he rebaited another pot, " what it would be like if the sea suddenly ebbed miles out, and left all this bare. There'd be some queer sights, I bet."

" We'd see that German submarine that was sunk with a depth charge just outside of here," said Henry. " And at least a dozen steamers that were blown up during the war."

" I've heard tell there was one of the ships of the Spanish Armada sunk off High Batts," said Marney. " It might be full of gold."

" Aye," said John. " And we might even see those damned lobster-pots of ours. Full of lobsters ! I don't think ! "

"Hold your jaw!" father rebuked smartly. "We know all about that without you reminding us. There's a Burnharbour boat coming down from the nor'ard," he added, looking suddenly in that direction. "We'll have to look smart, or he'll get his pots in on our ground."

We had nearly reached the end of the second fleet. The Burnharbour boat, a large motor-coble, was just north of Low Batts Point when, with the two fleets stacked from our bows to midships, we turned landwards. We recognised it shortly as the very boat which had been fishing on 'our' ground the day of the gale; but it had already started shooting, close in, but well out of our way.

I knew, however, that its presence had set my companions thinking. We shot our two fleets in silence; turned back to sea again, hauled the third fleet, and brought that close in. Then we set off for home. All three Lunns preserved that moody silence. The wind had freshened a little, and the moorland hills were garlanded with mist, yet there was still no indication of any drastic change in the weather.

"I wonder how the Fosdycks have done?" John remarked at last, as we drew into the Landing.

The Fosdycks, who had gone off the same time as ourselves at the south end of the bay, had been ashore only a few minutes; and Luke and Tindal were just carrying a basket on to the scaur.

"They've got one good basket of something," Marney said quietly, as they tipped it into a rock pool for cleaning. "They're going back for another."

We ran in alongside their coble, and by that time three baskets of fish had been carried ashore. Luke turned to greet us. He was actually smiling.

"Now, then," he said genially. "It's still keeping fine."

" Aye," Henry answered, " and it looks like lasting. You've done well this morning. What are they ? It looks as though you'd got some haddock from here."

" We've got nothing else *but* haddocks," said Luke. " There's only two codling among them. First good catch of haddock we've had this winter. I thought they'd all gone. But it seems they haven't."

It seemed, too, that for once the laugh was not on the Fosdycks, and Marney's comment, I thought, was distinctly sporting.

" They're a fine sample, too," he said, as we looked at them. " You ought to get a good price for them with all the Burnharbour boats lobstering."

As we parted on the top of the slipway, however, for our respective breakfasts, he gave me a private qualification to this remark.

" They won't do that often. It's only luck ; and if the weather would change, lobsters would be worth ten times as much as haddock."

John said nothing, but I imagined that he had at last discovered the true significance of Marney's subtle wish, as he took a quick glance back at the sea, which still gave no indication of the north-east gale that was to be blowing fiercely within an hour.

CHAPTER TWELVE

EVEN Henry had never known a gale blow up so suddenly and unexpectedly. We had planned to go out to the pots about eleven o'clock, after we had helped the Fosdycks launch up, and packed the crabs. We had scarcely begun the latter operation, when Marney gave a shout, and pointed to Low Batts.

" Look at it ! " he yelled. " The wind's turned north-east ! "

There was as yet no conspicuous change in the aspect of the sea, which was tolerably smooth, and of a uniform grey. The change was only atmospheric. The south-west wind had dropped almost twenty minutes ago, and the drizzle had ceased. Now the cloud-pall to the north-east had resolved into heavy dark billows moving rapidly shorewards across the torn sky. Before Marney spoke again, an ice-cold air current was playing fitfully on our cheeks.

" It's north-east, all right," he said tensely. " Shall we have time to pack the crabs ? "

We were all in the coble. We had just started to pack a barrel when Marney had first shouted. Henry and John were now staring towards Low Batts. John took the responsibility of answering Marney's question. He suddenly laid his hands on the engine casing.

" No. We haven't time," he shouted. " To hell with the crabs. Come on, all of you. Push the boat off, and let's get the pots out to deep water. We don't want to lose another lot. They'll smash up in half an hour, where they're lying now. For God's sake, come on ! "

Henry said nothing. For a minute longer he remained staring seawards. Then he climbed over the coble side. We quickly did likewise. The coble was barely afloat. We pushed her out until she was clear of the bottom and climbed in again. John had primed the engine. He gave the starting-handle a swing. The engine coughed, but it did not start. He opened the priming valves, squirted some more petrol into the cylinders, and again swung the handle. Again the engine coughed, but refused to start. John moved to repeat the process.

" What's up ? " Henry demanded, just a little tensely. " Are your tanks full ? "

Marney sprang to the petrol tank, and unscrewed the cap.

" Empty," he said laconically. " Give us that tin."

I seized a petrol tin from the boat bottom. It felt suspiciously light. It proved to be empty. There was only one other tin in the boat. It also was empty. Marney jumped out and ran up the scaur towards the slipway. The puffs of icy air had grown to a definite wind, before he was back, his face wet with perspiration. There was already a gleam of white, at Low Batts Point.

" Look lively ! " said father, who had not for a moment relaxed his seawards watch during Marney's absence.

Marney began to fill the tank. John again primed the engine.

" Let her have it," said Marney. " There's plenty of juice in now."

John " let her have it." This time there was not even a cough. He tried again, with no better result.

" Plugs must be fouled," said Marney. " Let's have a look at them. Where's the spanner ? "

John pulled out a box of very rusty tools from under a

seat, and began hurriedly to rummage among them for the desired tool. I observed a chisel which had been searched for urgently a week ago, but while there were many spanners, the required one was not there.

" It must have dropped under the bottom boards," said John, whose face also now dripped with perspiration. " I had it only yesterday."

We turned up the bottom boards without success. Then suddenly Marney leapt overboard again.

" Damned if I didn't take it to fix up our mangle last night," he muttered. " I won't be a minute."

He ran for the slipway. We waited for him in silence, gazing towards Low Batts. The sea had gone darker there now, giving a clear relief to the lines of broken water at the cliff foot. Wisps of white cloud were racing the heavier ones shorewards; there was the first suggestion of a counter swell farther out, where the line of the sea cut the sky.

Ten minutes passed before Marney, completely out of breath, arrived with the missing tool. John turned on him furiously.

" Next time you want a spanner for your damned mangle go and buy one. If we've lost those pots it will be your fault."

Marney said nothing. He looked distinctly chastened. John removed the two sparking plugs. They were both foul. He cleaned them, left them to Marney to screw back, and again primed the engine. He swung the handle then until he was exhausted; but the engine still refused to start. Henry, who very rarely interfered with the mechanical side of the boat, suddenly moved over and seized the handle. He gave it a couple of powerful swings. The engine started without a murmur. He moved back to the tiller. We began to move down the Landing. But we hadn't travelled a dozen lengths before we stopped again.

" She must be choked," said Henry curtly. " Take out the jet, and look at it."

The plug spanner did not fit the nut of the jet. John began another frenzied search of the tool box, and finally took from it a very rusty pair of pliers.

" I didn't borrow that spanner," Marney said revengefully. " I saw you nailing down a crab barrel with it a day or two ago."

Henry said nothing as he glanced alternatively at the engine, and the north-east sea. The ever-freshening wind had blown the coble almost to the shore again before John had removed the jet, blown through it, and screwed it back. The engine started easily. We turned again for the sea. It stopped before we had reached the posts. John removed the plugs. They were foul. He cleaned them, put them back, and once more we got under way. We had no further trouble with the engine. Like a capricious but good-hearted woman, it had indulged in a mood, and having exasperated almost beyond endurance, had decided to behave.

We could not have stood much more. Already we had lost a precious hour. As we passed between the posts the coble felt the swell, and there was no mistaking a northeast swell for a southerly one. No one spoke. We got into our oilskins, and squatted down as low as we could to protect ourselves from the freezing wind, and the spray which whipped over the bows.

Here, by a miracle, was the weather Marney had wished for. I saw no satisfaction in his eyes, however, as he looked ahead for the buoys. The seas were now breaking heavily

K

on the rocks at Low Batts Point. We had left the pots in less than three fathoms of water ; not more than a hundred yards from the rocks themselves. In calm weather it would take us two hours to haul them and move them out to the deep, muddy ground. It seemed now that in less than one hour, no boat of our size could possibly live in the water where the three fleets lay.

We started on the first fleet we came to. We had to haul stern first against the wind, and sea, and tide. The seas as yet were short, but they broke under the low coble stern, and sent torrents of freezing spray in our faces as we hauled.

" Never mind what's in them," Henry shouted to Marney. " Stow them well. That's the main thing. We'll have to take two fleets on board."

I was helping to haul. Marney himself gave a hand between pots ; but I noticed that when a pot with a lobster did come on board, he managed to get it out before returning to the ' tow,' again. And the devil was in that ' tow.' It seemed incredible that a ' string ' of lobster-pots, each weighing when soaked not more than twenty pounds, could put such a strain against the strength of four men. The rope was newly tarred, and was encrusted with sharp sand. It cut our wet, half-frozen hands like emery cloth, and one daren't leave go to protect them with the woollen mitts which even Henry and John wore in very cold weather. Yet one did not notice the pain then. We were all out, as men are in the fever of battle, and completely possessing us was a fighting exultation.

As each pot came on board, as each sea smashed in our faces, Marney shouted ; and it was like a war-cry, giving defiance to the storm. One ceased to think ahead, one lost all sense of danger. One felt in that rope the strength of the sea itself, and in each foot of it won was the thrill of victory.

We won that fleet, but it cost us an hour ; and before we had reached the first buoy of the second fleet, it had started to snow. Even the nearby cliff soon became almost invisible. The seas were growing longer and more danger- ous as the gale got into its stride. The weight of the pots, too, was narrowing our free-board ; yet their weight was not so perilous as their bulk. With one fleet on board, the stack was four feet above the gunwale. With half the second fleet in, it had risen another foot. The shape of the coble was such that it was impossible to prevent the stack swaying as we pitched and rolled. Soon Marney was obliged to give up helping with the ' tow,' in order that he could steady the topmost layer of pots.

I expected any moment while we fought the sea for that second fleet, to see Henry cut away. There was a period of nearly ten minutes, during a terrific hail-squall, when we merely hung on to the ' tow ' with all our strength without gaining an inch, with the spray driving continually over us ; there were times when I took the spray for green sea and believed that we were swamped. His knife was stuck in the gunwale close by him. When we were four pots from the end, a sea broke under our stern, lifted the boat up, and wrenched the ' tow ' clean away from us. I saw Henry's hand touch the knife then, but he did not grasp it. We got hold again, and continued hauling. We won that second fleet intact. There remained the third.

As the last pot came on board, and Henry started to haul the buoy rope in, John sprang eagerly to the engine,

" Shall we take these out, or shall we take them home, and make sure of them ? " he shouted.

" We're not going to chuck away a fleet of pots,"
Marney put in quickly, his eyes already on the remaining
buoys. " We're going to take these out, and come back for
the third."

" There'll be too much sea by then," John protested.
" I vote we make sure of these two. They might easily
shift in deep water if it gets much worse, and then it will
be another Muddy Dooks. What do you say, father ? "

Father was straining his eyes towards the buoys of the
third fleet, some distance to the north-east, but not quite
so close in as the first two had been. I knew what he was
thinking. We could haul that fleet now, but we could not
stow it. The coble already was perilously overloaded. If
we ran the other two out to deep water, there was a bare
chance that we could save the third, and take it home ; but
with a slight risk that we should lose the two deep-water
fleets if the gale was exceptionally bad. But if we went
home direct, then for a certainty there would be no time
to return for the third, which would inevitably be lost.
Would the first two be safe in deep water ?

Again Henry Lunn had to make a gambler's decision.
Yet he could not have guessed what ultimately hung upon
it. As the coble gathered way, he swung the tiller round
until we headed for the open sea.

" We'll chance it," he shouted. " If it gets no worse
than this in half an hour, we'll get that other fleet all
right."

I had imagined that during the last two hours I had seen
the limits of our own and the coble's power of endurance,
that only pure luck had saved us from being swamped.
The sea which rose as we turned head on to the weather,
put the boat almost vertically on its stern ; and it was
only a foretaste of what was to come.

" Hold on to them ! " Henry shouted, as we lifted.

We hung on. The whole stack of pots moved towards us. It was the reverse dip of the wave which stopped them from shooting over the stern, not our desperate resistance.

We had half a mile to go to reach the deep-water ground, from which, in tranquil weather, we had taken the pots that morning. Hitherto we had been in the comparative shelter of the headland cliff, and inside the main tidal current. In a quarter of an hour we were clear of the land, and in the worst section of that famous tide race, which Marney called Worry Guts. It was an apt name. On a calm day with a neap tide, it was enough to give a small boat an uncomfortable movement. What made it doubly dangerous now was that the tide had turned, raising a counter swell to that of the gale. The seas came on us with a corkscrew motion impossible to anticipate. That we weathered one of them was to me miraculous.

We hung on to the pots desperately, jamming our thighs against the coble seats. We pressed against each aftwards sway. We eased the corresponding forward movement ; but when they went sideways we were powerless, and only Henry's consummate seamanship saved them. It seemed to me that all the ferocious enmity of the sea had been transmitted to that stack of pots. They were alive. Their movement was brutal. The frozen netting of them cut our hands. The sharp corners of the weighted bottoms bruised us. And yet without them we could not have made a passage. The stack took the weight of the seas which were now breaking continually over the bow. The pots alone saved us from filling.

Under normal conditions we should have run out to the deep-water ground in less than ten minutes. At least an hour had passed when Henry gave a shout that was scarcely audible above the roar of the wind and sea. We were out of the tide-race. The seas now came only one way, but they were too dangerous for us to risk running with them. We turned to them head-on, with the engine slightly throttled. At that, they and the wind would move us south-west against the engine, fast enough to run the pots out clear.

We took up our positions for ' shooting.' The huge coil of ' tow,' already an inch deep in snow, lay to the starboard side of the coble. The individual ropes of the pots ran from it to the stack, at regular intervals. John stood near the coil, but near enough to the engine to reach the throttle. Marney remained amidships, ready for the actual shooting ; while I hung on to the swaying stack as best I could.

Marney threw the buoy overboard. He had already bent on the deep-water anchor, and he let this go. He seized the first pot and threw it clear. John seized the topmost coil of ' tow,' cleared it overboard, and shouted to Marney :

" Right ! "

A sea which broke clean over our bows leapt up and snatched the second pot as a salmon might snatch a fly. It left us breathless, but John did not falter in getting the ' tow ' clear away.

The ' shooting ' went on. We were steaming north-east, but travelling at least more than the equivalent of our engine speed south-west. We were moving homewards. One had a sense of home ; of the tranquil Landing ; the immobility of earth ; one had a thought of Marney's cottage, the darkness coming on outside, and inside the firelight. We were fighting the sea again, and we were winning. Two fleets were almost certainly safe. The third would be our hardest fight, but we should not have to cross Worry Guts with it. We would take it direct home. And more hung upon the issue of this fight than the saving of pots. During a temporary period of moderate visibility, we had caught a glimpse of that Burnharbour boat to the north, hauling its pots in the teeth of the gale. Involuntarily the thought sneaked through one's mind that the gale would end the glut of lobsters.

The ' shooting ' went on. The gale was steadily increasing in force ; but the stack of pots was as steadily growing less, and the movement of the stack was a little more controllable. We threw the last buoy of the first fleet overboard. We started directly on the second fleet. Should we have time to go in for the third ? It was snowing too heavily now for us to tell how much broken water there was where we had left it. With the stack apparently safer I started to help Marney by lifting the next pot, and moving it within his reach. We had shot half of the second fleet, when the coble, recovering from a sea which had put her nearly on end, struck another on the port bow, which came on board. I was standing on a seat with my body leaning against the stack, my hands reached out to grasp the next pot, when the sea came. I heard John shout, and I felt his shoulder against mine as he hung on to save the top row of pots from going overboard. The next moment I heard him shout again :

" I'm going ! I'm going ! " followed by an awful shout from Henry, " Eh ! John's overboard ! "

I had seen nothing. The sea had blinded me. And as the coble recovered, I lost my balance on the slippery seat, and rolled down to the starboard side of the coble close to Marney, who was desperately hanging on to the receding 'tow.' I struggled to my feet, instinctively seized the 'tow,' and leaned overboard. There was no sight of, John. I looked at Henry. He was leaning forward as far as he dare without leaving hold of the tiller.

" Can't you see him ? " he shouted in an awful voice. " For God's sake hang on."

We hung on. We tried to haul, for the thought automatically must have possessed each of us that John was caught in the rope of the pots which had gone. His felt hat was floating close to the bow.

" I daren't leave the tiller," Henry shouted, " propeller may hit him if we turn. Hang on. Haul if you can ! "

" Shall I stop the engine ? " Marney shouted.

" No. Haul. It's our only chance."

Another sea broke over us. The coble lifted, and wrenched the ' tow ' out of our hands. We felt blindly for it, and as we seized it, we heard another violent shout from Henry :

" There he is ! . . . There ! "

We left go of the ' tow,' but Henry anticipated us. He leapt from where he stood to the midship seat, leaned over the opposite side of the coble, and pulled John by his hair and shoulders into the boat. The next moment he was back at the tiller, measuring an oncoming wave.

" Go on shooting ! " he yelled.

We were aware that a miracle had taken place before our eyes : but we went on shooting. And by the time Marney and I had got the next three pots clear, John, still vomiting sea-water, was back in his customary position, and was clearing the ' tows.' We had no time for talking. Within the last few minutes the gale had reached a terrifying force. The land had cleared. The first sight of it was enough to show the impossibility of saving the third fleet.

We were lucky to have a straight run for home. We carried on. The last pot went overboard. Marney threw the buoy after it, and he made no gesture of disapproval as Henry turned the coble round for home. We looked instantly at John. He had collapsed on the engine casing. His teeth were chattering, his face was the colour of a corpse. Marney and I unfurled the coble sail and wrapped it round him. We pulled off his sea-boots and stockings, and rubbed his bare feet and hands with snow ; until at last we were relieved to hear him swear.

" Don't put any more of that damned stuff on me," he muttered between chattering teeth. " I'm cold enough without you making it worse. For God's sake give me a fag."

We were running with the sea and gale behind us. We managed to light him a cigarette, and then, swaying to the wild movement of the coble, we stared at him, while the full realisation of his escape slowly dawned on us : dawned on John, too.

" I went right under the coble," he chattered. " Right under her bottom. I saw the damned propeller spinning round. I tell you I went right under. God ! I'm damned well perished with cold. How far are we from home ? "

" We'll be in in ten minutes," shouted Henry, in an unusually anxious voice. " Get up and move about. Don't sit still or you'll die of cold."

" Then I'll damned well die," stammered John, with sudden asperity. " I'd like to see you running about in your bare feet in a snowstorm, when you've just been under a coble bottom. Do you think I'm a damned walrus ? Give me my sea-boots."

Clearly John was recovering.

" I hope you're satisfied," he went on savagely,

" praying for a gale. You've got it, haven't you ? Another fleet gone west. And the other two likely to go before this is finished. I tell you I'm fed up with this damned carry-on. I'm going to chuck it after this. I'm going back to sea. I'm damned well frozen inside-out."

We did not argue with him. In spite of his vehement protests, Marney and I continued to rub his hands and feet until the circulation in them was restored. Then we helped him into his boots. We were not aware that we had safely made the passage of the Landing mouth until Henry shouted to Marney to stand by the engine. The rollers were not yet so formdable as those we had tackled on that memorable occasion. Only an odd one was breaking right across, and father had timed his entry perfectly. The tide was half-way up. Marney throttled the engine. We ran into smooth water, and gently touched the bottom. Then Henry moved anxiously to John.

" Get home quickly, and get your things changed," he said. " Never mind the coble. The Fosdycks will help us up. They're coming down now. Can you walk all right ? "

From that moment I was left with no doubt that John at heart was a very true Lunn. He jumped up and flung the sail away from him.

" What do you think I am ? " he shouted angrily at his father. " Do you think I'm a damned kid, running home because I've got my trousers wet, and having the Fosdycks laughing at me ? They've got enough to laugh at without that, with those haddocks they caught this morning, and us very likely losing all our pots again. Come on. Let's get the wheels down. And you can all hold your jaws about me going overboard. I don't want to be the laughing-stock of Bramblewick ! "

CHAPTER THIRTEEN

THE gale lasted only until Wednesday night ; but in that time it did almost as much damage as the previous one had done. Four Burnharbour boats lost their complete equipment of new pots. Four boats lost at least half their gear. The boat we had seen just north of Low Batts lost three fleets out of five. We had definitely lost one ; for the wreckage of it was washed up on Low Batts on Tuesday. The safety of the other two was more than doubtful when we set off to haul them on Thursday morning. One of their buoys had been found near Garry Beck last night.

This was " snakes and ladders " with a vengeance ! There was no glut of lobsters now. The few which had gone to market on Monday (thanks to Marney, there were twenty-seven of ours) had averaged three shillings each. And here was fine weather again, an excellent market, if only we had the gear to fish with !

John, physically, was none the worse for his remarkable adventure. Mentally, its effect lingered ; and we were not a very cheerful company, although Marney seemed fairly optimistic as to our chances of finding the pots safe.

" The worst that can have happened to them," he said, " is that they've been scrubbed a bit, and that we'll have to waste time mending them. We didn't take them far enough out for my liking. They weren't so very far from the rock edge."

" We went far enough out for me," said John. " Next time I want a bathe I'll bring a bathing costume with me. And next time you pray for a gale I hope it's you who does the bathing, not me ! And I'll tell you what," he added. " If we *have* lost those two fleets, I'm giving it up for good. I'm damned well fed up."

" Lobsters may be back at three-and-six to-day," put in Henry very quietly. " It strikes me we're going to have another good week, if only we get our pots all right."

" Aye. If," John retorted. " You know what old Isaac says, ' Pots are all right, if you've got them. But they're no use when they're gone ! ' If. Always If ! If you'd taken my advice for once we'd have had those two fleets safe anyway. What's the use of lobsters bringing that price if we've got no pots ! "

Henry said nothing : but I knew that he was wincing. He had made that gambler's decision to try and save all three fleets. As a result John had been nearly drowned, and one fleet for certain had been lost. I saw more than an ordinary relief in his eyes when Marney shouted :

" Don't talk so damned daft ! There's the first buoy there, almost where we left it. There's the other two a bit farther south. It must be this fleet that buoy came off. Cheer up, John," he added as he reached for the gaff. " You'll be able to buy a trombone to go with your concertina next Saturday night. We're going to start coining money again."

" We'll wait and see," said John. " We haven't hauled them yet. Something must have happened to this fleet or its buoy wouldn't have gone. We'll wait and see."

We steamed up to the buoy. Marney gaffed it, and hauled in until he came to the ' tow.' John stopped the engine. We took up our usual positions for hauling. Marney beamed as he waited to receive the first pot.

" Come on," he shouted to his father and John, "let's get them up and into shallow water and the blue-backs.

I've got lobster fever again ; strong as ever. I told you we only wanted a gale to liven things up. Haven't you got the anchor off the bottom yet ? "

Henry and John were straining their utmost at the ' tow.' At a sign from Henry I joined them. The sea was quite smooth again ; there was no wind, and very little tide ; yet we could scarcely win a foot of the rope on board.

" There's something wrong," panted John. " Come and give us a hand, Marney. Don't stand there staring."

Marney obeyed.

" The anchor must be fast," he said with a suspicion of uneasiness.

" I don't think it is," Henry muttered rather gloomily. " I felt it come loose a minute ago. The first pot ought to be well off the bottom. But there's something wrong."

We took a short rest.

" I know what it is," said John. " The whole damned lot have moved, and got piled up in a heap. It will take us all day to clear them. I knew something like this was going to happen. Didn't I tell you ? "

We started to haul again. Obviously the pots were not fast to the sea-bed ; for with our united efforts we succeeded in hauling another fathom or two on board.

" We're not more than three fathoms from the anchor now," said Henry, " so it can't be that. I expect John's right. They're all tied up in a heap."

" Aye. And most of them will be smashed up too," John qualified. " We ought to be praying for another gale. This one hasn't done half enough damage."

Once more we were physically all out : but this time there was no sense of exultation. If the pots had moved, and become entangled in a ' heap,' for a certainty most of them would be damaged ; and instead of fishing with them we should have to take them ashore, and at least two days might be spent putting them in repair again.

We paused while we removed our coats and rolled up our sleeves. It took us fifteen minutes of terrific exertion to reach the anchor : another ten minutes before the first pot came on board. It was not damaged, however, and it contained nearly twenty crabs, which Marney, more respectful than usual, quickly removed before turning to the ' tow ' again.

" Crabs ought to bring a better price now," he said. " That gale will have improved things all round."

" Yes," said John. " I was just thinking the same. Wait till you see the next pot ! "

The next pot should have followed the first in less than a minute. At least five minutes elapsed, before Henry announced, gloomily :

" Here it is. There's two more with it, all tangled up."

" Didn't I tell you ? " said John. " They're in a hell of a mess. We'll be lucky if we get this fleet hauled by tea-time."

Marney leaned over the side and seized the first one. The ropes of the other two were laced about it in an indescribable tangle. I had to help him with it over the boat side. Its netting was torn in several places, and it contained one enormous crab.

Marney stood and looked at that pot curiously.

" Can't you reach the other two ? " said Henry. " Never mind that one now," he added rather crossly. " Hurry up. What are you staring at ? "

Marney was quite oblivious to his father's irritation. He was regarding the pot with increasing curiosity.

" Come on," snapped John. " Get hold of these other pots. What the hell's up with you ? "

Marney suddenly picked up the pot, and pushed it along the seat to his father.

" What's up ? " he echoed excitedly. " Have you ever seen that pot before, father ? "

It was Henry's turn to look astonished. He knotted the ' tow ' round a thole-pin, peered closely at the pot, then suddenly looked overboard.

" By God ! You're right ! " he muttered. " There's another ' tow ' there ! "

John turned, bewildered.

" What's up with you both ? Have you gone potty? There's only one old crab in the damned thing."

" There's more than an old crab," shouted Marney. " Look a bit closer, brother John. Look at those crab shells."

I was still as mystified as John. I examined the pot. The fact that in addition to the big crab, there were in it the shells of several smaller ones, and some empty whelks, did not immediately signify anything important. Then suddenly I saw John's gloomy face lighten with a broad grin of understanding.

" Well I'm damned ! " he muttered. " It's one of the lost pots from Muddy Dooks. Who'd believe it ! "

" That old crab would, I know," Marney answered. "He must have eaten off all his pals, since that first night in Muddy Dooks. Come on, you chaps," he added with wild excitement. " The whole fleet will be here. Very likely the other two. The whole lot must have drifted down in that gale, and we put this fleet right on top of them."

He leaned over the side.

" Aye," he shouted. " One of these is an old pot. They're *all* here ! Isn't that an old one, father ? "

Father also was peering overboard.

" Aye," he said, in a very shaky voice. " It looks as though we've fallen right on top of them, and with this fleet moving a bit, they've all fouled. It's almost too good to be real. . . . Come on," he added suddenly laying hands upon the knotted ' tow,' " there's going to be some hard work here. We'll be lucky if we clear them all by dark. Particularly if we do strike the other ; and there's no reason why we shouldn't."

" I don't mind a bit of work," said John, eagerly seizing hold of the ' tow.'

" Aye. And you don't mind a gale, and a ducking," said Marney, with quiet triumph, " when it turns out like this."

" I don't mind anything so long as we keep the laugh against the Fosdycks," John answered ; and, "God ! " he added, " if we get only two of the old fleets, we'll have as many pots as we can work."

" And lobsters fetching three-and-six," said Marney, lifting two more pots on board. " You'll be able to get wed on what we'll earn this week. Here we are ! Another old crab and a score of skeletons. I shouldn't have liked to have been a little crab in one of these pots. Fancy being eaten by your own mates. That big one must have all those others inside him. Didn't I tell you lobster pots were fine things for nature study ? I'm going to keep that one for my tea, if old Luke won't take it for a present. Next pot, please. Do you think we *are* going to find them all, father ? "

" I don't know," Henry answered quietly. " But it's a damned good job we didn't take the two fleets home, isn't it ? I'll be pleased enough if we only get one. It's a miracle, anyway."

It was a miracle. It took us until late in the afternoon

to haul, and clear the tangle, and to make temporary repairs to those few pots which were damaged. We did not take them into shallow water. But we had salved two of the lost fleets. We had four fleets to shoot on the lobster ground to-morrow morning, and the market looked like holding for at least another week.

Book   Two

CHAPTER ONE

It was a Sunday in early April. I had 'lunched' at Marney's. Amy had washed up and was in the bedroom, changing into her Sunday 'best.' Marney, already in his Sunday 'best' (blue serge trousers and jacket, new blue guernsey and smart black boots), was in front of the fire holding the baby, who also was in its Sunday 'best,' a one-piece knitted costume of blue with yellow stripes, which Amy, at Marney's special request, had made from a pattern presented with a popular woman's weekly.

Amy was going to have tea with a married sister, who lived half-way between Bramblewick and Burnharbour. She was to take the baby and catch the two o'clock bus. But there was still some doubt as to whether Marney would go.

"I don't like Sundays," Marney remarked, rather wistfully, as he listened to the sounds of drawers being opened and closed upstairs. "I never feel quite natural on a Sunday. Mind, I don't mind having a lie-in for once, particularly if it's been a hard week. But when you get up, and get into a pair of slippers, instead of your sea-boots, and shave, and put on your best togs, it's all like having something tight coiled round your neck. Aye. And it's worse still when you look out of the window, and see it's fishing weather, and know you're not going off."

"What have you done with my nail-scissors, Marney?" came a rather harassed voice from upstairs.

"I haven't had them," Marney bawled back. "Look in the top drawer."

" I've looked in the top drawer. That's where I've tried to hide them from you ; but I might have saved myself the trouble. What have you been using them for ? Where are they ? "

" I tell you I don't know. Have a look in the blue vase."

" I've looked in the blue vase. I'm going to miss that bus yet."

There was a noise of hurried tramping about upstairs. Then a silence, followed by an indignant shout.

" They're in your trousers pocket. All covered with tar. I do wish you'd leave my things alone. Nothing's safe from you. You're worse than a child of two."

" I didn't know I'd had them," Marney shouted back apologetically. " It must have been for splicing that clothes-line you begged me to put up for you. I'll clean them."

There was a silence, during which Marney glanced again wistfully at the back window. It was a lovely day. The sea was calm to the horizon. The gorse-fringed cliff of Low Batts was bathed in the warm spring sun.

" We ought to be fishing, a day like this," Marney muttered, *sotto voce*. " I wish we were off."

" What time's it got to ? " asked Amy from upstairs.

" It's half-past one. You've plenty of time."

There was a final slamming of doors ; then footsteps on the stairs, and Amy came into the room. She had her new coat on over a dark dress, and a charming little hat she had made herself. She had new shoes and silk stockings and there was no lack of sincerity in Marney's voice when he said :

" By Gum ! You look a treat. That coat *does* suit you after all."

" Don't talk so daft," Amy answered, quickly darting to the mirror in a vain effort to disguise that she was blushing. She made an entirely unnecessary adjustment to her hair ; then, her self-composure restored, she turned to Marney, and lifted the baby from him.

" Have you decided to come or not ? " she demanded. " I'm not going to miss the bus, waiting for you to make up your mind."

I could see that Marney himself was not at all convinced about the matter. He liked going out with Amy. But he hated anything in the way of formal calls.

" I'm either way," he said. " I'll come if you want, or I'll stay."

" You needn't think any one wants you," Amy answered rather tartly. " We can manage to get our teas without your assistance."

" I shouldn't mind if it was just tea. It's sitting there doing nothing all afternoon I don't like."

Amy was putting on the baby's hat, also knitted and " to match."

" Then why don't you talk when you're out ? You just sit twiddling your thumbs, and never uttering a word."

" I'd like to know when I get a chance to utter a word when you and your Molly get going."

" There's no call for rudeness," said Amy sharply. " I'll watch out you don't get invited there any more. Anyway, I don't want you to come.

Amy herself evidently was in two minds as to the desirability of Marney's company. She was intensely proud of him. She was not above showing him off to the world in her subtle way. But her sister's husband was a sailor, and away at sea. These occasional teas, at which Marney was not a success, were therefore predominantly feminine, and there could be no doubt that the presence of one male was a constraint. Besides, there was the baby to show off, a male without drawbacks. Yet behind all this the jealous lover's instinct was not completely dormant. She did not want Marney to go ; but she wanted him to want to go.

" If you're not coming with me, where are you going to ? " she asked.

Marney got up, and glanced through the window at the tantalizing sea.

" I don't know," he said nonchalantly. " We'll most likely go for a walk. We might go up Browe Beck, and see if we can get some daffodils. We can't sit inside, a day like this. I'd sooner by half take you for a walk though," he added. " You look champion."

That last remark satisfied Amy. She started to fuss round for her gloves and purse, pretending that she had not heard.

" Well, I'm not going to miss the bus for you. Only I'll expect you to meet me when I come back. And don't go and spoil your new boots, getting them wet and muddy. You can get your own tea, can't you ? "

" Yes. We can manage that all right," said Marney, with an eagerness which did not seem to be quite discreet. " There's some tarts and things somewhere, aren't there ?"

Amy turned to the pantry.

" I'll put some out for you," she said, " or there'll be none left for supper."

She did so : and then, with a harassed glance at the clock, she moved for the door.

" Don't get your clothes in a mess ; and don't forget the bus," was her parting admonition.

Marney closed the door and turned to me, smiling.

" God! I'm glad I got out of that," he said softly. " I just can't put up with sitting still on a day like this, and listening to two women yapping about nowt. I shouldn't mind if what they said was interesting. But it never is. Shall we have a look up Browe Beck? There might be a salmon in the big pool. It will be better than doing nothing, won't it? Come on, before everybody gets out for their Sunday walk. I'd put my old clothes on if it wasn't that we might meet somebody. I've got a bit of string and a hook in my pocket."

The tide was up. We had to walk round the back of the village and climb by a path round the edge of the hill where Henry's cottage stood, to the top of the low clay cliff which rises from the shores of the bay, forming a link as it were between the two Batts. From there one had a bird's-eye view of the village itself. It lay compact in a ravine whose north-east side was the protecting sea-cliff, and its cottages were so closely packed together the tiled roofs were almost continuous, making a great blotch of red against the blue of the sea : a red slightly veiled by a pearly haze of smoke. The full power of the spring sunlight was on the roofs, and made yellow flames of the gorse on Low Batts cliff. The fields sweeping inland were stained with the emerald green of new corn. There was warmth in the colour of the distant moors, and there was the magic of spring in the air.

We paused for a moment when we reached the top. We had caught sight of Henry, standing on that favourite look-out place of his, close by the warehouse door ; and as usual looking at the sea. He, too, was in his Sunday ' best.'

" Father feels the same as I do about Sundays," Marney remarked. " Look at him ! He's just wishing like

anything we were off hauling our pots. And he'd go, too,
if it wasn't what folks would say. Not that lobstering is as
good as it was early on," Marney added as we moved.
" I'm not grumbling, mind you. Prices have held very
well, and we're having a damned good season. But you
get sick of doing the same thing, day in, day out. I'd like
to try something else for a change. I'd like to have a go
for salmon this year. Salmon are better paying things
than lobsters if you're lucky with the weather. Only it's
expensive starting, and it's a very short season. And
father's all for going on with lobsters until cod start again."

I had suspected for a while back that lobster fever was
on the wane. We had, as Marney had predicted, ' coined
money ' with the providentially rescued pots. But the
Burnharbour fleet had not been so very long in starting
again ; prices had come down ; and while there had been
no sensational glut, our fishing had gradually settled to a
steady routine, without a single gale to make things
exciting. The Fosdycks, too, were now ' lobstering.'
We had so consistently beaten them that the game of
' turning the laugh ' had lost all flavour. We were
slightly bored with lobsters, but this was the first time
Marney had expressed himself definitely on the matter.

The path followed close to the cliff edge ; and there
were ploughed fields and pastures to the right of us.
Somewhere a lark was singing ; from a clump of beech
trees, at Bramblewick Hall, came the noisy chatter of
nesting rooks. Marney pulled a dead wheat-straw, and
chewed at it thoughtfully as he walked. Was it the excitement of a new fever I saw in his eyes ?

" It's a queer thing," he continued, " that neither
father nor grandad ever went in for salmoning. Of course,
before the war, there were more at it, and it left father a

clear field for lobsters. Then there used to be a lot of squabbling about berths. There's only about five places in Bramblewick Bay where it's worth while shooting a net ; and it's always been the rule that the first chap to get his nets in on a Monday morning keeps that berth till Saturday night. Last year there was only the Fosdycks fishing. They had the whole bay to themselves. They did very well. There was one night they made over thirty pounds. And they must have averaged at least eight pounds a night for a fortnight. I tell you salmoning is a paying thing if only you're lucky. I shouldn't mind having a go at it."

We soon reached the gap in the cliff made by Garry Beck. There was a shaley ravine immediately beneath us ; but a little farther up was the old water mill, and a wood which extended for half a mile inland.

" We'll come back by Garry Wood," said Marney. " We'll come back by the dam, and see if there's a water-hen's nest. But there's more likely to be daffodils up Browe Beck. Amy likes daffodils better than any other flowers except roses."

I suspected that the remark was an off-shoot from something a little less altruistic, working in Marney's mind ; and I was right.

" I've heard tell there's been one or two very good salmon seen up Browe Beck this winter," he continued. " They got up from the sea in those big rains. Someone told me they saw one weighing about twenty pounds. I wish we'd brought a bit of old net with us."

We climbed down the ravine of Garry Beck, and up the opposite side. Marney stopped to gather some primroses and violets, which he stuck jauntily in his cap. But his thoughts apparently continued on the subject of salmon.

" The worst of salmon fishing," he went on, as we reached the level of the cliff top again, " is the nets. The licence is nothing. Only a couple of quid. But there's coarse nets, which are fairly cheap, and aren't much good, and there's fine flax ones, which will catch salmon in broad daylight, but cost a devil of a lot of brass. Aye. And you've only got to get them in a little bit of rough sea, and they've gone like smoke. Salmon-fishing is more of a gamble than lobstering. . . . But it *can* pay—if you go the right way about it. And I'll bet that if we started this year, we'd do just as well as the Fosdycks. I wouldn't be surprised if we beat them. It's only experience that does it."

If I had doubted the onset of a new fever, I could not doubt it now. Marney had chewed the straw to its end ; and he lighted a cigarette.

" Old Luke can certainly catch salmon," he said. " But that doesn't mean no one else can, when they've got the right gear."

We reached the valley of Browe Beck. Like Garry Beck it was wooded to within a short distance of the sea : but there was no mill, and the wood, being very undergrown and boggy, was a wilder spot. We hurried down to the edge of the stream. There was a long pool here dammed by a mass of shingle thrown up by the sea near the mouth of the cove. The smooth surface of the pool was rippled by jumping salmon smelt. But we had bigger game than this in view.

We entered the wood ; and still keeping to the banks of the stream, moved on stealthily, speaking in whispers. In a strictly legal sense we were now trespassing, and the intent to poach was not absent from our minds. The wood was very still. The trees were not in leaf yet ; but most of them were thickly clad in ivy; and there was only a spattering of sunshine upon the dark, boggy ground. A wood-pigeon flew out suddenly with a terrific clatter from a mass of ivy; and Marney dropped his cigarette in fright. He did not observe a bunch of daffodils that he nearly trod upon: and perhaps it was tactless of me to remind him of the main object of our expedition.

"There'll be plenty more farther up the wood," he whispered. "Don't make a noise now," he added. "There might easily be a big salmon in the shallow end of the pool. That's where they lie; waiting for a spate to take them to the sea. If we go careful, we might easily get one."

The pool was quite distinct from the one which reached into the cove. It lay in the darkest part of the wood, where the stream narrowed down a shaley gorge, and fell over a cliff the height of a man. The walls of the gorge were overhung with a dense tangle of brambles, which gave us cover for our preliminary reconnaissance. Marney went first. He suddenly stopped and raised his hand.

"Shut up," he whispered tensely. "There's a big one there. Damn it, there's another. There's three!"

I squirmed stealthily alongside him and looked. Whatever scruples one had about the sportsmanship of catching salmon in any other manner than with "rod and fly" vanished in that moment.

We were primitive men in sight of game: and the technical illegality of our intentions merely made the sight more thrilling. The salmon lay, as Marney had predicted, at the shallow end of the pool; where the sun filtered down through the overhanging foliage, lighting a patch of warm amber mud, on which they basked, with scarcely a fin of them moving.

We stood watching them almost breathlessly for a full minute. Two of them were quite small ; but one the nearest to our own bank must have weighed at least ten pounds.

"If only we'd brought a net !" Marney suddenly sighed. "We could have got that big one easy as winking." He was silent for a time. Then he whispered, "I'm going to have a try for him, anyway. A hook's no good. We've got to frighten him ashore, and nab him before he gets back."

I waited, intensely interested to see how this operation was to be executed. Suddenly Marney pushed the coil of string into my hand and pointed below.

"You go back and come up the stream, quietly as you can," he whispered. "I can get down this side of the waterfall, and creep along a ledge. When I'm near enough, I'll suddenly show myself, and the chances are a thousand to one he'll be so scared he'll try to rush downstream, and go aground. Run for him then like hell, tie him up, and hold him till I come."

I had learnt to put complete faith in Marney as a fisherman, and I obeyed his orders implicitly. I retraced my footsteps through the jungle, until I was well clear of the pool, then jumped down to the bed of the stream, and worked my way cautiously upwards. Soon I saw Marney swarm down a network of creepers, just on the pool side of the waterfall. He alighted on a ledge, instantly went on his hands and knees, and began to creep, inches at a time, towards the unsuspecting fish. We communicated by signals. To me the fish was invisible. But Marney signalled to me to come nearer, and then, as he completed another section of his crawl, he pointed to the shallows, to indicate that they were still unalarmed.

What happened the next moment I could not clearly see, for I was attempting to look at two things at once. I saw Marney rise. I heard him give a shout, which I judged was part of his plan to frighten the salmon. Next I heard a heavy splash ; and I must have imagined that the salmon was working to plan. I had leapt to the edge of the pool before I realised that Marney was up to his waist in water, clawing with his hands at the ledge from which his feet had slipped. Before I had time to decide what to do, he was wading ashore.

He did not speak immediately. He stood and pressed his hands down the legs of his Sunday ' best ' trousers, and wrung the water out. He sat down then, and removed his ' best ' Sunday boots, tipped them, and wrung the water from his socks. Not until he was dressed again did he speak. He walked back to the pool and picked up his hat, which had floated to the shore.

" My foot must have slipped on that damned shale," he muttered. " It's those rubber heels. . . . Come on," he added with a shiver. " We'll not bother any more with those salmon now. We'll come up one night with a net. Fresh water's twice as cold as sea-water. Where was it we saw that bunch of daffodils ? "

We hurried back and found the flowers ; but it was an isolated bunch, and we were obliged to carry on a long way farther up the wood to find more. Marney had cheered up by then, but he was far too cold to be really happy. The sun had gone when finally we emerged from the wood about a mile inland. The sky was overcast. The air was very cold.

" We'll cut across the fields and down to Garry Beck," he said. " We might get a few more daffodils down by the dam. There's scarcely enough to fill a vase here. . . . I wish we'd got that salmon," he added. " I hate making a mess of a job."

We did not discuss that lamentable adventure, or the broader aspects of salmon-fishing again. The sudden fall in temperature was due to an easterly wind. Garry Wood was shrouded in a sea-fog when we reached the south edge of its valley. We could hear the dismal blast of the Kettlenab fog-siren.

" Thick weather," Marney muttered through chattering teeth. " It's come on damned sudden. I don't like fog. The only good it ever does is to put a steamer on the rocks and it isn't very often that happens now because of these wireless signals, that tell a ship almost exactly where she is, no matter how thick it is. It's a devil for lobster-fishing. You can't see your buoys. I hope it doesn't last."

If Marney had guessed the ultimate influence this sudden fog was to have upon our fortunes, he might have amended the last part of his remark. We moved very quickly into the wood, and struck the path which leads along the stream as far as the mill dam. It was a clean wood, this, of well-pruned oaks, and there was no undergrowth. But the fog, sweeping from the sea, made it darker than the wood we had left, and produced already the illusion of dusk.

" We'll not bother looking specially for any flowers," said Marney, as he led the way. " I've got to meet that damned bus, and I'm dying for a hot cup of tea. But we'll just see if that water-hen's nest is there this year again."

We were approaching the dam now. The wood was slightly denser. Suddenly we heard a shout. We stopped abruptly.

" Did you hear that ? " said Marney. " It sounded like——"

It was Steve's voice shouting :

" Marney ! You, Marney ! "

It came from a clump of willows just slightly ahead.

We ran. There was a willow-tree, with its trunk leaning out over the dark water of the dam itself, and at the very foot of this sat Steve, nursing his ankle, and looking very tragic.

Marney had completely forgotten his own discomfort. He went down on his knees beside his diminutive brother.

" What's up with you ? " he demanded. " What the devil are you doing ? "

Steve obviously was in very great pain.

" It's my ankle," he cried tragically. " I've gone and broken it. Don't touch it. It hurts too much. Just help me to get up, and I'll walk."

We did not demand further explanations then : they were unnecessary. A few feet above Steve's head in the willow was a water-hen's nest. We took off his boots (like Marney's they were new boots which no longer looked new). We pulled off his stocking. There was no sign of a fracture ; but there was every indication of a sprain. We rendered first aid with a wet handkerchief, and then Marney heaved Steve up on to his back. But Steve, with his ankle at least more comfortable, had retained his presence of mind.

" Eh ! There's my basket," he cried as Marney set off. " Don't forget that."

I picked up a basket, lying at the foot of the tree.

" Don't lose the daffodil that's in it ! "

I looked at the solitary daffodil the basket contained and assured Steve of its safety. We moved off in procession. Marney, who had been decidedly scared, now took up a very elder-brotherly attitude.

M

" What were you doing down here, any way ? " he demanded. " You know mother says you haven't to go near the dam."

Steve did not answer.

" Didn't you hear what I said ? " persisted Marney.

" Mother told me I could go and get some daffodils," Steve answered with a familiar defiance.

" Not by the dam ! "

" Well, there weren't any anywhere else ; so what could I do ? I didn't want to go back empty."

We had emerged from the wood on to a short path, which led to the top of the cliff again. The fog was so dense we could scarcely see more than twenty yards ahead. To the regular moaning of the Kettlenab fog-siren was now added the more distant and intermittent sound of steamers' horns, out beyond the invisible bay. The easterly wind was freshening. Marney's teeth were still chattering : but he pursued his stern judicial inquiry.

" You didn't come to the dam just for daffodils."

" I didn't know of any other place," Steve parried. " I daren't go to Browe Beck."

" You came to the dam to look for that water-hen's nest," went on Marney mercilessly. " You heard me talking about it the other day."

Steve was silent for a time ; then :

" It was an old one, anyway. There weren't any eggs in it. I wouldn't have fallen if I hadn't heard you two coming and thought it was someone else."

" Aye. You thought it might be father, didn't you ? You heard his belt-buckle rattle. There's going to be a row about this when you get home."

Again Steve lapsed into silence. We had crossed the first stile when he answered, suggestively :

" There won't be a row unless somebody tells."

" I'm not going to tell any lies for you, if that's what you mean."

" I don't want you to tell any lies for me," Steve rejoined quickly. " You needn't say anything. If you let me down at the bottom of our hill, I can hop home on one foot. You needn't come in. You needn't say anything."

" Aye. And leave you to lie for yourself ! "

" I shan't tell any lies. I'll tell them I fell. And so I did. They won't ask me if I've been bird-nesting, unless you tell them."

" And what about your daffodils ? "

Once more Steve was silent. Then he said, rather weakly :

" Well, I've got one, haven't I ? "

Marney did not answer. We reached the top of the village path. The village itself was completely invisible. The density of the fog was now accentuated by the approach of real dusk. Marney hurried. At the bottom we diverted towards Henry's cottage. The warehouse loomed out of the fog.

" Are you going to take me right in home ? " said Steve tragically. " I lent you the ' Grey Spider ' yesterday."

Marney put his brother gently down on to one foot.

" Can you hop ? " he said quietly.

Steve hopped.

Marney took his own bunch of daffodils, and divided them into two. He put half of them into Steve's basket.

" Go on," he said. " And don't tell any lies about me. I'm not in it."

Steve looked from the basket to Marney, as though he could scarcely credit his good fortune. Then he picked up the basket.

"I'll give you this week's 'Grey Spider,' to-morrow," he said with emotion. He turned, and hopped dexterously towards home.

"Come on," said Marney. "What time do you think it's got to?"

He swung round abruptly. The sound of the Bramble-wick church bells had suddenly joined the moaning of the fog-sirens.

"God Almighty!" he cried in alarm. "It's six o'clock and the bus gets in at a quarter-to. I'll have to tell Amy about Steve, and ask her to keep her mouth shut about it; or she'll play war about my boots, and missing the bus. We won't say anything about the salmon. Come on. She may be back. She might make us a cup of tea."

CHAPTER TWO

AT four o'clock next morning Bramblewick was awakened by the lifeboat gun. It was still dark. The fog was so dense one had literally to grope one's way down to the dock. Here two oil-flares had been lighted, showing the pavement from the lifeboat-house to the slipway top. The doors of the house were wide open. The flares gleamed on the lean blue-and-white bows of the vessel itself. Men were hurriedly strapping on life-belts ; and, under the stentorian command of Luke Fosdyck, moving to run out the launching-tackles.

There was no time for questioning. Men were scarce in Bramblewick. I had been one of the crew at the last practice launch ; and I seized a belt from the pegs that projected from the house wall inside. I turned to find Marney behind me. We helped each other with our straps.

He was excited.

" They say it's a steamer on Low Batts," he muttered tensely. " The coastguards found her. But she hasn't shown any signal of distress. It will be a salvage job, if only we get there first."

" Hurry up, lads ! " came Luke's voice from outside. " Are the tackles clear ? Give her a start. All together, now. There she goes ! "

The boat, on its terrifically heavy steel carriage, began to move slowly out of the house. We began to heave gently as far as the slipway top. Then with the hawsers round two posts, we eased her down the steep descent towards the sea. The sea itself was not visible yet. The wind, however, though still easterly, was only moderate. It seemed evident that we were not bound on any spectacular mission of rescue. Yet it was exciting. The voices one heard were all tense, even that of John, who was hanging on to the same hawser as ourselves. And Luke Fosdyck's voice had in it an entirely unfamiliar eager quality.

" Steady now. Don't give her too much way. Easy with your starboard wheels. Let her go a bit now. Easy."

The tide was ebbing and was half-way down the Landing. At the slipway bottom we halted, while the hauling-tackles were taken forward by the launching-party. I saw old Isaac at the head of the launchers carrying one of the flares and moving with the alacrity of a man of thirty.

" Give her way again," Luke Fosdyck bawled. " All together. Keep her south a bit. Pull at her. Pull."

The launchers had to haul waist-deep into the water, which brought the fore-end of the carriage awash. We had to climb aboard then, and ship our oars. The boat herself lay on a greased rail above the wheels, with a slight slope forwards ; and was locked to this by a steel pin through her keel. One of the launchers stood ready by the pin with a hammer.

" Are you all clear ? " bawled Luke.

A voice from the launchers shouted back :

" All clear."

" Then let her go."

The pin was knocked out. The boat began to move slowly down the rail : we hit the water : and Luke Fosdyck shouted :

" Pull ! Pull ! As hard as you can go. We may as well be in our beds if we're not there first."

There was, in Luke's excitement, a key to the excitement which possessed us all. The lifeboat's first clear function is the saving of life, if life is in peril. When life is not in peril, however, a stranded vessel is for the lifeboat-man a business proposition. Recognising this, the Royal National Lifeboat Institution permits its boats to be used for purely salvage purposes, on the understanding that a percentage of any money earned goes to the coffers of the Institution, and that the crew bears the cost of the launch, and of any damage to the boat and gear.

There was, it seemed, no life in peril now. While the Kettlenab siren, and the horns of distant steamers continued to blow, we heard no signal of distress. We were acting on 'information received'; we were 'job-hunting.'

We pulled our utmost. We quickly lost sight of the flare which old Isaac had carried to the extremity of the scaur. There were vague signs of daylight; but the fog was too dense for us to see the Landing posts. We felt the swell, however. We heard the breakers on either side of us. We knew soon, by the feel of the swell, that Luke, steering by compass, had changed our course north-east for Low Batts Point. He continued to urge us on.

" Give way to it, lads," he bawled. " She's a fair-sized boat, the coastguard says. She's lying close under the cliff near the point. We'll not be the only one after her. That damned salvage tug will be down on us soon. Pull away. First come, first served. We'll make some brass if we reach her first ! "

" That damned tug may spoil everything," confided Marney, who was rowing alongside me. " The company that owns her have agents everywhere, paid to telephone

when there's anything doing. There's one in Bramblewick.
I bet she's got her anchors weighed already."

"That damned tug" figured largely in coast politics.
It was stationed at the mouth of the River T——, some ten
miles north of Burnharbour, ready at a moment's notice
to steam anywhere, on the chance of picking up a salvage
job ; and by doing so had on several occasions succeeded
in "taking the bread out of local folk's mouths."

"I only hope it keeps as thick as it is," Marney added.
"She'll not come so quick in this weather."

"Aye. But it won't keep thick," said John from behind
us. "She'll be here all right."

We were a scratch crew. In addition to the three
Fosdycks, and the three Lunns, there was the landlord of
the Bramblewick Arms, the local fishmonger, the baker,
the foreman of the gas-works, an elderly joiner, and a
retired marine engineer. Henry was rowing on the next
seat aft. He was quiet. Somewhere deep inside him, I
knew, was a subtle resentment at being under Luke
Fosdyck's orders. But I knew, too, that nothing less than
a colossal act of bad seamanship on Luke's part would
have caused him to make this manifest. And Luke was a
good coxswain. In all the years that he had held office,
during which he had taken the lifeboat out in all conditions
of weather, one had never heard, even from the ' foreigners,' the faintest criticism either of his seamanship or his
courage. And here at present was only a moderately rough
sea that would not have kept the cobles ashore : and the
fog itself suddenly showed signs of clearing. Daylight
seemed to spring upon us at once.

"It's going to lift," said Marney. "But it may not lift
farther north."

"I'd like to see that damned tug go ashore in it," said

the elderly joiner. " Somebody ought to cut that telephone wire when there's a ship ashore."

" Land's clearing," shouted Luke excitedly. " There she is ! Close in to the cliff. And there's no other boat in sight yet. Pull ! We'll be there in ten minutes if you pull."

We glanced over our shoulders as we pulled. The fog had not completely gone. The village and the whole coast southwards was still wrapped in it, as with a vast layer of cotton-wool. But north-east, and to the horizon (where the sun was just rising), the sky and sea were clear. The steamer was lying just south of Low Batts Point.

She was not a very large boat. She turned out to be a collier, of about 2,000 tons, in ballast for Newcastle. But she was new and she was valuable. Such a vessel would be worth anything up to £15,000 ; and she was well aground.

The thrill which possessed one made no conflict with one's conscience. One did not think immediately of the personal problems involved in the stranding of a ship. If through our exclusive co-operation this steamer was re-floated, our services would be paid for in proportion to the ship's value ; a payment made, not by the owners, or the officers of the ship, but by that vague abstraction, the insurance company.

We pulled in within hailing-distance, then we eased down, maintaining just enough way to keep us head-on to the swell, which had noticeably grown since the break of day. The ship was lying almost broadside on to the shore, with her stern to the open sea and the swell. The tide was nearly down. On all sides the sharp edges of those famous rocks of Low Batts were becoming visible among the broken water.

Several men were standing on the ship's deck, looking down at us. Luke Fosdyck suddenly hailed :

" Ahoy ! Which of you's the master ? "

One of the men, very youthful, with a pale, haggard face, signalled with his hand.

" Here," he yelled.

" Do you want us to give you a help ? " shouted Luke.

The master made a negative gesture.

" I was going to wait till low water and see if her bottom's damaged," he shouted back. " It looks as though I'll want a tug."

Involuntarily we all glanced seawards. There was still no sign of any rival craft. And Luke was not discouraged.

" You'll not want a tug," he shouted. " We can take a kedge anchor out into deep water for you. If you're not holed you'll float before it's high tide again. If you heave on your kedge then, you'll get off without a tug. Why do you want to waste money on a tug when you can do the job yourself ? "

The master (we learnt later that this was his first voyage in command) glanced anxiously at the broken water that separated us.

" You'll have a job, to get alongside us for a kedge, among all those rocks," he answered. " How are you going to get hold of it ? "

" Leave that to us," was Luke's quiet answer. He waved his hand to the ship's bows, under which was one narrow patch of heaving but deep and unbroken water. " We can run in to your lee bow. If you can lower your kedge we'll do the rest. We'll have it out for you before the tide ebbs. You'll be off before it's full, and no tug to pay for. Will you take us on ? "

The master stared down at the sea. Then he turned to an older man alongside him, evidently the mate. We continued to keep the lifeboat head-on to the swell, while they carried on what apparently was a very earnest conversation. Looking at the pale, haggard face of that youthful sea-captain, one forgot, for awhile, one's personal anxiety as to the upshot of their discussion. Whatever explanation there was for the stranding of the ship, the captain legally was responsible. If much damage was done, a black mark would go against him in the insurance company's books. He might lose his berth. If the ship became a total loss, and negligence was proved, he might lose his certificate. If on the other hand he got his ship off undamaged, and without the heavy expense of a steam-tug, the fact would go a long way to mitigate any official censure. Could he trust us for successful co-operation ?

He suddenly turned from his companion, and for a while looked earnestly down at the broken water.

" I'll take you on," he shouted. " See what you can do."

CHAPTER THREE

THE kedge, which is an ordinary iron anchor, weighed a quarter of a ton. It had to be lifted by derrick from the ship's after deck, slung forward, and lowered over the overhanging 'shoreward' bow. We had to dodge in then, between the breaking seas and the half-bared rocks, and prepare to receive it. This we did successfully; but it was not the least perilous part of our task.

We were now within touching distance of the ship's side; and still pitching and rolling wildly. A seaman threw down a line and we made fast. We unshipped our oars. The anchor swayed above our heads, and about ten feet above average sea-level. But before it was lowered again, we rose up on a big sea, and almost crashed into it. As the sea fell we swung violently into the ship's side.

" Fend off ! " yelled Luke. " We've got to pay for any damage, remember. Fend off ! "

We fended off with our hands. We escaped damage, We rose again. Again it seemed as if the anchor would hit us. We missed it by less than a foot; and, the next time we rose, someone, standing in our bow, threw a bight of rope over one of its flukes, and made it fast. That some-one was Marney. He eased the rope out as we sank.

Luke, lifting his head upwards, shouted to the ship :

" Lower away ! "

" Make your sling fast as soon as she's deep enough," he shouted in the same breath to Marney. I observed that Henry, too, had moved forward, and had seized the rope. The anchor came lower. Watching his chance, the man above us in charge of the winch let it go until it disappeared from sight close to our bows. Henry suddenly made the rope fast. The anchor was slung from the lifeboat just deep enough to be clear of our keel, and of course clear of the sea bottom. It was a smart piece of work.

" We're all fast here," said Henry quietly.

Again Luke lifted his head.

" Let's have your wire now," he shouted.

Two enormous coils of wire hawser were lowered to us. We manned our oars again. But we continued to hang on to the ship's rope until there came a temporary easing of the swell : then we let go, and we began to move very gingerly round the ship's stern towards the open sea.

The lull lasted only until we got out of the shelter of the ship. We were broadside to the swell now. The weight of the anchor on our bows made pulling and steering doubly difficult. The first real sea we encountered broke clean over our quarter and drenched us ; and it would have smashed us back against the ship's hull, but for Luke's fine seamanship. Another sea broke over us before we were a length away. We missed one of the half-bared rocks by a matter of inches. But we cleared and paying out the hawser (one end of which was fast to the collier's winch) we toiled strenuously and slowly seawards.

It was gruelling work. The wind had freshened. There was a suspicion of north in it. The sea undoubtedly was growing. Yet our excitement was even more intense. The salving of that ship had become more than a business proposition, now that we had made a direct human contact with it.

There was nearly a quarter of a mile of hawser. We could not tighten it. But we laid it in a straight line so that the winch would have a fair haul when the time came.

When only a few coils remained, Luke gave a shout to us to redouble our efforts. His brother, who was for'ard, was standing ready with an axe.

" Let her go ! " Luke shouted.

Tindal slashed at the kedge sling. It parted with a crack. Relieved suddenly of its weight, our bows rose. The last coil of wire whipped overboard. And as it went, Luke waved his hand to Low Batts Point.

" There's that damned tug ! " he shouted.

A dark, rakish-looking craft, with a cloud of heavy black smoke blowing ahead from its funnel with the now unmistakably north-east wind, had just cleared the point. Someone swore.

But Luke gave a confident grunt.

" The skipper will not be fool enough to take that chap on until he's given the kedge a try. Pull your oars, lads. We can't do anything now but wait for high water. We'll pull close in to the ship, just to let any other boat see we're here. Then we'll have a sup of rum."

The tug was travelling at high speed. It had already changed its course shorewards. Before we had got back to the steamer, it had almost come abreast of us. It dropped anchor, and a stout rowing-boat, with two oarsmen and a man in oilskins in the stern, put off from it, and came quickly in towards the collier. When it was near enough the man in the stern stood up, and put a megaphone to his mouth. We saw the collier's captain signal his identity.

" Are you going to take us on ? " the man in the boat bellowed.

The captain did not answer.

" You're in a nasty spot," the man shouted. " It's going to blow up from the north-east. You'll lose your ship if you mess on with that kedge. This is the nastiest

spot on the coast in a north-east swell. You'd better give
us the word."

" He's taken us on : so you can get out of it," shouted
Luke suddenly. " First come, first served ! "

The tug-master took no notice of the interruption.

" Will you take us on ? " he yelled again. " You'll be
sorry you haven't, if you get piled up under that cliff. The
sea's growing every minute."

Again one forgot one's own anxiety in sympathy with
that young captain. One could see that he was hesitating :
that the tug-master's warning had told. He glanced seawards. Undoubtedly the swell was growing. He looked at
the bared rocks, at the kedge hawser, the slack of which
had now been taken up by the winch. Could he trust that
absurdly fragile-looking rope to pull his ship to safety ?

As though reading his mind, Luke shouted again :

" You give us a try first. He'll not go away. You can
take him on if the kedge fails. Wait till the tide gets up."

For a while longer the captain continued to look
apprehensively at the sea. Then suddenly he made a
negative gesture to the tug-master.

" I'll not say yet," he shouted. " I'll wait for high tide."

Old Luke grinned.

" And that will be six hours," he added to us. " Come
on, lads. The job's as good as done. We'll drop anchor and
have a sup of summat to keep us warm."

None of us had breakfasted. It had been warm work at
the oars. We were soaked with sweat and sea-water. The
wind now was bitterly cold ; and while the rum gave us an
immediate glow, its effect quickly wore off, and the wind
was freshening. The last remnants of fog had gone from
the moorland hills. There seemed every prospect of a real
' blow.' Before the tide had flowed an hour, the seas

were pounding high up the steamer's stern. Although an
examination at dead low water had shown that she was
undamaged, it was clear that she would not remain so
long, if the weather grew much worse.

The tug-master evidently had not lost hope of making a
job. He had gone back to the tug, but his boat remained
in the water. We envied him and his crew. We envied
even the men of the collier. From her galley we caught
the scent of frying bacon. Her decks were deserted, while
we huddled, hungry and wet and cold, in our wildly
pitching open boat. The foreman of the gas-house was
sea-sick. Avery Fosdyck had several violent paroxysms
of coughing. We cheered each other by speculating on the
financial outcome of the business. We were already
assured of receiving something. The taking out of the
kedge was a contract without conditions. Whether it
proved instrumental in saving the ship or not, the
customary fee was in the neighbourhood of seventy-five
pounds. But if it saved the ship, our claim would be for
the value of the ship against total loss, and the smallest
figure would be four hundred pounds. With thirteen of
the crew to share equally and allowing for payment to the
launchers, and a percentage to the Institution, we should
each receive about twenty-five pounds.

As John remarked, with typical gloom, " it sounded too
good to be true." Something, he said, would happen to
stop us earning all that money, and that most likely would
be the weather. Steadily the wind and swell increased.
Before the tide had half flowed, the seas were breaking as
high as the collier's stern. The captain and crew were on
deck again. The captain was pacing restlessly up and
down. We weighed anchor, and pulled about for half an
hour to keep warm. We came back, dropped anchor, and

waited another hour. There was still an hour to high water. The seas were now lifting clean over the collier's stern. Her fabric was shaking.

Suddenly Luke waved his hand to the tug.

" She's weighing anchor," he shouted. " Come on. We'll do the same."

We weighed anchor. The tug was coming slowly in, stern first.

" Why the hell can't that chap see he's not wanted ? " growled the elderly joiner.

" Never mind him," Luke answered gruffly. " If the captain only does what we tell him, and doesn't get frightened, the tug won't earn its coal. Now, lads. Keep her head to the swell."

Luke turned to the ship, which was now shaking continuously to the pounding seas.

" Ahoy ! Captain," he shouted. " You're not far from floating now. Start heaving on your winch. Take no notice of the tug. He's only out to make a job of you. Start heaving ! "

The young captain signalled in acknowledgment, and signalled to the mate who was standing by the winch on the forecastle deck. Clouds of steam came from the winch. The hawser tightened. We watched breathlessly for the ship to yield. But she gave no sign of movement in the desired direction.

" Keep at it ! Keep at it ! " yelled Luke. " There's an hour yet to high water. Keep at it ! "

Meanwhile the tug had crept in until her stern was so near the collier a line could easily be thrown between them. Her master was on the bridge. Suddenly a tremendous sea caught the collier's stern, swept over her after deck, and sent a shower of spray as high as her bridge.

N

The tug-master shouted through his megaphone.

" Are you going to wait any longer, captain ? Another sea like that and you'll be past my help. You're driving in ! You'll smash up to-night for certain. We'll have a hawser on you in two ticks if you say the word ! "

"Take no notice of him ! " yelled Luke.   " Keep heaving ! "

The face of the young sea-captain was deathly pale. Another sea crashed over the stern.   The whole ship shuddered and we heard the awful sound of metal grinding on rock.   Her stern perceptibly moved shorewards.   We saw him take a quick glance at the hissing winch, and the kedge hawser :   then at the tug, where a seaman stood ready with a coil of line in his hand.   Another sea broke. The captain glanced again at the winch.

" Keep at it ! " bawled Luke.

" I'm warning you," bellowed the tug-master.

The captain turned abruptly. We did not see him signal, for he was hidden temporarily by a shower of spray. But we saw the coil of line thrown from the tug ; we saw the collier's seamen haul it until they got the end of the tug's hawser to which it was made fast. We saw the tug-master signal to his engineer to go ahead.

None of us spoke. We watched the tug move seawards, paying out its still slack hawser ; and before that hawser ever did tighten, before the tug had brought an ounce of its energy to bear upon the stranded ship, the latter seemed to lift bodily under a terrific sea.   Her head, obedient to the pull of the winch on the kedge which we had laid, moved slightly seawards. She became inert again. But almost instantly she lifted to another sea. She actually rolled :   and then her seaward movement became continuous.

We saw her captain seize the engine telegraph. We heard the muffled clang of the engine. Luke shouted to us :

" Pull—pull."

We had to pull our utmost to get out of the way as the collier with her kedge hawser cast off, and, under her own power, moved towards the open sea. But we pulled like beaten wearied men. We stopped automatically as we cleared. We saw the collier cast off the tug's hawser. The tug steamed off. The collier swung round to her course, at full steam ahead. And then somebody shouted angrily :

" *We* got her off. That damned tug didn't. He never got his damned hawser tight."

There was a chorus of imprecations.

" The damned chap ought to be shot ! "

" He did his best to frighten that young skipper out of his wits."

" If only the damned fool had left it to us ! "

" It was the kedge. She was moving before that chap ever got his hawser on board."

" Somebody ought to cut that telephone. He wouldn't have come but for that."

" We ought to claim full salvage anyway. The tug did nothing."

" He'll get everything. Just because he got his hawser on board. That's the law."

" The damned law ought to be altered."

Legally, it seemed, the fact that the collier had got off without the tug's actual help had no significance. A contract was implied by the securing of the hawser, to which obviously the collier's captain had agreed.

Henry Lunn, I observed, said nothing.

John said :

" I knew that chap would do it on us. It's daylight

robbery. Twenty-five quid. Dangled in front of our noses and then whipped away. That tug will claim four thousand quid for doing nothing."

Luke did not swear. He was glaring darkly at the swiftly receding collier, and suddenly he growled :

" Come on. Pull your oars, and let's get home."

We manned the oars, and pulled shorewards. By the time we had reached the Landing posts the collier and " that damned tug " had both disappeared behind Low Batts. And it was not until then that Marney indicated to me that his own philosophic equilibrium was restored.

" Well," he said, " I'll bet we're not the only ones fed up with what's happened. I should think that young skipper is gnashing his teeth that he didn't wait another minute or two. I'd rather be me than him. We'll make five quid apiece for that kedge, anyway. . . . And I know what I'm going to do with mine," he added tensely. " I'm going to start salmoning. I'm going to buy some nets."

Book Three

CHAPTER ONE

" AYE," said Marney to his father. " It's easy enough for you to sit there on your backside, chewing sweets and finding fault. But the proof of the pudding is in the eating. You'll get a surprise if we land back with a score of salmon to-morrow, and beat the Fosdycks for a start."

" I should be surprised," said Henry ironically. " And I'm not finding fault. I'm only telling you you might just as well try and catch salmon with a bent pin, as try with nets like those. I don't know much about salmon, but I know they're not daft enough to shove their heads into a net that's thick enough to stop a submarine ! "

We were on the warehouse hill in the sunshine of a perfect July day. John and I were helping Marney to lace a new net on to a corked rope, a section of which was tied between two of mother's clothes-posts. Three other nets, which were completed, lay on the ground close by. On one of these sat Henry, with a jaunty white cotton hat on his head, and a bag of sweets on his knees. Nell was curled up asleep on the ground beside him.

" It's not my fault they've sent the wrong nets," said Marney. " The sample I ordered was only half as thick as these. And I'd have ordered flax, if they hadn't cost so much."

" Why didn't you send them back ? " said Henry.

" Aye. And wait another three weeks for the right ones to come ; and then likely as not find they were no better. I tell you it's no use crying over spilt milk. You're not in this job. And it doesn't make things any better for you to

keep saying the nets are no good. They're salmon-nets.
And it's my belief they'll catch salmon almost as well as
any other nets, if only we go the right way about it. You
stick to lobstering, and don't interfere."

Henry grinned.

" You'd have done a damned sight better if *you'd* stuck
to lobstering, and put that salvage money into buying
some new lines for next cod season, instead of chucking it
away. I tell you salmon fishing at Bramblewick is a waste
of time and money."

Henry, from the first, had been strong in his condemn-
ation of Marney's new venture. We had, only three weeks
ago, received ninety pounds for the salving of the collier.
It had worked out a share of about £6 per man. We had
each subscribed towards the purchase of the nets and
licence, but Marney had insisted in defraying the biggest
part of the cost. And now, having waited nearly three
weeks for the nets to come from a manufacturer in the
south of England, they had proved to be coarser even than
the cheapest of samples he had selected from.

" I tell you again," Henry went on, "salmoning's no
good : even when you do get the proper gear. If it had
been any good I know grandad would have tried it."

" There were more folks at it when he was fishing,"
Marney put in quickly. " You're old fashioned. That's
what's wrong with you. You won't do anything grandad
didn't do. You ought to realize that times change. I don't
think you're a bit more modern in your ideas of fishing
than Luke Fosdyck when it comes down to it. You
wouldn't have started lobster fishing early if I hadn't given
you lobster fever."

" I thought it was me who gave you all lobster fever,"
put in John.

" It wasn't either of you," said Henry, quite nettled. " I never had lobster fever as you call it. We started lobster-fishing early because cod were no good, and lobster were likely to bring a good price. If there'd been plenty of cod, and a market for them, I wouldn't have changed. And it's not likely I'd want to go in for anything so daft as salmoning when there's still fair money in lobsters. Aye. And there'll be more than only fair money in it, when all the Burnharbour chaps get salmon fever, as you call it."

" It strikes me," said Marney, " you've *got* salmon fever, only you won't admit it."

" I haven't got salmon fever ! Or any other sort of fever," father retorted.

" Then I have," said Marney. " And I'm going off to-night whether we get this net finished or not. We're not going to let the Fosdycks have it all their own way. There they are. They're off now ! Just so that they can pick the best spot ! "

We looked down to the Landing. The weather was sufficiently settled now for the boats to be left at anchor all night. The three Fosdycks had appeared walking down the west scaur, each carrying on his back a bundled net. They had brought in their lobster-pots two days ago, and launched up their coble. The anchored boat opposite which they put down their loads was about the same size as the *Emma* ; which was also lying at anchor near the motor-coble.

" Look at them," repeated Marney, " *they've* got salmon fever all right. Luke's been as frisky as a damned goat the last few days. He actually spoke to me this morning. I shouldn't have been surprised if he'd bought me a packet of fags. Do you think I'm going to stand by and see them

coining brass ?   I tell you they'll have the laugh on us
properly the next two months."

"I've no doubt they will," said Henry dryly, as he
turned to look at the net. "And so will everyone else
when you chaps start salmoning. You're lacing that net
nothing like close enough to the corks," he added.
"Salmon will get through there easy as winking."

"You seem to know a lot about what salmon can do,
and what they can't do," Marney retorted : continuing,
his task. "Any one might think you'd been one."

"I don't pretend to know anything about salmon,"
Henry answered, quite calm again. "But I fished for
herring before you were born : and I've seen herring swim
up a net, until they've found that gap between the net top
and the corks : and go through like eels. There's not much
difference between herring and salmon, when all's said
and done. They're both fish."

"Then, if that's so," said Marney, "I should think
you'd do better than the Fosdycks if you got a start."

Henry took another sweet, and looked to the Landing.

"I don't say I would," he remarked with a peculiar
thoughtfulness. "I don't say I would. But I reckon
there's no more in catching salmon than any other sort
of fish——"

"——so long as you have the right sort of nets, and lace
them on the right way," Marney completed. "Well," he
added, "we don't want you to start salmoning, so you
needn't think we do. We can manage by ourselves, can't
we, brother John ? "

"It will certainly be a change from hauling pots," said
John. "But I tell you straight, it's an experiment so far
as I'm concerned. And if it isn't a success soon, I shan't
go on with it. *I* don't want the Fosdycks laughing at us."

" It will be a success," Marney answered. " You'll have salmon fever as bad as I've got it, before the end of this week. And I bet father will be wanting to join us, to learn how it's done. . . . Hallo ! " he added. " Here's old Isaac coming up. Now we'll get some more expert advice."

Nell, with a growl, got up. Isaac's two cats leapt complacently on to a wall near the warehouse : and Isaac himself came towards us. In his eyes was that inevitable ironic amusement. The hill, however, and the heat, had left him slightly breathless ; and Marney got in an anticipatory shot.

" Now, Isaac. Have you come to tell us there's going to be a gale to-night ? "

" No, I haven't," Isaac answered, quite alertly. " I've come to see if you can lend me a bit of pot twine. I've run short."

" Sit down here," said Henry, getting up, and moving towards the warehouse. " I've got a bit somewhere."

Isaac did not sit down. He stood and watched us.

" So you're making some lobster-pots ? " said Marney.

" Aye," Isaac answered. " I'm making a score. I've made eighteen already, but I've been thinking I needn't have troubled. I'll lose them all the first time it blows north-east. I might make a few shillings out of them first, but it will be a wonder."

" When are you going to put your boat down ? "

Isaac was still looking at the nets ; and the amusement in his eyes was growing.

" To-morrow, if it keeps fine. I've put another coat of tar on her this morning. . . . So you're going to try salmoning ? " he added, with a chuckle which made me feel for Marney's nerves, already worn by his father's merciless criticism. " You've not going to have many break through, with thread as thick as that ! ''

Marney did not answer. But John did, with a surprising sharpness :

" No. We're not going to have many fish break through. And we're not going to have our nets torn to bits first time there's a swell. We've got these nets to last.''

John was distinctly cross, and I was glad that Henry returned with a good-sized ball of twine in his hand. " Here you are, Isaac,'' he said. " Will this be enough ? There's plenty more if you want it.''

Isaac chuckled his gratitude ; and by this time Marney had recovered his composure.

" Where are your gulls to-day, Isaac ? '' he demanded. Have the cats eaten them ? They look a bit fatter than when I saw them last.''

Isaac's sense of humour had its limitations.

" Those cats would as soon start on me, as touch Joey and Charley. They're nesting. That's where they are. They've got mates, and they're nesting in Low Batts Cliff. I'll not see them for a month very likely. And then if there's nobody about, they'll come for a bit of fish, and they'll bring their mates and young ones with them. That's what they did last year, and the year before that. I see Luke and Tindal are getting off early.''

" Aye,'' Marney answered, without glancing to the Landing where the Fosdycks were now preparing to start.

" Their nets are fine enough,'' Isaac continued, with an unconscious want of tact.

" Aye,'' said Marney quietly. " But the worst of fine nets is that you've only got to have 'em in a bit of swell and they're finished.''

" It doesn't matter whether they're thick or fine when it blows a north-easter," Isaac answered. " It doesn't matter whether they're salmon nets or lobster-pots. They'll go ! "

No one spoke for a full minute : then Marney said :

" Well, it looks like keeping fine now, anyway. . . . We'll give you a hand down with your boat to-morrow, if you let us know when."

The atmosphere had grown tense ; and it was not relieved very much when Isaac departed.

" It's a pity some folks can't mind their own business," John growled. " What the devil has it got to do with him, whether we've got thick nets or not ? "

" He fairly gives me the pip with his croaking," said Marney. " I wish Nell had worried his two old cats for him."

Father made no comment. He had sat down again, and was looking rather wistfully out across the sea. Suddenly he shouted :

" By Gum ! That was a big one jumped ! Just outside the Landing posts. Look. There he goes again. It's a real salmon that, not a salmon-trout."

We stopped our task to look. We missed the fish, but we saw the ripples on the polished sea, left by its leap.

" They've been jumping all day long," said Marney tensely. " Salmon and trout. I've never seen so many. I wonder where the Fosdycks are going ? I hope they're not going on to Browe Beck sands. It looks as though they were."

The Fosdycks had left the Landing, and were rowing steadily south.

" There's better places than that," said Henry, still looking seawards.

"It's the best spot in Bramblewick Bay!" Marney contradicted. "Easily."

"There's several better spots!"

"Where?"

"It's better just this side of High Batts, in Spinney Hole. And I bet Luke's going there now."

"A fine place to lose your nets if it blows," put in John.

"I tell you there isn't a finer spot on the coast than Browe Beck sands," Marney maintained. "And that's where we're going to-night, if the Fosdycks don't take it."

"Then you'll be a bigger fool than I thought you were," Henry put in hotly. "Unless they've taken Spinney Hole."

"What do you know about salmoning anyway?" was Marney's retort.

"I know as much as you do. What do you know?"

"I've kept my eyes open. I kept them open last year when we were lobstering and they were salmoning. I know where they caught most fish."

"And so do I," said Henry.

"Then you'd better come and show us," Marney quickly parried.

Henry, distinctly discomforted by that remark, got up.

"I reckon my time will be better spent in bed," he said. "I'll leave salmon fishing to those who know all about it."

"And that's the wisest thing you've said this afternoon. You stick to lobsters. You do what grandad did, and his grandad before him."

Henry grinned, but it was with an effort. He did not mind being bested in an argument, but the imputation that he was old-fashioned never failed to rile him. He turned to me.

" Come on. We'll leave them to it, and have a last look at the pots. You can give us a hand up with the lobsters when you see us land back," he said to Marney. " We'll have to have something to live on, while you two chaps are amusing yourselves."

CHAPTER TWO

IT had been agreed that for the present I should help Henry with the pots, while John helped Marney. But for me, the temptation to join the first salmoning expedition was irresistible.

It was shortly after ten o'clock when we rowed out of the Landing in the *Emma*. Passing the posts, we turned immediately south, close in to the shores of the bay. Father had shown a complete apathy to the expedition. We had done quite well with that final haul of pots ; but after we had landed, and the lobsters were packed, he had gone home, and according to John, was going to bed early.

" He's got the sulks," was Marney's shrewd comment. " If he hasn't got salmon fever, he's sickening for it. I'll bet he hasn't gone to bed at all. I bet he stays up half the night on the hill-top, wishing to God he was with us. Well, serve him right. A chap ought to say what's in his mind. If he wanted to come he should have said so."

It was now almost dark. There were stars but no moon. A faint warm wind, scented with mown hay, blew from the shore. Over land and sea hung the glamorous hush of a midsummer's night.

" It's ideal," said Marney excitedly. " Couldn't be better. It's dark enough, and there no phosphorescence, as there usually is on a warm night like this. I reckon coarse nets will catch salmon every bit as good as fine ones in the dark. And say what you like, there's not a better spot anywhere than Browe Beck sands. It's a bit of luck the Fosdycks have gone to Spinney Hole."

"They caught some salmon at Browe Beck last year," said John, "and no mistake. But they caught plenty at Spinney Hole, too. I don't care where we go so long as we have a decent haul, and not have the Fosdycks laughing at us. I tell you, again, I'm not going to mess on long at this game if we don't do well."

"You leave that to me," Marney said confidently. "We're going to do well."

The Fosdycks had been anchored under the northern wall of High Batts all evening, and it was evident that they were going to set their nets in that sometime perilous cove for the night. The method of fishing employed along the whole of this reef-bound coast was to anchor the nets across the inlets of the numerous lagoons, almost at full tide, and when the tides started to ebb, row down each lagoon in turn, striking the water with a heavy pole known as a ' blasher.' Hauling as a rule was done at daybreak.

The Broad inlet among the scaurs which was known as Browe Beck Sands was admirably suited to this method of fishing. To the south of it were about a dozen long scaurs running parallel to the coast. The lagoons between them were deep, and were a favourite summer haunt of salmon and salmon-trout. With four nets it was possible to make a trap across the whole series of lagoons from high-water mark to low. We pulled into the shore, and dropped the anchor-stone of the first net in less than a foot of water. Then we began to ' shoot ' across the ends of the now sunken reefs.

Marney did the shooting. We did not speak while this was being done. We made as little noise as possible with

o

the oars. Our nerves were keyed up, as though we were
hunters stalking a shy, suspicious quarry, that would take
to flight at the faintest indication of our presence. When
Marney came to the last anchor-stone, he actually lowered
it into the sea so that it would make no sound. And he
waved to us then to sheer off and row well away from the
line of nets, as though he had an idea the fish were
watching us ; making an intelligent association between
ourselves and the trap we had surreptitiously laid for
them. We rowed north, and then shorewards ; and at
last dropped anchor. The tension to a degree was relaxed ;
but when Marney spoke it was in subdued tones.

" You can't be too careful about salmon," he said as he
lighted a cigarette. " They say they're the most timid fish
that exists. They'll take fright at anything."

" I only hope they'll not take fright at our nets," said
John. " I wish to God we'd got finer ones. I still think
we'd have done better if we'd taken father's advice and
sent them back. I don't always agree with what he says,
but I think he's right this time. It'll not only be the
Fosdycks who'll be laughing at us if we don't get a
catch."

" Now, don't *you* start," said Marney sharply. " You
wait and see what happens when we haul. We'll not blash
until nearly low water, so you can go to sleep if you want
to. I'm going to see if there's a plaice or two knocking
about. We're on sand here. There ought to be a few
good ones. I've got a few worms I pinched out of a tin of
Steve's, when he'd gone to school. He's got a line set
somewhere."

John yawned. He moved for'ard, sat down, and began
very methodically to wrap the sail about his body. Then
he stretched himself along the seat, and made a final

adjustment of the sail so that it completely enveloped him, and gave him the appearance of a corpse ready for sea-burial. I joined Marney in the stern. By the glow of our cigarettes we baited two hand-lines, and lowered them over. In a few minutes, John was snoring lustily.

I had guessed that Marney was not so confident as he professed to be.

" If there's one thing I can't stand," he said shortly, " it's waiting. Now some people, like our John there, when they've got to wait for something can go to sleep and never think at all until it happens. But I can't stop thinking. I can see those nets now as a fish would see them. I can just imagine I'm a salmon, swimming along looking for crabs and other things to eat, and suddenly hearing a great *crack* of a fisherman's blashing-stick on the sea above my head, and starting off like hell ; and then suddenly coming bang up against a net. Now it stands to reason that if I see a net, and *know* it's a net, I'm not going to try and poke my head into it. So I start back. And then I hear another *crack* ; and that makes me think I can't get back that road. So I find myself up against the net again. Well, this time I swim along it trying to find if there's a hole big enough for me to get through. I go backwards and forwards, up and down, and while I'm doing that comes another *crack* ; and this time I'm so frightened, I take a chance and go full speed ahead, and I get caught. . . . . But then that's only one way of thinking. I shouldn't see that net at all if it was a fine net. I'd get caught first time. And if it was a coarse net, like those of ours, I might be more frightened of it than by the noise I heard, and not get caught at all. . . . ssh ! I had a bite then."

Marney hauled his line in. There was nothing on it. He

re-baited it with another of Steve's worms, and let it go back. Then he continued :

" I hate waiting," he repeated. " I hate not knowing. Now, it's different when you're reading something. Like the ' Grey Spider,' for example. Then it's not knowing that keeps you interested. It's when you've got a feeling that things aren't going to turn out well that upsets you. I was like that when our kid was born. Everybody said it would be all right ; and Amy herself was as cheerful as if she'd been going to the pictures. But I nearly went out of my head that night ; just waiting, waiting, and not knowing. I couldn't rest ; I couldn't do anything but smoke fags. I smoked over a hundred. And when her mother called to me that it was all over, I thought she meant it was all over with Amy, and I broke out into a cold sweat from head to foot. I didn't feel a bit better even when I heard the kid screaming. I tell you there's nothing worse than waiting. I'd rather die a dozen times over. . . . That's another nibble. I think I'll see if the bait's still on."

We fished for an hour, but without success. We saw the distant village lights and the lights of farmsteads go out one by one, until at last the whole coast between High Batts and Low Batts was without sign of habitation, and loomed obscure and desolate against the stars of the west. We saw the lights of steamers moving slowly along the seaward horizon. Once we saw the faint flicker of a light near the foot of High Batts, and Marney said :

" There's old Luke, lighting his pipe " ; and he added rather thoughtfully, " There's no doubt Spinney Hole's a good spot for salmon ; but I'll not believe it's better than this spot till it's proved."

The remark was a certain clue to Marney's state of mind.

He could better his father at an argument, but he could never in his heart lose the profound respect he had for his judgment in matters relating to their common craft. Marney was uneasy. It was with an obvious effort to bolster up his own cracking confidence that he said :

" I don't think it really matters a bit our nets being so coarse when it's as dark as this. I shouldn't be surprised if we do very well. If only we hadn't got to wait such a damned long time before we knew."

We had to wait until after midnight before the tide was low enough for the ' blashing.' We wakened John, whose temper was not improved by the discovery that he had been sleeping with the iron head of the boat-hook under his ribs. We weighed anchor and rowed seawards to the outer buoy. We ' rounded ' it and turned landwards, inside the line of nets. We then proceeded to ' blash ' each lagoon in turn ; John and I rowing ; Marney hitting the water with the blashing-pole, first at one side of the boat, then at the other.

" We'll give them another hour," said Marney when we had finished. " If there are any fish they'll be in by then, or not at all. We ought to get a dozen, anyway. I'll be surprised if we don't."

" I'll be surprised if we do," growled John. " I'll be surprised if we get a fish. I believe I've got a hole in my side with that damned boat-hook."

" We'll bring a feather-bed for you to-morrow night," said Marney tartly. " You can say your prayers, and then I'll tuck you in."

We rowed back to our old position. John once more wrapped himself up in the sail. Marney and I lighted cigarettes, and we made ourselves as comfortable as we could in the stern ; but we did not attempt to sleep. It was a long hour ; and John's steady snoring did not tend to ease Marney's state of mind. It was with a distinctly savage voice that he shouted at last :

" Come on there, John. You're worse than Kettlenab fog-horn. We're going to haul. It will be daylight in another hour."

There were already signs of dawn. The stars in the east were losing their brilliance. The profound shadows of High Batts were perceptibly growing lighter. We rowed in silence to the outermost buoy. Marney seized it, and as we put the stern of the boat towards the shore and ' backed,' he began to haul.

We did not speak once throughout the whole operation, which occupied less than half an hour. There was nothing in the nets. They were as clean as when we had shot them. The end stone, and part of the first net we had shot, was aground ; and we had to wade out and carry them in. But we did this hurriedly. In our minds was now a common, all-obliterating thought—the Fosdycks.

Day was breaking. A streak of pale orange divided the eastern sky from the level line of the windless sea. A colourful half-light glowed on the face of High Batts, and penetrated the lingering shadows at its foot ; where without difficulty we could distinguish the Fosdycks' boat moving north.

" They've hauled, and they're pulling back for all they're worth," said Marney. " Come on. We've got to beat them in."

John took a pair of oars, Marney and I one each. But we had a start of half a mile, and we took things easier as we drew near the Landing posts. Marney's interest then became suddenly concentrated on the shore.

" There's no sign of any one about," he muttered.

" And it's a damned good job," growled John. " Let's moor the boat and get straight up, before any one sees us. We're going to be the laughing-stock of Bramblewick, if any one does."

" I'm going to wait at the slipway top and see how the Fosdycks have done," said Marney. " We don't know that they've done any better."

" We haven't set them a very big job, have we ? " John growled back.

" I'm going to wait," repeated Marney.

The tide was down. We landed, and moored the *Emma*.

" Leave the nets," said John. " We'll come for them later. I want to get home before father's up. I don't want the job of breaking the glad tidings to him until I've had my breakfast, and I'm feeling a bit stronger."

We walked swiftly up to the slipway, but we halted near the breakwater ; and John, in spite of himself, halted too. The Fosdycks were already through the Landing posts. They rowed their boat aground. Avery got out and took the anchor ashore. Then he returned to the boat, and we saw Luke hand to him a long, gleaming object that was unmistakably a fish. Luke held out another. Avery, completely laden, waded ashore. Tindal got out, and leaning into the boat, lifted out two others. Luke was already reaching down for more.

" They haven't done better than us, have they ? " said John with bitter sarcasm. " That's only six they've got."

" They've been among them all right," said Marney. " God Almighty ! How many more ! "

We had counted twenty-three when Luke threw an empty basket ashore, and got out to help Tindal and Avery wash the catch.

" It must be a very poor spot for salmon, Spinney Hole," said John with a supreme irony as we turned. " I wonder what gave father the idea it was better than Browe Beck sands ? He must have been dreaming."

" If I was as funny as you," said Marney, " I'd send myself up to *Comic Cuts*." But to me, as he parted, he said in a tense whisper, " If we don't beat the Fosdycks at salmoning before the summer's out, I'll chuck fishing for ever."

CHAPTER THREE

WHEN Henry and I returned from the lobster-pots that afternoon, old Isaac was waiting on the slipway with Marney and John. The *Nil Desperandum* was ready to be launched.

Even old Isaac was uncertain as to the age of that venerable boat. Originally she was the ship's boat of a schooner which had been broken up at a northern port ; and she had been sold to a retiring Bramblewick sea-captain who, on his last voyage down the coast, put her overboard near Low Batts, where one of the Fosdycks was waiting to tow her ashore. That sea-captain used her as a summer pleasure-boat for at least fifteen years, and he had been dead twenty !

The *Nil Desperandum* (Isaac had adopted that name from the ' motto ' of the *Nancy Price*) had to be handled very delicately. There was not, in her whole structure, a piece of planking, or rib, or timber which had not been spliced or patched. Her keel was in four sections and so infirm that had she been suspended at her stern and bow alone, she would have broken in two with her own weight. It was Marney's theory that she had no wood whatever on her bottom ; that it consisted only of a crust of successive applications of tar, in which was imbedded strips of canvas, oilcloth, bits of rope, even brown paper. Yet Isaac apparently had every confidence in the seaworthi-ness of his craft. It was the launching which was perilous.

She was lying at the back of the lifeboat-house. We had to lift her carefully, as if she had been a grand piano, on to the launching wheels belonging to the Lunns' small rowing-boat. Then we moved her slowly down the slip-way, and deep into the water, so that she would float off the wheels without friction. Old Isaac made his painter fast then ; and we helped him to put the first consignment of six lobster-pots on board. There was not room for more.

" It will very likely be the last I'll see of them, when I shoot them," he said. " I'm going to put them just by the Landing posts. It's the nearest place where there's lobsters, but it's the first place for the seas to start breaking, when it blows up north-east. So I expect I'll lose them."

None of the Lunns commented on this characteristic remark. One had been aware since our landing of an electric family tension. They had not spoken to each other. Henry who, while at sea, had not volunteered a single remark upon our night's failure, stood watching Isaac make his final preparations for departure as though he were absolutely unaware of his sons' existence. John's face wore that familiar expression of gloom. Marney sucked nervously at his cigarette, and stood swaying from one foot to another, in a way which clearly indicated that he was very uneasy.

We watched Isaac get in, and start to row down the Landing ; then suddenly Henry turned, as though to go homewards. And Marney spoke in peculiarly subdued tones.

" How many did you get, father ? "

Henry did not stop, but he slowed down a little. We fell into step with him.

" Thirty-eight," he answered laconically. " We've put them overboard until evening."

We had moored the coble, and come ashore in the little

boat, which was now being kept afloat by Steve. Our catch had been left in a basket, let down into the water from the coble, so that the lobsters would keep alive until it was cool enough to pack them. It was a very hot day.

We walked in complete silence up the cliff lane. Henry went straight indoors. I climbed with John and Marney to the space by the warehouse, where the unlucky nets were spread out to dry. John and Marney had evidently just started on the task of 'sorting' them when old Isaac had requested help with his boat.

They fell to again, maintaining that tense silence. It was very hot, yet the air was dry and stimulating, with no indication of thunder. As far as eye could reach there was not a cat's paw of wind on the sea. There was mist on High Batts, but it was the mist of sheer heat, and its cliffs trembled through it like a furnace wall. An immense flock of gulls was wheeling above a mackerel shoal close in to Low Batts where the buoys of our lobster-pots were clearly visible. Old Isaac had nearly reached the Landing posts.

Marney was not looking directly to the sea. But I knew that he was observing it out of the tail of his eye. A salmon jumped, not very far from Isaac's boat. I knew that Marney saw it. I knew that he was aware of the shoal of mackerel. The mackerel were hunting a shoal of herring fry, which in vast numbers come close in to the coast in very fine weather. Their presence was considered one of the surest signs that salmon and salmon-trout would be in shallow water within reach of nets. Yet Marney said nothing. He did not even speak when the Fosdycks appeared on the scaur with their nets. He took not the slightest notice of his father, who shortly strolled up to his customary look-out position.

Nor did Henry take the slightest notice of his sons. He had changed his sea-boots for carpet slippers. His cotton hat was pulled low over his eyes. He stood with his hands thrust in his trousers pockets, his back towards us. Isaac had started shooting. The Fosdycks were carrying their nets into their boat. The gulls were still visible. Within the last two minutes I had counted no less than seven salmon jumping within a half-mile radius of the Landing posts. Yet John and Marney continued the sorting of the net. Henry continued to look seawards, seemingly with complete indifference. Then suddenly Marney broke that no longer bearable tension. He turned almost savagely on his father.

" What are you standing there for ? " he demanded. " Just staring and saying nowt. If you've got anything to say about last night, why don't you say it, and get it over ? "

The warmth of that outburst seemed to take Henry off his guard.

Without looking round, he said, quite meekly :

" I'm saying nowt because I've nowt to say."

" I bet you're thinking plenty," put in John.

" Aye," Henry answered, with more confidence. " I've got plenty of thoughts."

" Then why can't you say what they are ? " Marney pursued. " Are they about salmon, or lobsters, or hens, or what you're going to have for your tea, or what ? "

Henry turned, and suddenly there was no meekness in his voice.

" I'm thinking about those damned salmon that are jumping," he said, " and you chaps ashore, still meddling on with your nets. You ought to have had them sorted an hour ago. Look at the Fosdycks. They've wasted no time over it. They'll have another twenty-four salmon to dangle in front of your noses to-morrow morning."

Marney was staggered, but only momentarily.

" I thought you said the nets were no good."

" They're good enough, if you know how to fish with them," Henry retorted hotly.

" You didn't say that yesterday," put in John.

" Never mind what I said yesterday. It's what I'm saying now."

" Well, what *are* you saying now ? " Marney demanded. " You're no more fed up than I am we didn't get any fish. If the nets are no good at night, it's a damned certainty they're no good by daylight, and with the water as clear as this. Why don't you say what you're really thinking ? "

" I've told you what I'm really thinking," Henry answered in slightly quieter tones. " If you're going to catch salmon, you ought to be at it, and not let the Fosdycks get out first and take their choice of berths. I know where they're going now. And if I'd been salmoning I'd have been there an hour ago with my nets down, and never mind whether they'd catch anything by daylight. But they'd have been shot so that they'd catch something at night."

I saw Marney take a shy glance at his father. But he was too subtle to show that he had diagnosed Henry's very obvious complaint.

" And where are they going to ? " he said quietly. " Spinney Hole ? "

The Fosdycks were now rowing down the Landing, drawing near to old Isaac, who was returning for his second consignment of pots.

" They're going north," Henry answered. " They've got their eyes on those gulls. They'll be shooting just this side of Low Batts Point to-night, not so far from our pots. And that's where I'd have been before now, if *I'd* been salmoning."

" Well, you're *not* salmoning," said Marney subtly. " We had to wait ashore for you to come back, so we couldn't have gone off sooner. And I wouldn't have gone there anyway. There's better spots than that. We might even try Spinney Hole. What do *you* say, John ? "

John grinned. Perhaps he knew what was coming. That Marney knew, I had no doubt whatever. Henry had turned abruptly to look seawards. Then he as abruptly swung round again, and he took the net from John's hands.

" Go down and tell mother to get tea ready sharp," he said, in a voice that was unmistakably tense with salmon fever. " Tell her to put something in a tin for supper. You can go to the pots to-morrow. Look sharp ! " And to Marney he added : " You'd best go and get ready too. We'll finish the nets. We'll be off in less than half an hour."

It was a victory for Marney. He had an intense affection as well as an intense respect for his father. From the first he had been uneasy about Henry's non-participation in the salmoning venture. But he gave no outward sign of his subtly achieved victory now. His tact was superb.

" I *am* ready," he said quietly. " My grub tin's in the *Emma*. There's only this net to be sorted. If you like to go and have your tea, we'll finish it, and have them all in the boat by the time you're ready." And he added, with a glance seawards, " You're right about the Fosdycks, father. They're going north. Gum ! That was another salmon jumped. The bay's alive with them."

CHAPTER FOUR

I met John at the slipway at six o'clock next morning. Both the *Emma* and the Fosdycks' small boat were at anchor again ; but it was not until we had got the coble under way for the lobster ground that John deigned to answer my inquiry as to the result of the night's fishing.

" I don't know how they got on," he said grumpily. " I heard father come in, and I thought I heard him go to bed about half-past four. Then, about five, I heard him washing and moving about downstairs ; and when I got down I was just in time to see him going down the cliff steps in his Sunday clothes, and in a hell of a hurry. I don't know what happened. It's all a mystery to me. I looked in the warehouse, but I couldn't see any fish in it. They wouldn't leave them in the boat. There's a bus for Burnharbour at six o'clock. They *may* have got some fish, and he may have gone down to market with it. But I don't see why he should have put on his Sunday clothes for that."

John, at best uncommunicative in the early morning, was more than usually so after making this tantalising announcement. The three fleets of pots (we had one ashore in reserve) were now being left close in all night ; and with the weather still calm, it was easy work hauling them. We got nearly sixty lobsters. But lobster fishing had completely lost its thrill, now the spell of salmon fever was upon us. While we hauled, scarcely a minute passed but what we saw a salmon or a trout leaping somewhere on the mirror-like surface of the bay.

As we turned homewards we saw old Isaac hauling his pots near the Landing posts. His two gulls were on the gunwale of the *Nil Desperandum* not a yard away from him : and as each pot came on board, and Isaac cleaned it, the gulls thrust their beaks out for the old bait he offered them in turn. But they flew away as we drew near. We asked him how he was doing. He gave an ironic chuckle.

" I've only got one," he shouted back, " and it's only got one claw. There used to be lobsters here, but there aren't any now. How many salmon did your chaps get last night ? "

" I don't know," said John. " Did you hear how Luke got on ? "

" I saw 'em putting three boxes on to the carrier's cart," Isaac answered. " I should say they'd have about thirty, but I didn't trouble to ask. There's Joey and Charley come for a bit of fish. They haven't brought their mates, it seems. They must have left them sitting on the eggs ; slipped away on the sly."

We landed. Marney was waiting for us. He looked very tired, and more worried than I had ever seen him look before.

" Do you know where father's gone ? " he shouted to John as we waded ashore.

" No, I don't," John answered. " He went off in his Sunday clothes about half-past five. And that's all I know about it. He must have gone for the bus. How did you get on ? "

" We got three trout," Marney snapped. " The Fosdycks got thirty-five. Come on. Let's get the lobsters up and packed. I wonder what the devil's up with him ? "

" He's maybe got another tooth aching, and gone down to get it out," suggested John, as we set to, putting the lobsters in a basket.

" He never spoke a word to me from the time we started hauling," said Marney. " All his teeth might have been aching at once. We had two nets at Browe Beck and two at Spinney Hole. There wasn't a fish at Spinney Hole. We got those three in the first net we shot at Browe Beck. The only thing I'm pleased about is that we got ashore before the Fosdycks."

" They've got the laugh on us now, and no mistake," said John. " I wish to God we'd never started salmoning at all. We're only making fools of ourselves ! "

" Then we'll go on making fools of ourselves," Marney snapped. " I'm going off to-night if I've got to go by myself. I've carried all the nets up, and got them spread out. I've never known father act so daft. Where the devil *has* he got to ? "

It was late in the afternoon when the mystery of Henry's disappearance was solved. The day was hotter even than the last two had been. The sun shone with a tropical intensity. There was no wind. We had sorted three of the nets and were at work on the last one, with our backs to the cottage, when we heard familiar footsteps. Henry, still in his Sunday ' best,' and looking extremely hot and uncomfortable, had walked up to the cottage door, and set down in front of it a large brown-paper parcel.

" He's back," said Marney. " Now we'll know what's up."

Henry had already taken off his hard felt hat. Mother had come to the door. Henry peeled off his best coat and guernsey, and handed them to her : then he took

P

hold of the parcel, and came up the warehouse hill.
He still looked uncomfortable. His face dripped with
perspiration. He walked as though his feet were much
too large for his ' best ' Sunday boots. But there was a
peculiar excitement in his eyes and in his voice. He
put down the parcel and waved his hand to the pile of
nets.

" You can stop that," he said. " We're not going to
waste time putting those damned things in the sea
any more."

John and Marney stared at him in silence ; but in
Marney's eyes already was the dawning light of com-
prehension.

" You can stop that job," Henry repeated. " You can
start stripping the lot."

" What are you talking about ? " said John. " What's
the joke ? Is there a prize offered ? "

" If there was a prize, I should think you'd win it,"
said Henry dryly, as he sat down on his parcel, and took
off his " best " boots. " Go down and ask mother for my
slippers. And ask her to make me a cup of tea. And don't
stand there gaping. We've got to get those thick nets off
the corks and sinkers, and get these on them, before
to-morrow."

John said nothing more. He went off on his errand.
Marney was staring eagerly at the parcel, which Henry,
with an exasperating indifference to our feelings, continued to sit on.

" Where have you been, father ? " said Marney.

" I've been to Sledburgh," Henry answered, rubbing
his swollen toes. " I went to Burnharbour, and caught a
bus that took me all the way. They're handy things,
aren't they ?—these buses. It used to take us all day to

get to Sledburgh by train. And they're so cheap, too. About half the price of the railway fare.''

" You didn't go to Sledburgh just to find that out," Marney interrupted impatiently. " You could have seen it all on the notice-boards. What *did* you go for ? "

" I went to see grandad," Henry went on smoothly. " He's not too grand. His eyesight's about gone. He didn't know me until I spoke. I doubt very much if he'll see the summer through."

" Poor old grandad ! " said Marney very sympathetic- ally, but without taking his eyes from the parcel. " What had he got to say about salmoning ? "

" He had nothing to say, because I didn't tell him. It wouldn't have done him any good the way he is to have been told about last night, and the night before, and how the Fosdycks have got on."

" Then where did you get any nets from ? There's no one sells nets at Sledburgh. What sort are they ? Are you going to keep them wrapped up like a Christmas present for nobody to see ? "

" They'll take no harm for staying wrapped up," said Henry mercilessly. " We'll get these damned submarine nets stripped first. I got 'em from the missus of a chap who died last year, just before salmoning began ; and he'd never used them. I got 'em middling cheap, too. If they'll not catch salmon nothing will."

John returned with father's carpet slippers and an apron. " Mother's going to have your tea ready in a minute," he said. " And she says you've got to put this apron over your best trousers, if you're going to mess on with the nets."

John, apparently, had been doing a little private thinking during his absence, for he added :

" What have you got in that parcel ? What's all the damned mystery about ? "

Henry, taking a sardonic delight in our growing curiosity, slowly drew the slippers on to his feet, pressed his fingers all round them, as though he were trying on a new pair ; then got up, strode about in them, as though he had been in a boot-seller's shop, and at last bent down and started to unknot the many strings with which the parcel was tied.

We all three automatically offered him our knives. But he waved us back.

" Never cut a piece of good string," he admonished. " You may be wanting it next minute. Aye," he went on, wrestling with a knot, " grandad's aged since I saw him last. But he still doesn't look eighty-four. You wouldn't think he was a day more than seventy."

" You'd better by half cut it," said Marney.

But Henry was too excited himself to continue exasperating us. He suddenly gave the parcel a squeeze, and slipped the strings off. The nets were visible.

A woman would not have examined a piece of exquisite lace with greater æsthetic emotion than Marney did that shapeless bundle of net. He lifted a piece, and stretched it daintily between his hands. He rubbed a piece of the thread between his fingers. He put the same piece between his teeth, and chewed at it. He took a handful of net and inhaled its oily aroma, as one might inhale the perfume of a rose. Then in a profoundly excited voice, he said :

" God ! They're beauties ! I've never seen such nets. I didn't know they could be made so fine. It's pure flax that, I know. There's not a thread of hemp or cotton in it. And ready oiled, too. God ! They'll catch salmon. They'll catch anything ! "

" They'll not catch salmon until we get them shot," said Henry with a sudden briskness, as he turned to the pile of coarse nets. " Come on. We've got to get these stripped, before we can start putting the new ones on. We can give up any idea of going off to-night. These are going to be laced on properly. But we'll be off to-morrow dinner-time at the latest. And that will be long before the Fosdycks are ready. We'll have our choice of berths."

" There were thousands of salmon jumping this morning when we were off," said John as we set to work. " Thousands ! "

" Salmon have been bringing three-and-sixpence a pound all week at Sledburgh," said Henry. " Trout two-and-nine."

" Those three we caught ought to make thirty bob then," said Marney. " The Fosdycks must have made more than twelve pounds. I tell you it's a paying game is salmoning, if you get the right gear and you're lucky with the weather."

" Are you coming for your tea, father ? " came mother's voice from the cottage door. " Remember you've got your best trousers on, if you've started working."

" Damn it ! " said Henry, slapping his thighs, " I was wondering why I couldn't find my knife. I'll be back in a minute," he said to Marney, " and you can leave the nets alone while I'm gone."

" If he hasn't got salmon fever now," said Marney, as soon as father had disappeared, " it's something very like it."

" I've got it myself," said John. " You *can* get salmon fever when you've got nets like these to work with. . . . But they'll want some looking after," he added. " It won't take much of a swell to make a mess of them."

"Shut up. It'll keep fine like this till the end of the summer," said Marney. "And by that time it won't matter if we lose them or not. They'll have paid for themselves a hundred times over. We're going to coin money—I tell you. Coin it!"

CHAPTER FIVE

THREE of the new nets were completed when we stopped work at dark, and only a short section of the fourth remained to be done in the morning. Henry and Marney would again take the *Emma*. They would leave before dinner-time, and, according to the prevailing conditions of sea and the weather, shoot the nets in the most favourable spot, and hang on to that spot until night. They would put each other ashore for a meal, for the local salmon fishery by-laws prohibited that anchored nets should be left unattended. John and I were to take charge of the pots.

But we had not reckoned with our old enemy, lurking furtively as it were, with concealed weapons, under that tranquil, star-lit, summer sea. A thunderstorm broke over Bramblewick shortly after midnight. It raged violently for an hour. Then it abated, and without a warning a strong wind started to blow from the east. By dawn the bay was white with breakers.

We had known long before dawn that we had lost our lobster-pots. It would have been quite impossible to find the buoys in the dark and get back to the Landing before the mouth of it was barred. The Fosdycks had been fishing at Browe Beck sands. At the first puff of east wind they had hauled and rowed their hardest for home. All the boats then had to be hauled up to the dock. The *Nil Desperandum* again was safe in her winter berth, and Isaac too had lost his pots. He took that loss with his usual ironic humour. He had known that they would go in the first rough sea ; and, anyway, he had done better with them than with the ' last lot,' for they had given him one lobster, even though it had ' only one claw.'

We had lost our pots. Our new salmon nets were ready. The wind blew from the east across the turbulent waters of the bay which only yesterday lay like a mirror under the midsummer sky. And it was old Isaac's opinion that the wind would gradually back north-east and that it might blow for several days, before the sea was smooth enough for fishing again. He recalled a summer when it had blown north-east for seven consecutive weeks, and the salmon fishers had never wetted their nets. The season ended officially on the last day of August.

I went round to Marney's after dinner. I was surprised to find him shaving, with Amy fussing about with his best clothes.

" Have you heard ? " said Amy in rather important tones.

I had not. Amy looked even more important.

" Father's had a wire from Sledburgh," she said. " Grandfather Lunn is very ill, and they're expecting the worst. Father and Marney have to be off at once."

" Why can't they say he's dead ? " put in Marney, desperately scraping at his chin. " Everybody knows what ' expecting the worst ' in a telegram means. They'll have sent off another by now."

" They only do it so that it won't come as a shock."

" Who's going to be shocked ? When everybody's been expecting the old chap to peg out the last ten years ? "

" Everybody's not like you," retorted Amy. " Some folks are decent."

I could not see Marney's face properly, but I could tell

that he was deeply upset, and that he was trying to disguise this fact in a very familiar way.

" I don't see how you make things decent by mooching round with a long face when somebody's dead. We've all got to die some day. And when a chap gets to his age, and loses his sight, and he's got to stay in bed, I say it's a mercy when he is dead, and folks ought to be thankful he's out of his misery, and not sorry for it. . . . Damn it ! That's the third time I've cut myself. What have you done with the towel ? "

Marney had turned from the looking-glass, pressing a finger on to a bleeding patch on his chin.

" I've put it straight in front of you, if only you'll look for it," said Amy, moving to his assistance. " You'll have to hurry up if you're going to catch the bus."

Marney seized the towel.

" For God's sake stop yapping ! If I'm going to miss the bus, your yapping won't stop me. I tell you I wouldn't go at all, if it wasn't that we couldn't go fishing. I hate this sort of carry-on. It's all pure daftness ! "

Amy looked profoundly shocked.

" Daftness ! " she echoed. " I think you ought to be ashamed of yourself, talking like that about your own grandfather. I don't know how you dare. . . . Your shirt's lying on the bed. I'll keep your boots down here for you. I hope you won't manage to get yourself in a mess before you arrive. I hope you'll look decent, if you don't feel it."

I did not see Henry before the two of them set out on their pilgrimage to that distant village to which old Marney, like a weary exile faithful to some precious memory of his youth, had retired when his fishing days were over. Marney was right about the second telegram.

Grandad had died at midnight. The funeral was to be to-morrow.

John did not go. The buoys and 'tows' of the lobster-pots might be washed ashore, not irreparably damaged, and there was the fourth salmon net to be finished. And it appeared that grandfather had many times expressed a wish that Marney should be present at his funeral. He was the old man's favourite grandson.

The wind got round to the north-east by evening. It was not a gale ; but it more than maintained the easterly swell. It was still blowing next day. Henry and Marney got back about seven o'clock. I went round to Marney's about nine, and found him, with his coat and boots off, but still in his best trousers and guernsey, sitting staring into the fire.

Amy was washing up the supper things. The baby was in bed.

"I'm glad you've come," she said to me, glancing in Marney's direction. "He's just about giving me the creeps, sitting there so dismal."

Marney did not look up, but he said, dismally enough :

"Aye. You wouldn't be very cheerful if you'd seen what I've seen to-day."

I sat down. Marney spoke very slowly, still staring into the fire.

"If you'd seen poor old grandad before they put him in his coffin ! And if you'd thought how he used to show you how to splice a rope, when you were a kid, and make pots, and lines, and whip hooks on to snoods. I'll tell you straight, I was as near crying as makes no matter. There never was a finer chap put to sea than poor old grandad. He knew everything there was to be known about fishing. He'd go out in any weather. Nothing frightened him."

Marney still gazed into the fire.

" Nothing ever frightened him," he repeated. " And to see him all dead and done with, and that damned coffin waiting for him. . . . And it was shaped like a coble too. I couldn't help but notice how it was shaped like a coble. Aye. And that made me think of the times he used to lift me into his coble, when I wasn't big enough to reach up to the gunwale. And there they were ! Two chaps in black, like two old crows, waiting to lift him in."

" They gave him a grand funeral," put in Amy, in a voice tense with morbid excitement. " How many did you say there were ? "

" Well over a hundred," Marney answered. " Everyone in the place turned out for it. And with it being bad weather, all the fishermen were there. But I tell you, I'd rather die myself than go through that again. And seeing them lower him down into the grave. And that brass plate on his coffin. That got me worse than anything. MARNEY LUNN. . . . *same name as me.*"

Marney suddenly seized the poker, and stabbed savagely at a lump of dead coal, as though it symbolized for him all the dark horror of his experience.

" I tell you what," he said abruptly. " When I die, I hope I'm drowned at sea, and my body never washes up at all. I don't want a damned funeral. . . . For God's sake give us a fag ! I wish to God we could go off fishing to-night. I wonder how long this damned north-easter's going to last ? "

The wind did not increase in force. The weather generally, while unseasonably cold, was bright, with blue skies and brilliant sunshine. But the rough sea, just rough enough to bar the Landing mouth and hold up all fishing, continued through ten days of that short salmon season.

Then, at night, the wind veered north-west, and finally west. It blew a half-gale for a whole morning and late into the afternoon, then dropped, leaving the bay as tranquil as it had been before the east wind came.

CHAPTER SIX

I HAD gone to Burnharbour that afternoon. When I returned it was to find that Marney and John had already set off in the *Emma*. Henry, two days ago, had developed a poisoned thumb, the result of an old prick from a gurnard he had been cutting up for lobster-bait. I found him on the warehouse hill. But he was sitting on the grass, nursing his bandaged hand, which obviously was causing him very great pain. I could see the *Emma* half-way to High Batts. The Fosdycks were only just moving out of the Landing.

Henry looked depressed. He had been profoundly upset by his father's death. The loss of the lobster-pots, the run of bad weather, and the pain of his hand, had all rattled him ; and now, his having to stay ashore, while Marney and John made a belated trial of the new nets, obviously was straining him to endurance-point. But he was not jealous of them. He hated inactivity. He wanted to be ' off.' I recognised all the symptoms of repressed salmon fever.

" They're going to Spinney Hole," he said, very quietly, but tensely. " I fancy the Fosdycks will go to Browe Beck sands, seeing our boat's beaten them. It's a damned nuisance my thumb getting like this. I shouldn't have minded the pain, if only it had been my other hand. But a chap's no good in a boat with his right hand useless. I should only be in the way. Fancy having to stay on shore, doing nowt, with the weather like this. If they don't come back with fifty salmon to-morrow, they ought to be ashamed of themselves. If only the weather keeps like this ! "

With the complete fall of the west wind the weather had become very warm again. But the air was fresh ; there was no suspicion of cloud. Everything seemed to point to an ideal night for salmon fishing. I had arranged with Marney that if he went off in my absence I should walk along the beach about dusk, bring him his supper, which Amy would give me, and stay to see the nets hauled. I sat down with Henry. He offered me his bag of sweets, and became expansive.

" Aye," he went on, " it's the same with salmoning as it is with any other sort of fishing. It all depends on the weather. But it's worse with salmon fishing. It's got to be fine, or it's no good. at all. And that's why father never bothered with it. It never is fine weather for very long on this coast. Look how it came on last time. And it might just as easily do the same thing to-night."

Was it a case of sour grapes ? I saw Henry glance vindictively from the alluring sea to his bandaged hand. Then he turned again. Steve was coming towards us, carrying a coil of fishing-line.

" Eh—father," he said. " These hooks you gave me are too big for plaice. Haven't you got any smaller ones ? I've got some worms. If I set this line down the Landing to-night, I might easily get a plaice."

Henry's expression had lighted up a little. He reached out his good hand for the line, and at the same time brought the bag of sweets to Steve's notice.

" Who told you they were too big ? " he demanded.

" Marney," Steve answered. " But he's very likely lying," he added philosophically. " Marney will tell me anything. He told me there was a big sole on my line last time I had it set. I ran down as fast as I could go, and found out he'd put an old boot-sole on one hook. And he's always pinching my worms, no matter where I hide them. You've got some real plaice-hooks in the warehouse. Can you let me have a few ? "

" I've been looking for those hooks for a month now," said father. " Where are they ? "

Steve disappeared into the warehouse, and returned quickly with a paper packet.

" Here they are," he said briefly. " I only want twelve."

Henry had already got his knife out, and, working awkwardly on account of his thumb, began to remove the condemned hooks. But Steve protested.

" I can do that. You'll be making your thumb worse. I only want twelve hooks. I can whip them on myself."

Henry grinned. The fates, it seemed, were conspiring to thwart all kinds of activity for him to-day. He surrendered the line, and Steve expertly began the removal of the hooks. Suddenly Henry reached out his hand, and seized the end of a rather grimy, but familiar, periodical which the action of bending had caused to project from his son's trousers pocket.

" What's this ? " he demanded sternly. " Another of those blood and thunders ? "

Steve took the discovery with a calm which suggested that he had already exhausted the number of its " Grey Spider " thrills.

" It isn't a blood and thunder," he said, pursuing his occupation. " It's the same as the one you took away before, and you read to mother, only the stories are farther on. You'd best not go and burn it. I've promised to lend it to Marney."

Henry did not answer. He was studying the illustrated

cover. Steve gave him a surreptitious glance. Then opened the packet of hooks.

" I think there ought to be sixteen hooks on this line, instead of twelve," he said quietly, and with an uncanny echo of Marney. " It stands to reason there's more chance of getting a fish, more hooks you have. I'll take them out now, and put them in my pocket, so that I won't lose them. I'll put the rest back where I found them."

Henry had opened the ' blood,' and had started to read. Steve carried on in silence. I looked across the bay. I watched the *Emma* draw close in to the foot of High Batts. I watched the Fosdycks arrive at Browe Beck, creep in to the beach, and begin to shoot their nets. I saw a shoal of mackerel and a school of porpoises far out beyond the Landing posts, and a salmon jumping even inside the Landing. But it was not until I became aware of a peculiar, dark-grey mass of cloud rising into the blue of sky above High Batts, that I felt really justified in distracting Henry's attention.

Instantly he was alert, and looking south.

" It looks like a thunderstorm," he said with concern. " I hope it doesn't mean another blow."

CHAPTER SEVEN

THAT mass of cloud swelled slowly upwards, and spread east and west until it occupied the whole southern wall of the sky. Then, towards evening, a mist began to creep along the slopes of the moorland hills, and the last trace of blue sky and the sharp contours of that mountainous cloud-mass disappeared. It was as though the lowering sun had already set; but the air became warmer, oppressively close. There was not a breath of wind.

I went round to Amy about half-past nine. It was then nearly dark. She had the lamp lighted; and with the baby sleeping in her arms was sitting in front of the fire-place, where the primus stove was roaring lustily under the kettle. A meat-pie, a pile of cheese-cakes and an empty beer bottle were on the table, along with Marney's grub tin.

" I'm just going to make the tea," said Amy, putting down one of Marney's stockings she had been darning. " Isn't it close to-night? I'm certain we're going to have a storm of some sort."

She looked tired; and as she made the tea, she said uneasily :

" I wish father was with Marney, instead of John. John makes Marney twice as reckless by trying to make him more careful. I'm certain we're going to have a storm. You'll have to tell Marney the milk's gone sour with the heat, so he can't have any in his tea. He hates condensed milk."

Amy filled the bottle, wrapped it round with a piece of

flannel, and packed it and Marney's supper in the tin. I prepared to go : but before I had opened the door there was a heavy clap of thunder. Amy, putting the teapot away, nearly dropped it from her hand. But the baby had not opened its eyes.

" There you are," she said, rather faintly. " I knew it would come. I do wish they were ashore."

As I stepped out I was greeted by a savage lightning-flash, that could not have been far off, for the report of it followed almost instantaneously. A deluge was falling before I reached the dock. Remembering that I had left my oilskins in the warehouse, I hurried across to the cliff lane, and almost collided with Henry, who was hurrying down. A flash of lightning illuminated the dock as he shouted gruffly :

" Here's your coat, if that's what you're going for. Let's get into the lifeboat-house shelter."

Again the thunder-clap followed almost instantaneously; and there was another dazzling flash before we reached the shelter. We halted, and looked seawards, waiting for the reverberating noise of the double explosion to die away.

" You needn't bother going along the shore," said Henry then. " Both boats will be coming back. It's going to turn real dirty. Glass has dropped nearly an inch in the last hour. If it doesn't blow, it will be a wonder to me."

As he spoke, a gust of wind swirled a torrent of rain into the shelter. The next lightning-flash showed the lines of rain driving up the slipway from the sea.

" It's east," Henry muttered. " Same as it was last time. But it may fall away when the rain stops. It goes all ways in a thunderstorm. I hope they're hauling their nets, anyway. It's a bad spot to be caught in where they are now."

I could not see Henry's face. The darkness between the dazzling flashes of lightning was that of a cellar ; for it was now past ten o'clock, and the Bramblewick street lamps are not lighted during the summer months. But I knew from his voice that he was seriously worried. Suddenly he said :

" I've come without any matches. Have you got any ? "

I gave him a box. The wind was still blowing in gusts, but its direction was consistently east. The rain made it impossible to see much farther than the slipway top when the lightning flashed.

" It's coming in foggy, too," Henry shouted. " I'm going to light the lifeboat lamp."

There was a gas lamp with red panes on the highest part of the breakwater. It was masked north and south, so that an incoming boat, picking it up, was certain of its bearings for the Landing mouth. I gave Henry my oilskin to put over his own like a cloak. He dashed out, and a minute later I saw the splutter of a match, and then a tiny permanent gleam that showed the lamp was lighted. He came back. It was not until then that I remembered his bad hand. He, himself, apparently, had forgotten it.

" It's blowing east all right," he said. " They'll be hauling and making for home if they've got any sense. We'll go down soon and see if there's any sign of the Fosdycks. They'll be in first."

We waited. The thunderstorm seemed to be passing over, but there was no diminution in the rain, and the wind was soon blowing in violent squalls up the slipway. Shortly we were joined in the shelter by old Isaac, in an oilskin smock and a very tattered sou'wester.

" Now then," he said. " It looks as though it's coming on bad again. I thought it would. Coming hot like it did this afternoon. It's a good job I didn't put my boat down. There'll be one less for us to pull up. Have you heard any sign of them yet ? They'll not be troubling about salmon in this weather. They'll be lucky if they save their nets. Marney and John are at Spinney Hole, aren't they ? "

" Aye," said Henry. " Luke's at Browe Beck."

" Spinney Hole's a bad spot with an east wind."

" Aye," Henry answered steadily. " But they should have had plenty of time to get their nets and pull out of it, if they'd started to haul straight away. It's coming on thick like this that I don't like."

" It's stopped thundering, anyway," said Isaac, for once almost optimistically. " We'll know soon if it's only a thunderstorm or a real easterly wind."

We did know soon. In less than an hour it was blowing a half-gale from the south-west. Above the sound of wind and driving rain we could hear the ominous roar of surf. We had left the shelter for the lee of the breakwater wall. Henry had fetched a lantern from the coble (which was still launched up) and he had lighted it. But seawards it revealed nothing but a wall of fog and driving rain ; which beat almost horizontally on the panes of the red signal lamp above us.

We did not speak any more. Each of us realised the peril which threatened the two returning boats. If the wind continued to blow as it was doing now for another hour, the seas would be breaking across the Landing mouth and they would inevitably be cut off. To beat seawards again, once they had committed themselves to an attempted entry, would be impossible.

Suddenly Henry shouted :

" Listen ! Wasn't that an oar ? "

I could hear something faintly resembling the sound of moving oars. We moved out of the lee of the wall ; Henry leading with the lantern. We heard the unmistakable sounds of a boat ; then, voices.

" It's the Fosdycks," said Henry.

The tide was ebbing. By the time we had reached the edge of it, the lantern gleamed on the Fosdycks' boat, moving slowly in to the scaur. Henry and I waded in. Luke got out and came towards us. One could not mistake the sincerity of the concern in his voice when he shouted :

" Are they in yet ? "

" No," said Henry.

" It's time they were, then," said Luke gruffly. " It's not far from breaking now. It took us all our time to find our way between the posts. We couldn't see the lamp until we were through. We had to cut away from our last net."

Luke and Avery got out, and pulled the boat into shallow water. We stood together in the pool of light thrown by Henry's lantern, all staring towards the sea.

" When did you see them last ? " said Henry.

" We never saw them at all after it started to thunder. They were moored close in with their nets. We started hauling straight away. I should think they'd do the same. But they'd have to cut. They'll have to be here soon if they're to get through. . . . We'd better get our boat hauled up while we're waiting. It's going to get worse than this before it's done."

There was, in the business of hauling up the Fosdycks' boat, a temporary anodyne to our anxiety. We helped to carry up the nets first. Luke brought another lantern. Despite the abrupt termination to their night's fishing, they had caught one good salmon, and nine fair-sized salmon-trout.

" It seems as if there's some fish about," said Henry.

" Aye," said Luke. " We'd have had a good night but for this coming on. That lot won't pay for the net we lost, though. It was a new one, too. But I reckon your boat and your lives are worth more than your nets and anything that's in them. I only hope your lads are thinking the same, and not trying any daftness. It's a bad place, is Spinney Hole."

We shared that hope ; but we shared the fear of Marney's recklessness. There was still no sign of the *Emma* when we had finished the hauling. We returned to the lee of the breakwater again. Suddenly we saw the gleam of another lantern moving down the dock. It was the chief officer of the Bramblewick coastguards. He came down, and spoke to Luke abruptly.

" Are there any salmon-boats off from here ? "

" There's one boat," Luke answered. " It ought to be back now. Henry Lunn's two sons."

" There's a special gale warning come through by telephone," the officer continued quickly. " There's been a very bad affair at Burnharbour. A coble capsized hauling its nets just by the piers. Two men gone. Brewster, I think their name is. There's about five boats still out, and some of them this way. The motor lifeboat's out, but I fear it will be too thick for it to be of any use. Where were the Lunns fishing ? "

" Under High Batts," Luke answered.

" There'll be no need to ask you to keep a look-out for those Burnharbour boats then, if you're still waiting. I'll telephone to the High Batts watch-house about the Lunns. But there'll be watchers all along the coast to-night."

The officer turned up the slipway again. The rain was easing off a little now, but the wind was strong as ever, and the roar of the sea was steadily growing louder. It was still very thick.

" Lifeboat's no good a night like this," said Luke, half turning to Henry. " What do you think ? "

" It would be worse than useless," Henry answered quietly. " If there's anything to be done it will have to be done from ashore. If they're not back in half an hour, I'm going to walk on to High Batts. If they thought it was no good trying for home, they might have chanced it and run ashore."

" It sounds as though it was breaking across the Landing now."

Henry did not answer. He stood, holding the lantern, staring immovably towards the invisible sea. Then another lantern gleamed in the dock : and Amy, with a shawl over her head, came down to us. She did not speak. Henry turned and said quietly and steadily :

" Eh ! You ought to be in bed with your bairn, not prowling about down here this time of night. There's no need for you to get anxious. They've scarcely had time to pull down yet from High Batts. Go up and see if mother's got some tea made. Take your bairn with you. Tell her we'll all be up very soon."

There were too few of us men for one to go back with Amy. I saw her give Henry a peculiar disbelieving glance, which expressed better than words her profound anxiety. Then she went ; leaving us to our vigil. Another fifteen minutes passed. Then Henry said, very quietly :

" They'll not try to get into the Landing now. They'd

not see the posts unless they ran into them. They've either come ashore, or gone out a long way, and dropped anchor until daylight. I think I'll go along to Spinney Hole."

" Then we'd better split up," Luke answered. " If Isaac will stop here, one of us will go as far as he can north, and the others will keep along the scaur-ends. That will be better than us all stopping together. They'll not come in to the Landing now for certain."

CHAPTER EIGHT

I went with Henry. We walked directly to Garry Beck Cove. Then we struck down across the baring scaurs to low water, and followed the irregular, spume-fringed margin of the sea to Browe Beck Sands. We did not speak. Our ears were strained for the sound of a boat or voices. The rain had ceased, the wind, it seemed, was slightly moderating, but the fog continued thick as ever, and the roar of the sea was very loud.

Henry carried the lantern. Without seeing his face, I could feel his mind as one can feel the electric tension of a thunderstorm. We had hope. It came from our confidence in Marney's seamanship : but weighing against this was the knowledge of his contempt for danger. They were new nets. His reputation as a fisherman had been challenged by our initial failure. There had been this ten days of exasperating idleness : and, up to the time of the storm, the weather conditions had held high promise of a catch which would once more turn the laugh upon the Fosdycks. Haunting one was the memory of that first tussle with the long lines and the north-easter. Would Marney cut away from those brand-new nets, when probably there were fish in them ?

We crossed Browe Beck Sands. We followed the outermost of the reefs which towards High Batts curve in to form the cove of Spinney Hole. We saw nothing. We heard nothing to strengthen our slowly weakening hope that they had come ashore and were safe. We reached the bluff from which on that wintry day following the first

shooting of the lobster-pots Marney and I had our first
view of the beach where we had found the buoy ; and we
had just rounded it, when, simultaneously, we caught
sight of something very white lying in the wash of the
receding tide. It was moving.

For an awful second I thought it was the naked limb of
a man, for Henry obscured my view as he ran forward.
But I saw before he shouted that it was a salmon still
feebly alive. It was lying in about five inches of water.
Henry waded in, and holding the lamp in his bandaged
hand, lifted it with the other. I saw then a fisherman's
gaff sticking into it.

" It's one of our gaffs," said Henry, with an awful
quietness. " Aye. It's got H.L. on it. That means they
were hauling close in."

He put the fish down.

" Come on," he said. " Look about, and see if there's
anything else."

I dared not think what we were looking for. I only
knew that something very drastic must have happened to
have made Marney lose his hold of a fish like that. We
searched the entire beach of Spinney Hole, from high-
water mark to the margin of the savage sea. We found
nothing. We heard nothing. With the wind south-east,
they could not, if they had tried, have gone further south.
Henry gave me the lantern and picked up the salmon, and
we started back for home. We walked in silence still
keeping to the margin of the tide. There could be no
doubt now that the wind was falling. The sound of the
surf, too, seemed to be growing less. But while there were
vague indications of approaching dawn, the fog was thick
as ever.

We had reached Garry Beck when we heard Luke

Fosdyck's voice ahead of us. We were within speaking-distance before we saw the gleam of his lantern.

" They're not ashore yet," he said gruffly. " Have you seen any sign of them ? "

" We only found this," Henry answered, indicating the fish. " It's got one of our gaffs in it. They haven't come ashore. If nothing bad's happened to them then they must have pulled out clear of the seas and dropped anchor. We'll not know until it's day."

We walked on.

" The wind's dropped, anyway," said Luke. " The sea's going down. I think we'd best get the lifeboat off, soon as it looks like daylight. It's not so far off now. It would be no use until then."

" No," Henry answered. " We're more use ashore while it's thick like this. There's nothing to do but wait for day. Has the coastguard been down again ? "

" Aye. He's telephoned all along that your boat's still out. Three Burnharbour boats are not back yet. It's old Ned Brewster and his brother that have been drowned."

We reached the slipway. Isaac was standing there alone. Henry turned to me and said in an undertone :

" Go up and tell mother and Amy we're still waiting but that the wind's dropped and the sea's going down. Tell them we think they're lying at anchor outside, waiting for daylight and the fog to lift. Don't say anything about those Burnharbour chaps being drowned. Look sharp back. You may be wanted."

I found Amy with mother. The baby was asleep in mother's arms. I gave them Henry's message. Amy said nothing. Her face was white and drawn. She glanced at me as she glanced at Henry, and I had the sensation that she was looking straight through my eyes, sharing that

vision which had haunted me since we had found the fish :
of the *Emma* capsized, and Marney and John lying dead
on the shore at dawn.   But Mrs. Lunn's face, although
deathly pale, was expressionless, enigmatic.   She said, in
her quick, fussy way :

" Eh—it's a good job the wind's dropping.   It did come
on sudden, didn't it ?   They'll have gone off to sea.   That's
what they'll have done.   They'll be riding at anchor till
daylight.   It's a good job they've got plenty of clothes
with them.   I always say to Henry and John, ' Take plenty
of clothes with you, no matter how warm a night it is.
There's no telling how the weather will change.'   Will you
have a cup of tea ?   We've just been having a sup.   I want
Amy to go to bed, but she won't.   I keep telling her it's no
good worrying.   Worrying does no good.   They'll not take
any harm, I know.   Marney's nearly as good a fisherman
as father is.   And I've waited for father many a time,
worse nights than this."

I left them and hurried back down the lane.   The wind
had dropped completely.   It was now nearly dawn.   I saw
that the lifeboat-house doors were standing open as I
went through the dock.   It was low water.   I found Henry
and the Fosdycks at the extremity of the west scaur.   The
fog was still very dense but, judging by the sound, the sea
had moderated to little more than a heavy ground-swell.

" It's for you to say, Henry," I heard Luke Fosdyck say
as I drew up.   " There's still a heavy sea on.   I'll fire the
gun now, and we'll be off in ten minutes.   Or we'll put
your coble down.   Although I still don't think either's any
use until there's more light or the fog lifts.   We might
search about for hours, while all the time they're close in,
and needing us.   If they anchored they'll take no harm
now."

There was no antagonism now between the two men. All that enduring jealousy and resentment of Luke's was sunk in a common cause against the sea. One felt that he was completely sensitive to Henry's feelings ; and that he was extending towards him a sincere sympathy. It was the same with Tindal, and Avery too, although they said nothing. And in old Isaac's continued silence, one sensed an attitude warmer than his customary one of ironic detachment.

Yet Luke's sympathy, if wholly sincere, was strictly relative to the occasion. He believed, as we each in our hearts believed, that the *Emma* had been capsized. We suddenly heard from the direction of the invisible Landing posts the faint sound of oars. None of us spoke, until, unmistakably, it came again. And then Luke swung round on his heels and said, almost savagely :

" It's them ! We're not going to stay and launch up now. They can stand by their boat until the tide flows it to the slipway."

" Aye. You needn't trouble about that, Luke," Henry answered in a shaky voice, " It's been very good of you all, doing what you've done."

The three Fosdycks went. Old Isaac remained. The sound of oars drew nearer. Suddenly the shape of the *Emma* loomed out of the fog. We saw Marney and John unship their oars, and then stand up as the boat came aground. They got out stiffly, and pulled the *Emma* close in. Then Marney came towards us. And as he did so, all the emotions that Henry had repressed throughout that dreadful night seemed to explode.

" What sort of a game's this you've been playing ? What the hell have you been doing ? Haven't you got a ha'porth of sense between the pair of you ? "

Marney stopped, staring sheepishly at his father.

" What have you been doing with yourselves ? " Henry went on, his voice shaking with rage. " What the devil have you been playing at ? Why didn't you cut your nets and come in while you had a chance ? Haven't you got any sense at all ? . . . For two damned pins I'd lay into you both with my belt end. I'll teach you."

Marney did not answer. His eyes were bloodshot. His face was red and caked with salt. He looked completely nonplussed. And it was John who answered, in a voice not a whit less angry than his father's :

" What the hell are you tearing your hair about ? " he demanded. " Talking to us as though we were kids. Do you think we were going to cut away from a set of brand-new nets with fish in them ? It's you who ought to have a bit of sense. If you want to know what we've been doing, come and have a look in the boat bottom, and don't talk so daft. I bet you wouldn't have cut away."

" Aye. Come and have a look," said Marney, turning back to the boat.

Henry emitted a savage grunt. But he waded in with us, and stared at the pile of fish lying in the *Emma's* bottom.

" Twelve salmon and thirty-three trout," said John triumphantly. " As well as a dozen damned fine cod. Spinney Hole was alive with fish. They were after a school of herring smelt. We got the nets right round them. I bet you'd have cut away. Now what about the Fosdycks laughing at us ? How many did they get ? "

" You can shut up about the Fosdycks," Henry answered in suddenly subdued tones. " They've been walking up and down all night watching for you chaps to come in. Where have you been ? "

" Riding outside the Landing, of course," said Marney.
" There was nothing else to do with it being so thick. We
couldn't let you know where we were ; how could we ?
. . . God ! We'd have got a hundred salmon if it hadn't
come on to blow. I lost the gaff in one that must have
weighed a score of pounds. We shipped a sea just as I
was lifting it in, and I had to leave go."

" Aye. We got that one," said Henry, almost calm
again. " It washed up in Spinney Hole, and it weighs
about twelve. . . . How many cod did you say you'd
got ? " he went on quickly. " That's a fine one there."

" There's one bigger than that," said John. " If they're
coming close in we ought to be getting our lines ready for
when salmoning closes."

"Aye. But it hasn't closed yet," cried Marney. "There's
three weeks before cod fever begins. Come on. Let's get
the fish up and the boat launched. I want my breakfast.
I'm as hungry as hell ! "

Marney bent into the boat and lifted out one of the cod.

" Eh ! " he yelled to old Isaac. " Do you want something to make a fish-pie with ? "

Old Isaac chuckled.

" Aye," he answered. " Throw it ashore ! "

THE END